ONE MORE TIME

D0029687

ONE MORE TIME

CELIA MAY HART

APHRODISIA

KENSINGTON BOOKS
http://www.kensingtonbooks.com

KENSINGTON BOOKS are published by

Kensington Publishing Corp.
850 Third Avenue
New York, NY 10022

Copyright © 2007 by Celia May Hart

All rights reserved. No part of this book may be reproduced in any form or by any means without the prior written consent of the Publisher, excepting brief quotes used in reviews.

All Kensington Titles, Imprints and Distributed Lines are available at special quantity discounts for bulk purchases for sales promotions, premiums, fund-raising, educational or institutional use.

Special book excerpts or customized printings can also be created to fit specific needs. For details, write or phone the office of the Kensington special sales manager: Kensington Publishing Corp., 850 Third Avenue, New York, NY, 10022, attn: Special Sales Department, Phone: 1-800-221-2647.

Aphrodisia and the A logo Reg. U.S. Pat. & TM Off.

ISBN-13: 978-0-7582-1922-0
ISBN-10: 0-7582-1922-9

First Kensington Trade Paperback Printing: December 2007

10 9 8 7 6 5 4 3 2 1

Printed in the United States of America

With thanks to
John, my aviation consultant and friend.

Any mistakes found regarding aircraft and the flying of them
are because I didn't pay enough attention.

1

Abby Deane nudged the yoke, banking her plane to the left. Looking out the side window, she spotted her new home, a sprawling ancient mansion dating back to the Tudor period, added to over the ages.

Her new home. Away from the pointless distractions of men, men who were so commitment phobic, wanting only a quick shag. Thank heavens for modern invention. She owned a potpourri of devices designed to please her. Who needed a man in the twenty-first century?

Ever since she'd given up on the heartbreakers, her life seemed less off-kilter. She hoped this new job would rebalance her life. The toys'd definitely help.

With a grin, she checked her instruments and glanced ahead, squinting in the sunlight even though she wore dark sunglasses. Puffy cumulonimbus blocked her vision of the private airstrip ahead.

Circling, she slowed the Beech Bonanza into its gliding speed. She guided the plane into its descent, checking the altimeter until she broke clear of the cloud cover.

She blinked. The airstrip had vanished. She glanced to the left and the right. Had she flown over the strip? Nope, nothing.

Just below the cloud cover, she circled, searching.

What the—A runway didn't just disappear.

This one had. All she saw were mown hayfields and green fields of grazing sheep.

The engine cut out, sputtering. She checked the fuel gauges. Not even close to empty. She throttled back on the engine and gave it power again, to no avail.

Her forehead tightened. She took a deep breath. No need to panic. She knew how to make an emergency landing. She'd practiced it before.

She leveled the wings, aiming for a mown hayfield. She lowered the landing gear. At least she wasn't far from the hotel. If she managed to land in one piece, she'd walk over. If not, someone from the hotel would see her go down and come to her aid.

Checking her seat belts, Abby glided in. The plane touched down, not skewing, but bouncing over the dirt ridges and truncated hay stalks.

The plane rolled to a stop. Abby sagged in her seat. Her seat belts relaxed their grip. A bone-deep ache radiated through her, a counterpoint to her thundering heart. Without further thought, she evacuated the plane. She stood at a safe distance, but the plane rested, still and silent.

She returned to the plane, reaching for her toolbox. She touched the right-hand engine and snatched her fingers back. Cold. That wasn't right.

Abby sighed. Both engines felt like they hadn't run at all. Weird. She'd never experienced anything like this before. She'd have to contact a mechanic to repair her plane.

She unloaded her luggage, hoisting the wheeled bags over the rich black dirt to the field's edge. Through a small gap in the tall hedge surrounding the field (presumably hiding the spoils of hay from the adjacent grazing animals) Abby spotted a dirt track.

That should take me to the main road, she thought.

Two bags, one laptop, a large purse, and a long tube holding her copies of the hotel plans. She sat on the biggest bag to wait for assistance to arrive.

And waited.

Half an hour later, Abby came into sight of the hotel, her future home. Her future home with useless staff to fire. It didn't matter that her boss had agreed to keep the original household staff. Someone must have seen her plane in distress. Why hadn't anyone come to her aid?

And this drive . . . Gravel made a nice crunch under a car's tires, but dragging heavy wheeled bags over it for a quarter mile was not so much fun. The other quarter mile had been nothing but dirt.

That had to be fixed. Hotel guests may not be inclined to travel to a boutique hotel all on dirt road. She thought of flying stones scratching a BMW's paint job and shuddered.

No, that had to be rectified at once. Well, once she'd hired new staff.

She noted the shuttered windows on the house and at once forgave the staff. Keeping the windows closed preserved the restoration's freshness. That's why they didn't see her go down, and her landing had been practically silent.

Speaking of silence   a breeze brought the sound of baaing sheep, the rustle of leaves from the giant trees lining the drive. No sound of civilization reached her ears. Not the dull roar of the M3 highway, which was only a couple of miles off.

Abby shrugged, shifting the tube strap on her shoulder. Maybe the house blocked the sound.

She reached the grand front entrance. Two giant oaken

doors, formidable and highly polished. Abby nodded in approval. The staff were doing superb work. Such attention to detail.

Leaving her luggage at the foot of the broad stone steps, she slung her purse over her shoulder. She ascended and rang the bell, an old-fashioned pulley. Another nice touch. With the hotel's official opening, those doors would stay wide open and welcoming.

She leaned backward, surveying the facade, approving of the sparkling windows and pollutant-free bricks.

A creak warned of the opening door. They polished the doors but didn't oil the hinges? Abby repressed a sigh of irritation. So much to be done.

The door opened a crack.

Some welcome. Abby huffed. "Are you going to let me in?"

A deep baritone voice answered: "Who are you?"

"Your former boss if you don't let me in," Abby snapped.

The pause from his end only maddened her further. "A woman?"

She hauled the door open, ready to give him a piece of her mind, and stopped dead. Her jaw sank and she closed her mouth with a snap.

Before her stood a gobsmackingly handsome man. She registered that much before his odd attire caught her attention. Perhaps it was the dark vee of chest hair poking out from his crumpled white shirt. Or the supertight breeches that let her know, despite the buttoned-up flap, that he was a well endowed guy. Very well endowed.

She cleared her throat. "Definitely your former boss. You're fired."

"Fired?" The man might look gorgeous but apparently he lacked in the brains department. "I do not work for you."

That gave her pause. Was this Lord David Winterton's son?

She modulated her tone. "If you are not on my staff, who are you?"

He smiled, a broad smile that must have broken many a heart. Abby steeled herself. Not hers. "I'm just passing through."

Her eyes narrowed. "Trespassing? And my staff let you?"

"There's nobody here but me." He surveyed her, wholly uninclined to leave her property. His eyelids lowering, his stern gaze turned his brown eyes into angry dark specks. "You don't look like the sort who possesses staff."

Abby's blood boiled. "You bastard." She pushed past him and into the house. Where *was* her staff?

In the middle of the large hall, she stopped, her sneakers squeaking on the marble tile floor. She frowned, surveying the space. "Something isn't right . . ."

The idiot man came up behind her. "I'm glad you're acknowledging that at last."

Abby ignored him, looking at the tiled floor. "For some reason, I thought this was linoleum in the pictures, but it's real marble."

"Linol-what?"

Abby made a slow turn. "It's in awfully good condition for an ancient floor."

"Ancient." He sounded doubtful.

Along the wall stood a delicate side table. The piece belonged in a museum, not a busy hotel hallway. On it, a single gold tray contained a scatter of ivory cards. Her breath caught in her throat. "That—that's not supposed to be there."

She reviewed the hallway. Had she gotten it all backward? "Where's the reception desk?"

"Madam, you are not making any sense." Abby turned and saw his tense stance, his arms akimbo. "This is not a hotel."

She frowned right back at him. "It is. I'm the manager."

"You?" His rich voice held a note of derision. "A woman?"

"Oh my God." Abby drew herself to her full height, a full foot shorter than he. "Just get over yourself. This is the twenty-first century!"

"It's 1807," he said, his voice quiet. His brown eyes pierced her.

She tried to ignore the discomfort. "Don't be ridiculous." She put distance between them, looking for a telephone. If this guy got dangerous . . ."I don't have time to mess about in some fantasy role-play."

"It's not a fantasy," he insisted. Truly, it was a shame someone so good-looking was also so deluded.

"Look, mister." Abby folded her arms and glared at him. "It's time you took a hike. You're trespassing on private property. Do you want me to call the police?"

The man didn't move. "You're a hard woman."

She'd heard worse.

With no phone in sight, Abby fished out her mobile, hitting speed dial. "I warned you." She ignored his sudden, ashen expression. If he did a runner, so be it. She put the mobile to her ear. Hearing nothing, she frowned. "Hmm, must've lost the signal."

"What . . . what is that?" His stilted voice broke into her musing.

So he hadn't run. "Can you give the old-fashioned thing a rest, please?"

He sighed, throwing up his hands. He stalked off into another room and returned with a newspaper. "It's a couple of months old, but look." He thrust it at her.

She picked it up. "So the date is 1807. It's a nice printing job. It's amazing what computers can do these days." She tossed it back at him.

He caught it one-handed. "You're not making sense."

Abby sighed. "You're still here? Let me find a landline . . ." She wandered off. According to her blueprints, they'd turned this room into an office.

A small sitting room, definitely feminine, greeted her. "But . . ."

What was going on? How could all the work she'd seen in photographs be undone? Had she fallen victim to some kind of scam?

She looked up. No ornate ceiling rose, no electric light. Only a few sconces with candles attached to the wall.

Abby trudged back into the hallway. "I—I don't understand . . ." Her intruder crouched by her bags. Bags she'd left outside. Her eyes narrowed. "What are you doing?"

"Trying to figure out how to open these trunks."

"That's my private property." Abby advanced, pausing when he stood his ground.

"I merely sought to discover your identity. You need your family."

"I need you to leave this house." Abby sucked in her breath. This house where nothing seemed right. "Why have all the renovations been undone? What's happened?"

"Madam, I am sorry for your insanity, but it seems you've regained your senses for the moment. I can see you know there is something not quite right with you. Who are your family? Where do you live?"

"I'm supposed to live here," Abby replied dully. "This is supposed to be my new home." She took a deep breath. "Is it really 1807?"

"I showed you *The Times*," he replied.

The breath whooshed out of her. "I'm not insane. Look in my bag. You'll see that this is 2007."

Crouching, he grinned up at her. "You are an extremely stubborn woman. Although, I will admit you do have unusual items in your possession." His voice sounded strangled. "I'm almost inclined to believe you. That . . . thing . . . you spoke into."

"My mobile?" She tossed it to him, still keeping her distance, and he examined it.

"What is it made of?"

"Plastic and metal, mostly. Are you going to open my bag or what?"

He shot her an annoyed glance. "How *do* you open this thing?"

Abby knelt beside him, at once aware that this stranger was no skinny geek. He was built. The muscles practically popped from his thighs. He seemed so . . . so big.

"It's a zipper," she told him, demonstrating its function by opening the bag partway. "I think it was invented in the twentieth century."

He grunted, tugging on the other zipper. He flipped back the lid. White shirts lay in neat stacks, in between which lay flat navy blue shoes and impeccably rolled black trouser socks.

"Don't even think of rifling through my underwear."

"Wouldn't dream of it, my dear," he murmured, lifting and setting aside her shirts with precision. His lips curved. "Well, well, well . . ."

Abby wanted to curl up and die. She shut her eyes, sinking back on her heels. Why hadn't she stopped him? Because she thought he had her other bag. *Oh, no no no no.* What a way to get started with her staff—or whoever this person was.

"I recognize this," he said. She cracked open one eye to see him squeezing a large synthetic dildo. "Not made of this stuff though. Wood or ivory, yes." He cocked his head. "Do the other items serve similar purposes?"

Her cheeks burned and she nodded, not daring to look at the extensive array of toys she'd brought with which to amuse herself.

"Interesting."

That was the understatement of the year.

"Never seen the like of these before."

"Just . . . just put them back," Abby gasped with a weak wave at her bags.

He chuckled. "Well, now that we've discovered that at least your luggage is from the future—"

"You are a very stubborn man." Her words didn't have their usual force.

"—I believe you may stay."

"So very kind of you," she muttered, tossing her shirts back into the bag and zipping it up. Standing, she hauled the bag upright.

He rose also. "Perhaps it's time we introduced ourselves, given that we lack a common acquaintance to do it for us. Very well, twenty-first-century woman. Do they have names in the future? Mrs.? Miss?"

Abby gave him her best level glare. "Ms."

"Mzz?" His forehead creased.

"Ms. Abigail Deane," she told him, choosing to ignore his puzzled expression. "And you are?"

"Mr. Hardy, Myles Hardy. At your service." He sketched a brief bow. "Now, what are we going to do with you?"

She had no idea. *I don't belong in 1807. What's going to happen to me?* She eyed Myles Hardy. *Can I actually rely on him?*

"No need to look so scared," Myles soothed, stepping forward. He paused at her involuntary retreat. "There's nobody in this house except you and me."

"That's meant to reassure me?" she braved. She eyed her handbag on the floor. If she could just get her hands on that can of mace . . .

"It gives us time to figure it all out. How you got here; how we can send you back."

"What is this 'we' business?"

"I was about to add 'and help you fit in here,' but if you don't need my help . . ." He backed off.

Abby loosed a huffy breath. "Look, thank you, but how can I trust you?"

"You can't." His broad mischievous grin did something unexpected in her belly. She banked down the surge of attraction.

Not again, and certainly not now. "If you wish to manage on your own . . ."

"No, no," Abby said hastily. "I'm sorry. I'm used to shifting for myself."

"Must be some future." Myles grunted as he picked up her other bag. He set off down the hallway. "What is in the cylinder?"

"Blueprints." Abby slung the cylinder strap over her shoulder, followed by her large handbag.

"What?"

"House plans," she translated. What else didn't they have in this time?

Myles glanced over his shoulder, pausing for a moment. "You don't say," he drawled. "They might be most amusing to examine."

"Hardly amusing." She fired her patented glare at his back.

He caught her glaring, and his boyish grin widened. So much for cowing him. "Forgive me, but how often does someone get a look into the future?"

"Two hundred years into the future. Maybe I shouldn't. If you invented things before your time . . ." She dragged her suitcase after her, following Myles to the foot of the stairs.

He ascended the staircase.

Abby looked up. The dark mahogany wood stairs rose from the hallway floor, splitting at a landing to run along the walls on either side of her. "I don't suppose elevators have been invented yet."

He grinned, stopping to look back down at her. "No. Leave your trunk. I will carry it for you."

"No. I can manage." She gritted her teeth. She could rest on the stairs.

Myles sprawled on her bed. Abby eyed him out of the corner of her eye. Was he trying to show off his body? If so, she was too wrung out to notice the way his open shirt revealed a sun-browned chest or the way his breeches clung to his calves, his thighs, his . . . his groin.

No, really. She didn't notice a thing.

Not. A. Thing.

She dumped her bag. Her muscles ached with lifting her weighty suitcase up the stairs. She hadn't wanted to scar a single inch of the wood.

Myles patted the mattress. "Come, sit down. You look all in."

She was. Abby settled on the edge of the mattress, looking over her shoulder at him. "Is this your room or mine?"

He chuckled, a rich lighthearted sound. "It could be ours."

Abby snorted. "Ha! In your dreams."

"I am not familiar with that phrase, but I think I understand." He rolled off the other side of the bed. "I'm sure this has all been a great strain on you. Indeed, it is much to take in. Rest. I'll find some clothes more suitable than your current attire."

He bowed and left the room.

Abby shrugged out of her beat-up leather jacket, tossed it across the room, and slumped back across the bed. She sank into the mattress. No box springs. She sighed.

And slept.

Some hours later, she woke. A dull red and orange glow filled the room. Abby rolled over and found Myles Hardy seated in a chair by the window. She scowled. It hadn't been a dream.

"You look so sweet when you're asleep," he drawled. The tube containing the blueprints rested across his parted knees. "Pity you don't stay that way."

She stuck her tongue out at him. "If you're trying to charm me into your bed, you're doing a piss-poor job of it."

He recoiled. "My God, you're common."

"Thank you." She slid off the bed and tapped the cylinder. "I suppose you want to take a look at these?"

His guileless grin shone up at her. "Yes, please."

"Is there any food to be had?" Abby reached for her leather jacket, hanging off the back of his chair. She glanced down at his upturned face and paused. Her breasts, covered by an old tight T-shirt, hovered just above his mouth. Before she stopped herself, she evaluated the kissability of his lips. Their rating soared at the realization that he wanted to taste her breasts. The tip of his tongue touched his upper lip. "I'm starving."

She straightened, swerving away and shrugging into her jacket. Abby smirked to herself. She didn't know what it was about this man. OK, she did. He was smirky and snarky. He might be her only ally in this time. Why not enjoy it?

He caught her arm, forcing her to face him. "I don't know if you are considered common in your own time, ma'am, but may I suggest that you take care with how you flaunt certain of your qualities, or—"

She glared up at him. "Or you'll what?"

"Or I'll this." Myles hauled her against him, grabbing the back of her neck and pressing his mouth against hers. His rough, heady kiss demanded a response. She fought that instinct, fought him, trying to push him off, and yet still he kissed her. Her actions brought their groins together, and the line of his stiffening cock made itself known.

With a groan, he thrust her from him. "I'll not take you unless you're willing," he growled.

Abby rocked on her heels. His absence shocked her in a way it shouldn't have, given the brief time she'd known him. She put her hand on her hip, posing. "Then you'll have to be a good boy before you'll get any of this."

He growled. "Let's eat."

A tightening in her belly answered him.

He led the way downstairs to the kitchen. He scrounged through the pantry, pulling cheese from one cupboard, bread from another, a few apples. "It's not much, I'm afraid. You're lucky I remembered to go down to the village this morning." He handed her a knife. "Cut the bread, if you please."

Abby perched on a stool and started slicing the still-fresh bread. "Lucky? Do you forget?"

"Part of my nature, I fear. I am a scientist."

Abby lifted both brows. The typical stereotype leaped into her mind: a pocket protector loaded with pens, glasses, unruly hair (usually white), absent-mindedness, and a lack of social skills. Myles Hardy didn't fit that description at all.

"Are you sure?"

He looked up from slicing cheese. "I study in the field of archaeology. I discover ancient works of art. Have done since I graduated from Oxford."

"Like that Elgin Marbles guy?" Abby munched on a makeshift sandwich.

He grimaced. "Not quite that big. That's why I—" He bit down on a hunk of cheese.

Her curiosity peaked. "Why you what?"

Myles shrugged. "What about you? You manage hotels? That's not a job I'd consider for a woman."

"My choices in this time being a wife, governess, or whore?" Abby sniped.

"Forgive me, but no self-respecting woman would choose to work."

"Boy, do you have a lot to learn."

His lip curled. "I think it is you who have the adjustment to make. You are in my time, not I in yours."

She grimaced. "I suppose that means I have to take up wearing corsets and long skirts."

"If you want to stay outside an insane asylum, I'd recommend it." He grinned at her. "Besides, I bet you look pretty in a dress."

Abby gave him one of her long looks that terrified her employees. Pretty in a dress? Did he think he'd get away with such simple flattery? His grin just grew wider. She changed the subject. "I thought a house was supposed to be teeming with servants? Don't they make your dinner for you?"

He shrugged. "They're on holiday." He managed a weak smile. "In my work, I find them too distracting . . ."

Something didn't sound right. Abby had heard worse stories from employees. "Is this usual?"

"Every now and then they get on my nerves. Move things, organize my papers—"

"You have papers? I'd like to see them."

Myles shifted on his stool. "I doubt you'd be able to understand them . . ."

"I have a university education." She smirked. "Which college did you go to? Mine was Magdalen."

His jaw went slack. "You—you went to Oxford? They let women . . . ?" He rubbed his chin. "Incredible."

"Not so incredible if you want to get into my pants, hotshot," Abby jabbed. She stood. "Let's see your papers. I'm done eating."

Myles didn't move. "They're private."

Abby folded her arms. "But notes that will lead to publication, right? How private can they be? I'm not going to steal anything from you. I'm hardly in a position to, after all."

He tore off a corner from the loaf of bread, rolling it with his fingers.

"Myles." Her fingernails drummed on her leather jacket sleeve.

His cheeks flushed. "Why do you insist in calling me by my Christian name?"

"It's your name, isn't it?" His measured gaze set her on edge.

She wasn't about to stop calling him that. He hadn't answered her original question. "Myles?"

He sighed, pushing back from the kitchen table. "Maybe tomorrow." His lips formed in a thin-lipped smile. "I'm not used to sharing."

She understood and eased up, unfolding her arms. "Fair enough. I don't suppose you have any wine to go with that bread and cheese? I'm parched." It was after sunset, why not?

His smile grew warmer. "I'm sure we can find something." He edged around the table and tucked her arm into his. "Will wine suit you or do future women drink something stronger?"

Abby chuckled. "Let's just start with the wine. You're not getting me into your bed by getting me plastered."

They sauntered down a hallway, the lemon walls glimpsed in the lamplight. Abby wondered who had lit all the candles. She spoke her concern aloud.

"I did, while you were sleeping."

He guided her through another door and into a grand drawing room. He released her to cross to the far wall, heading for a decanter glinting with a dark red liquid. He didn't seem to notice her awe.

"This is beautiful," she breathed, drinking in the rich fabrics and delicate furnishings, all in wealth of red and gold. "I wonder what happened to all of this stuff."

Myles paused in mid-pour. "It doesn't stay in the house?"

Abby pressed her lips into an apologetic smile. "I'm sorry. I didn't think. The idea that so much changes can't be pleasant."

He finished filling her glass and handed it to her. "It's not, but I am curious. Do you know what happened?"

"I expect it was the—" she broke off, biting her lip. "No, I can't tell you. Sorry. I've read enough time travel books to know that some things just can't be shared."

His shrug was almost too casual. "Time travel is common in the future then?"

She laughed. "No, it's fiction." She swirled her wine, watching the amber color dribble down the glass sides. She sipped her wine. "Hmm, this is good."

"Truthfully?"

"Yes, the wine is very good."

"That is not what I meant."

Gulping down her wine, she drew away from him, settling on the edge of an ornate brocade and gilt sofa. "Myles, I don't know how I got here. I don't know how I'm going to get back." She took another gulp of wine.

"Please, do not worry about it. I'm sure we'll find some solution." He sat next to her and patted her jean-clad thigh.

She glanced sidelong. He was even handsomer in profile, drinking his glass of wine. His nose hooked a little, giving it an interesting-looking bump. His lips . . .

The rim of his crystal glass concealed his lips, but she remembered them, and she liked how they'd felt against her own.

She recovered her senses. "Very kind of you, but we need to look at the worst-case scenario. What will happen to me if I'm stuck here?"

He reclined against the sofa back, smirking across at her. "I might be able to think of a few things . . ."

She rolled her eyes. "Oh, you're incorrigible." She toyed with her half-empty glass. She'd thought of a few things as well. Whatever happened to wanting balance in her life? She felt unhinged.

"So I've been told." His heated gaze warmed her.

"And it works for you?"

His grin grew wider. "Absolutely."

2

"I may be the first to so disappoint you." Abby set down her glass and rose. "It's getting late and it's been a trying day. I'm going to bed."

"Ah, yes, about that." Myles Hardy didn't seem inclined to move.

Abby frowned down at him and waited him out.

"There's only one bedroom made ready. The one I sleep in and the one you napped in." An uncertain smile hovered about his lips.

"So?" Abby shrugged. "You sleep on the sofa or I do. I don't care which."

Myles rose, gathering her loosely in his arms. "There's room enough for two," he murmured, bending his head toward hers.

She held him off, even though her chest tightened with anticipation. "I should refuse you. I don't know you. I don't know if you are even clean."

His eyebrow quirked.

"That's not what I meant, but you do need to bathe more often. I meant disease."

"Not got the pox or syphilis, never had." His hand captured her chin. "Satisfied?"

He thought it that simple? "I don't just fall into bed with anybody . . ." Why was she even considering him?

"Have you ever thought that you came back in time just for me?" he cooed.

Abby blinked. "You're a virgin?"

Myles choked. Triumph soared in her breast at scoring a hit. "No," he got out. "But there's never been that special person . . ."

She caressed his cheek, feeling the day's stubble tickle her palm. "Myles Hardy," she breathed, "you are a charmer of the worst sort."

"Thank you, Ms. Deane." His mouth quirked. "Perhaps it would be better if I spoke plainly."

"I haven't run screaming from the room yet," Abby reminded him. She didn't like his line, but he was one handsome devil. Bad for her in every way, except maybe one.

"The truth is I want you. I've wanted you since your insolence to me in the hallway. I've never met anyone with such fire and life. When I watched you sleep, I saw those curves you keep hidden under that male attire. I wanted to touch them, burned to touch them, in fact . . . I want you plain and simple. Plus," he added, "you possess some very interesting items. I'd like to see how they work. I'd like to try them on you."

Abby's insides turned liquid. His words filled her mind with images of Myles teasing her with one vibrator, then a dildo, and then . . . She shivered. That's not why she'd bought them. "I don't think that's a good idea."

His knowing smile let her know she'd lost this round. He dipped and brushed her lips. "There's no telling when you'll be whisked back to your own time. Why not make your stay enjoyable?"

No commitment in other words. But his words gave her pause. "And if there's no return trip?"

He sucked in his breath. His wide eyes crinkled into charm. "You have my solemn promise that I'll take care of you. You look capable. You might be a great help in my work."

"You'd employ me?"

"Of a sort." He sighed, stroking her lower back. "It wouldn't be fair to cast you out into a world you have only read about in books. I'll help you, and when you're ready, you can leave or stay, your choice."

Abby took a shuddering breath. "You'll . . . you'll do that?"

"Ms. Deane, at some point you're going to have to trust me. I am a gentleman and I do not go back on my word."

She'd heard something about honor back in the day. "I don't have a whole lot of choice, do I?"

"I'll give you as many choices as you need." His brown eyes sparkled. "Such as, which of your modern tools do I get to play with first?"

Abby laughed. His carefree attitude dispelled her fears like magic, but in the midst of this impossibility a part of her remained aware of the consequences. She'd always coped being left behind before, she'd be able to do it again. She hoped.

She managed a smile, watching Myles's expression softening. "Shall we start with the basics? My dildo?"

"I admit to having experience of this item." He kissed her forehead.

Abby smirked. "Should I ask in what way?"

Myles choked. "You have a wicked mind, Ms. Deane."

She grinned back at him. "You have no idea."

"After seeing those items, I am not surprised." He drew nearer and kissed her. It was no gentle kiss, but a scorching merging of mouth against mouth. His desire infected her, washing through her senses, drowning any remnant of uncertainty. Her decision made, Abby gave back as good as she got, twining her arms around his neck and drawing him closer.

Their bodies slid together. Abby rubbed herself against his

hard body. He was all her erotic dreams come to life . . . Maybe she *was* dreaming . . .

Myles's teeth grazed her lower lip, sucking it into his mouth before releasing it. "We're never going to make it to the bed at this rate."

"Conventional fellow, aren't you?" Abby teased, tweaking his rather large nose. The sudden image of his nose rubbing against her clit stole her breath. A soft moan escaped her lips.

"Need I remind you of what else is upstairs?" he crooned, stroking her cheek. "Something other than the dildo?"

"How about a vibrator?" Did she just say that?

"Mmm. Whatever that is, it sounds perfect."

Perfect. The word rang throughout her brain while they headed upstairs to a room that was suddenly *their* room.

This wasn't what she had planned at all. Some of the sputtering candles had given out, plunging parts of their path into impenetrable darkness.

She stumbled and his arms tightened about her, his mouth hot on her neck. She stilled in his grasp, her focus crashing to only his hands and mouth.

How could it be perfect? He was a man. Did she need to say any more?

Myles kicked the bedroom door shut. "Open your wretched trunk," he growled in her ear, guiding her toward her pile of luggage.

She sank to her knees. Her hands trembling, she unzipped her suitcase. How could she let herself open up to this practical stranger?

Uncovering her collection of sex toys, she retrieved her vibrator of choice, a sleek pearlescent tube curved at one end. Was she really going to go through with this and submit to the charms of this man?

Abby turned, shuffling on her knees, to tell him she'd changed her mind.

Myles reclined on the bed, butt-naked. She'd been so lost in her own fearful thoughts, she hadn't heard him undress. She gummed her lower lip. What magnificence!

Those structured genteel clothes concealed masculine perfection. A flat washboard stomach, muscled thighs below a semierect cock that stiffened further when her gaze fell upon it.

In short, he was built. None of her past lovers came close to this gorgeousness. It was shallow to consider only the physical, but, umm, it was a big consideration.

Not small by any means.

"Umm, you didn't waste any time." To hell with her doubts about a man's trustworthiness. She'd have to surrender her sisterhood card if she turned down this hunky specimen.

She waggled her vibrator. "I'm not sure I need this."

He smirked. "Show me how it works."

Abby sat on the edge of the bed and thumbed the dial on the bottom of the vibrator. A low whirring sound filled the air.

"What is that?" he whispered.

"Shhh," she hushed him. If she were to do this, she'd go all the way and be her assertive self. If he didn't like it, too bad.

She held it above him and then lowered it to his thigh, letting him feel its vibrations. He twitched but remained still. "Part your legs," she murmured.

"I'm not used to taking orders."

"You and me both." She smiled. She'd dealt with macho men before. She relished the challenge. "Trust me."

He gritted his teeth, closed his eyes, and moved his knees apart.

"Myles, there's no need to think of England." She trailed the vibrator farther up his thigh. Trust a man to deny his true feelings. The vibrator would coax the truth out of him, at least for now.

"I'm not," he ground out, every line of his body rigid. "I'm trying to maintain scientific objectivity."

Abby choked back her laughter. The vibrator tip slid along his inside thigh until it brushed his balls.

Myles let the air out in a whoosh, his cock jerking in eager response. "Sweet mercy!"

"You like it?" she cooed, letting the vibrator tip rest fully against his balls.

"Mmm."

She only needed to take one glance at his cock to see it hard and raging red. She teased the vibrator across his balls, varying the pressure.

"Oh God," he groaned. "If you don't stop I'm going to burst."

She spared him, switching off the vibrator. "That didn't take you long."

"It's been awhile," he admitted. "A whole two days since I've, ahem, taken matters in my own hands."

She rolled her eyes, smirking.

Myles sat up and took the vibrator from her. "How does it work?"

"You just turn this," Abby demonstrated. "The more you turn, the more intense."

He wiggled the dial back and forth, the sound changing as he turned it up. He turned it off and set it aside. "Do you know, Abigail, that you are a dreadful tease." Myles leaned in, capturing her in his arms.

His bare chest pressed against hers, and even through her layers of clothing, his heat reached her. She skimmed over his muscled biceps, amazed at how built he was. She'd attracted her share of geeks in her time, but this geek?

Like no other.

Abby canted her lips toward his. How could she resist?

He accepted her blatant invitation and covered her mouth with his. His kiss burned, and if she thought she'd turned molten at the sight of his rising cock, she'd been sadly mistaken. Her senses dissolved in flames at his kiss.

She wanted this impossible, impossible man. Wanted him with a burning need that scared her. Myles was a stranger; maybe that was why it was so easy to give into this fantasy. Maybe she crashed her plane and she dreamed the whole thing.

His hand slid beneath the cotton fabric of her T-shirt. He palmed a breast over her bra, and a fresh heat surged through her. She dragged her teeth across his plump lower lip.

Myles moaned. He returned the favor, flicking his tongue over her upper lip.

Abby let go long enough to shrug out of her leather jacket, melting in their shared heat. She wriggled out of her T-shirt, wanting flesh on flesh.

His hand slid around to her lower back, finding bare skin. He broke the heady kiss, leaning back to survey her. "No stays?"

"Bra." Abby guided his hand up to the clasp. His fingertips smoothed over it, examining it by touch, tweaking at it.

Abby sighed, impatient. "Here." She reached behind her, arching her breasts into him, and flicked the hooks free. The bra soared to land on a piece of luggage.

His hand slid down the curves of her back and she shivered. His mouth possessed hers again, the pressure of it bearing her down onto the mattress.

She lay beneath him, his weight upon her, their lower limbs tangled. He moved against her, his groin grinding against her still-clothed one. She moaned, matching his each thrust. Oh God, she wanted him, wanted him with an urge she hadn't felt since she lost her virginity.

Myles made a space between them. He unfastened the button on her jeans and unzipped them like he'd been doing it all his life. Between them, she wriggled out of them, pulling off her sneakers in the process.

"It'd be much easier if you didn't dress so mannishly," he grumbled.

"Even with a corset?" Abby laughed and drew him onto her again. Her hands roamed his body, unable to find a single square inch not devoted to fine, corded muscle.

They moved together. His cock slid along her wet slit, teasing her swelling clit with its blunt head. So good, so intimate. He reminded her how good it felt, being with a man. She writhed against him, arching her hips, wanting his cock inside her, wanting the feel of that first pressure against her aching hole.

He groaned into her mouth. His parted lips slid from hers and down her arched throat. He nibbled at her tender skin, one roaming hand palming her breast, her nipple pushing hard against him. He tweaked that nipple, rolling to one side.

"You're so beautiful," he murmured, nuzzling the sensitive, soft skin. "I want to see you. I want to see all of you."

Addled by desire, Abby arched her back. She *was* on display. What was he talking about?

He reached behind him and retrieved the vibrator. A soft hum filled the air. "Show me," he whispered. "Show me everything."

Trailing the vibrator across the top of her breasts, Myles circled one nipple, drawing the tip ever closer to the puckered nub.

Her breasts swelled, heated. Her nipples enlarged and reddened. The slightest brush with the vibrator made her gasp.

An aching awareness edged her skin. She lay back and let him play with her, play with the vibrator. Her body responded in the way it always had, coming along under the oscillating tip, but an added excitement built.

Touching herself with a vibrator wasn't anything like having somebody else in control of the sex toy. She shuddered at each touch, releasing soft moans. When she was alone again, assuming the batteries hadn't gone dead by then, she'd remember this moment, this night and relive it when touching herself.

Myles nudged the vibrator down the valley between her breasts. Abby cupped them, bringing them together, massaging the vibrator as if it were his cock.

The thought leaped into her mind. *Not nearly big enough.* She smirked, gasping as the vibrator slid down her belly. It nudged her pubic curls.

"Now I know how to wipe the smile off your face," he purred, his dark eyes boring into her.

She huffed, rolling her nipples between her fingers. "That's not the only way. Being incredibly annoying also works."

"Now, now," he cooed. "Remember who has your modern toy." He trailed the vibrator down her thigh, away from her melting core.

Abby parted her legs further, giving him a full view of her wet, pink cunt. Her cunt lips pulsed in need. "Myles, please . . ."

"Very well, Abigail." He took her hand and put the vibrator in it. "Show me. Show me how this pleases you."

Her eyebrows rose. "I'm sure you know."

He grinned down at her. "Let's just say I have a very good idea . . . but I want to watch."

"All right." Abby broke from his embrace and piled the cushions behind her. Myles moved down to the opposite end of the bed, making himself comfortable with the piled-up comforter.

Abby parted her legs wide, running her fingers along the outside of her slit. She combed away the damp curls, revealing the pink almond shape of her cunt. Myles sucked in his breath. Abby smiled, enjoying his reaction. It gave her a sense of power, of being in control, even though she most definitely was not.

She lay the vibrator along the length of her wet slit, moving it up and down in a slow motion. Her wet coated the vibrator.

Turning the curved end inward, she flicked the dial up a notch and sighed at the increase of rubbing against her opening.

But not there yet. Not yet.

Abby slid it up to her clit, brushing it with the lightest of touches. Back and forth, up and down, she guided the vibrator around her engorged clit, lifting it off when the pleasure threatened to grow too great.

Myles watched, his lips parted. Abby saw the wonder and desire on his face. A deeper answering warmth formed inside her.

She dipped the vibrator down into her hole and in deeper, twisting to find that sensitive spot inside that drove her crazy.

She found it and forgot all about her audience. She moaned, arching her back, teasing her G-spot until she drew near climax. Her moans grew louder and louder and—

Myles's large hand clamped down over hers. He drew the vibrator out of her and turned it off. She heard it clatter on the floorboards. "Not without me, sweet Abigail . . ."

He crawled over her.

She stared up at him, breathless. "Abby. Call me Abby."

"Abby." He groaned the name. "Sweet Abby."

He slid into her, smooth as silk.

Feeling him fill her and stretch her, she moaned. "Oh God, Myles." He felt huge, he felt heavenly. Every inch of that gorgeous cock slid inside her.

He held her, his cock buried deep inside. Abby stared up at him and caught her breath. His gaze was so intent, so wide-eyed.

"Oh," she breathed.

"Oh," he returned, with a whisper of a smile.

He moved within her, withdrawing and drawing in again. Each surge rendered her breathless. She clawed at his back, striving for the release she'd almost achieved solo.

Her cunt clutched his cock, squeezing around him as he

pounded in and out of her. None of the initial gentleness from the beginning remained. He too strove for release.

The bed shook, the headboard bumping against the plaster wall. His cries rose to match her keening ones. For Abby, nothing existed but him above her, him in her, and the sweet fiery elixir exploding through her body.

She hung on, the climax washing through her, blinding her to all else but the weight of her lover and the slick friction within.

Abby expected him to finish, but he continued to power into her, long steady strokes that filled her and kept arousing her to new heights.

Panting, she clutched him, her climax spiraling higher. She came, screaming a wordless cry. He stilled above her, riding out her orgasm.

He surged into her and she let out a disbelieving yelp. She blinked, staring up into his face, a face lost in wonder. His gaze focused and she held it as a third climax surged through her.

Myles's cock slid from her and her breath rushed in, almost sparking another release. Grunting, Myles took his massive cock in hand and pumped it, the dark head playing peekaboo with the uncircumcised skin until he groaned and his white come spurted over her belly.

She watched, taking shuddering breaths through her open mouth. She'd never had a first time with a man like this before. It seemed too perfect.

He sank to her side, taking in deep, shuddering breaths. "My apologies, I do not have any cundums to hand."

"Condoms?" Abby hazarded a guess, her limbs filled with languid ease. "I appreciate your concern but I take care of my own birth control."

His brow crinkled. "How?"

"The pill, a medicine," she clarified. "Although I only have a couple of months supply left." She winced. Would they still be together in a couple of months? The puddle of his semen on her belly started to harden. "I need to clean up."

"There's a washbowl over there." Myles waved toward the window.

Abby washed up. She stepped away from the washbowl to find Myles waiting his turn. She let him clean, straightening the rumpled bed.

After blowing out the candles, he climbed in beside her. "I must confess this awkward," he murmured, extending an arm to rest her head on his shoulder.

She accepted the invitation. "You're a love 'em and leave 'em kind of guy?"

"Ahh . . . Not exactly. It's just that the women I usually bed—"

"—Expect you to leave something on the bedside table." Abby wondered if he included her in that number, or if this was payment for his protection.

"Er, um, yes." The heat of his embarrassment warmed her cheek.

"I'm a working girl, but not that kind of working girl."

"Life must be quite different in the future."

Abby sighed. "You have no idea."

Abby woke. She rolled over and reached out for Myles's warm body, finding only cool sheets. She blinked awake. Had the whole thing been a dream? A quick glance revealed no light switch by the door.

Damn.

She rose, checking her luggage to find it exactly where she left it.

Except for her manor blueprints.

She frowned. Why had Myles taken them?

Dressing in fresh shirt and trousers, Abby wished for a bath. She seemed to remember baths were avoided in this time.

Damn.

She went downstairs and managed to find the kitchen by herself. The smell of frying eggs and bacon greeted her. "Yum," she said, perching on a stool at the broad kitchen table. "You cook too?"

Myles turned from the massive fireplace. Abby tried not to think about the beautiful Aga stove that should be standing there. "It's basic campfire cooking."

He dished up the hot breakfast beside freshly sliced bread. They ate in companionable silence. After satiating her hunger, Abby put down her fork. "Why did you take my blueprints?"

Myles chewed on his last bite of ham and took his time in swallowing. "I thought there might be something bothering you."

"You didn't answer my question." Abby folded her arms.

"I wanted to look at them." He gestured to the door behind her. Abby looked over her shoulder and saw the tube was still sealed and leaning against the lintel. "If you clear the table, I'll spread them out here. The light is good."

Abby didn't move. "Why do you want to look at them?"

"I'm merely curious about the evolution of this house."

"Maybe—" After last night, she ought to believe him, but . . . Abby rose. "Maybe if you let me look at your scientific papers, I'll let you look at the blueprints. Just don't take anything of mine without asking again, OK?"

"OK?" Myles sounded out the letters. "I won't remove anything belonging to you."

"And the papers?"

"What is your interest in them?"

She shrugged. Her interest stemmed from his evasiveness about them. "It's history. Old science."

He sniffed. "I don't think I'll allow you to look at my papers if you're making fun of me."

Abby raised her brows. "Then you don't see the blueprints."

"I'm stronger than you." He folded his arms, flexing his biceps.

"I'd like to see you try," she retorted, stung.

Myles cast a longing gaze at the blueprints cylinder. "Very well, the truth. There are no scientific papers here."

"You are not a scientist?"

He took a deep breath and slowly exhaled. "This is not my house."

It took her a moment to process the words. She started. "You're a burglar?" How strange that neither of them belonged here.

"No," he snapped. His tone softened. "No. This house used to be in my family about two hundred years ago. Then the Civil War happened, and my family were, *are,* royalists. Even after the monarchy was restored, we never got our house back."

"So where are its occupants?" Abby buried her disquiet about sleeping with a man she didn't really know. Too many assumptions led to trouble. Especially with a man who lied so easily.

"London."

She forced a casual air. "Do they know you're here?"

Myles shook his head. "They pay everyone off and lock the house up with just a caretaker."

Abby rested her hip against the table, regarding him. "It's a nice story, Mr. Hardy, but why are you really here?"

"This house has something I need, something that rightfully belongs to my family." Controlled passion filled his voice. "And I intend on getting it back."

"You sound pretty passionate about that." She tested him. "What are you looking for?"

"You sound rather relaxed regarding the matter. Why aren't you hysterical?"

"I don't get hysterical," she snapped. He'd avoided answering her questions again. "But I'll get mad if you don't start talking."

"Such an unusual way of speaking." He smirked. "So uncouth."

She glowered at him. "How long have you been looking for this object?"

"About a week." He seemed comfortable in answering that question at least.

"And doesn't your family legend tell you where the thing is hidden?"

"Hid," Myles absently corrected. "There are clues . . . but it's an oral legend passed down over time, never written down." He sighed. "My grandmother taught it to me. The only problem is, age has unhinged her, and I only met her for the first time a month ago. She spoke nothing but gobbledegook."

"That's rough," Abby observed, unsympathetic, "and you think there might be a clue in the blueprints, like the location of a priest hole for example?"

Myles's brown eyes lit up. "That's exactly the kind of thing I'm looking for. You know where it is?"

"Sure," Abby cooed with a false sweetness. "Which one?"

He gaped and Abby laughed.

3

"There is more than one?" Myles's deep voice rose a couple of notches. His boyish excitement shone through his sparkling eyes. "Will you show them to me?"

Abby's lips twitched while she tried to assume a stern expression. "On the blueprints?" she pursed her lips. "If you hadn't stolen them . . ."

"Not stolen, borrowed." His sweet boyish smile turned a little desperate. "Abby, please. Did last night mean nothing?"

That washed the humor away in a flash. "You seduced me to get at the blueprints?" she squawked.

Myles ran a hand through his loose brown hair. "I didn't need to seduce you to gain access to those plans. All I needed to do was wait for you to fall asleep. Which you've done twice so far."

Abby folded her arms. "I don't believe you."

"Honestly, I didn't really think of it until this morning." His suntanned skin flushed, showing red at the vee of his open-necked shirt. Under her dark-eyed glare, his eyebrow quirked and he kept his boyish smile. "Maybe a little bit." He shrugged, his eyes dancing. "It's the way I am. I see an opportunity, like this empty house . . . It is an instinct."

He came around the side of the kitchen table. "But Abby—"

"Don't call me that," she snapped. He expected her to believe that rubbish?

"Abby," he persisted, his voice going down into a delicious burr that made her knees weak. "Abby, if I did not desire you, if I were not intrigued by you, bedding you would never have crossed my mind."

"I'm not sure whether I should be flattered or insulted for the rest of my sex." Abby didn't back down. "You can't come waltzing along and expect to get everything your way." She stormed toward the door and snatched up the tube by the strap. "It doesn't work that way."

Myles yelled after her. "Does that include not helping you in the year 1807?"

Damn. Abby paused just a few steps outside the doorway. Slowly, she pivoted.

"You need me. I need you. I swear I didn't seduce you, Abby. I thought we made a mutual decision last night to share the same bed."

Abby let the tension escape with a long sigh. He was right. She'd wanted it as much as he did. A gorgeous, sinfully sensual man like Myles Hardy? What woman in her right mind would refuse him?

"You're right." She walked up to him, the tube still slung over her shoulder. She caressed his cheek, feeling the warmth from their bodies collide. His heated gaze, wariness warring with hope, met hers. "If I ever find out I'm right," she breathed, "you're a dead man."

His eyes flashed with humor. "Duly noted," he replied, straightfaced.

Abby stepped to one side, flipping open the tube's cap. Myles hastily cleared the plates, giving her room to spread out the blueprints. "There you go."

He bent over the blue-inked drawings, his fingertips gliding above the paper's surface. She watched him puzzle it out, propping her hip against the table's edge.

He flipped one sheet over and then another. "Is this one?" he said finally.

Abby leaned over to take a look. "Yup."

Myles grinned up at her. "Shall we take a look?"

She shrugged. "Sure. I don't have anything else to do."

Casting a long look over her figure, he replied, "We do need to find you something decent to wear."

"What's wrong with this?" Abby knew the answer while she pretended to look shocked. Skirts. Long, obnoxious, *hobbling* skirts. "I don't sew," she warned him, not waiting for him to answer what he must've thought was a rhetorical question.

"We'll find something later," he declared with confidence. He tucked his arm under hers. "Now, if I understood the plans correctly, this is near the old chapel?"

"In the corridor," she affirmed.

He bounded away, stopping in the doorway. "Will you come?"

His infectious enthusiasm made Abby grin back. "I thought we might do that later." She winked.

Myles wagged his finger at her. "Naughty girl."

Nobody had ever called her *that* before. She ought to be offended. She ought to put this politically incorrect man in his place. She ought to—

He disappeared down the corridor. Abby followed.

In the hallway outside the chapel, Myles stared at the wood-paneled wall, the wood darkened with age. "This chapel doesn't look like it gets much use."

Myles didn't look at her while he spoke, his hands running over the paneling. Abby watched him search for the catch that would reveal the hidden priest hole.

"It has to be hard to find," Myles muttered, more to himself than her. "The Protestants turned a household upside down if they had the slightest suspicion that a Catholic priest hid there. So the catch won't be easy to find."

He reached high above and down where the mopboard ran along the black-and-white marble-tiled floor.

He took a step back and glared at the wall. "It's here somewhere."

Abby agreed. "We turned it into a small closet for the Chapel Bedroom."

He directed his glare over his shoulder at her. "You knew all along?"

She grinned at him. "I like to see a man at work."

Grunting, he brushed past her and into the small chapel. Abby followed. She saw by marks in the layers of dust that Myles had searched in here before, particularly around the altar area. She settled into a pew, resting her arm on the back of it and her chin on top of her elbow.

"This is the common wall," Myles said, surveying it. In here, stonework replaced the wood paneling. Frowning, he approached it, running his fingers across it. He tapped a stone block.

"Hollow," he declared. "This isn't stonework, it's wood made to look like it. They even added grit to make it look real." He glanced over his shoulder at her. "I suppose you know where it is?"

She raised her arms in defeat. "I've only seen a photo. I can tell you where it is in location to the bed, but the chapel seems to be lacking that at the moment."

Myles's lips twitched. "Indeed." He turned back to survey the wall. "I guess it's up to me."

He knelt on the floor, examining the floorboards, tracing a

line from the floor to the false wainscoting. At the very bottom, where the mopboard would run, Myles pressed against a small stone.

The waist-high secret door swung wide, revealing a dark hollow. Ducking, Myles stepped in and looked back. "Coming?"

Intrigued, Abby followed him. "Have you found your object?" She peered over his shoulder into the small space.

"It's not out in full view. It wouldn't be, else the Catholic priests holed up in here would've found it and destroyed it."

"What if they got bored waiting for the Roundheads to leave?" Abby stepped into the small space, using the little available light to peruse the rough brick walls. "A few of these bricks are loose." She glanced over her shoulder at him, startled to find him so close.

He smiled down at her, an easy, lazy smile that speeded her pulse. She stared up at him, mesmerized by his sheer masculinity. No man had ever had that effect on her. She almost forgot to breathe.

"We can look," he breathed, not unaffected. "A priest may do nothing but pray in silence until the family released him. Moving the bricks? The noise might bring his death."

Abby faced away, reaching out to the bricks. The red clay crumbled against her fingers. Despite the almost nonexistent mortar, the first brick she tried refused to budge.

"Let a man take care of it." Myles attempted to move her aside but she stood her ground, bracing against both him and the walls.

"You are incredibly sexist." Abby tried another brick.

"Men are stronger than women." He softened his words with a smile, but it didn't conceal his matter-of-factness.

"Not all men, and not all women." She made a face at him.

Myles leaned in, his head bending down to hers. "But this man, and this woman."

She had to own the truth of that. Her lips parted, drawing

breath to speak, and his mouth came down upon them. Despite his claims of greater strength, he gentled his kiss, caressing her mouth with a delicious, tender warmth.

Her back pressed against the ancient brick, the corners digging into her. Her fingers curled into his shirt, gripping hard. She opened her mouth to him, letting him delve inside. The taste of him, the scent of him, the touch of him, sent her head spinning.

He moaned into her mouth, pulling her from the brick and onto him. Through their clothing, his hard cock rubbed against her belly. She wrapped her legs around his waist, opening herself to him.

Myles broke off the kiss, pressing his mouth against her neck. His breathing sounded loud and rough in the enclosed space. "If you weren't wearing those damned strange breeches . . ."

Abby choked off a laugh. "We're not here for—for this." No matter how much she wanted it. She unhooked her legs from his waist and slid down his body. "Don't we have some precious artifact to find?"

"It can wait," Myles growled. "It's too dark to see in here anyway." She sensed more than saw his wolfish grin. "Might as well enjoy it."

She clasped her hands behind his neck. She had all the time in the world. No deadlines to meet. She needed only to find her way in the world. With or without the gorgeous hunk of flesh in her arms.

Right now it was with. And Abby didn't mind that at all. "Might as well," she purred, drawing his head down to hers. She kissed him hungrily, grinding against his engorged, trapped cock.

Myles moaned, pushing her against the brick wall, humping her and rubbing his cock through their clothing. She sobbed, hanging on, surging against him, every sense and nerve ending alive.

Her breath came in gasps. The sounds of their striving echoed faintly from above. She paid no heed, tearing at his shirt, wanting flesh against flesh. His shirt ripped, and frantically, she tore at it until the waistband of his breeches prevented her from going any further.

"You are wild," he murmured. His mouth slid along her neck.

"Can you keep up?" she teased, squeezing her legs tighter around his waist.

"Just watch me," he murmured, his voice low and sexy as hell.

"We need," she said, pulling away from his hot mouth, "to get naked."

"Are all modern women this frank?" he asked, letting her slide from him and unfastening his breeches.

"No." She shimmied out of her trousers and panties, kicking them free of her feet. "I guess you just got lucky."

His chuckle made her want to cream. "That I did."

He was on her, ripping her blouse open, the tiny plastic buttons pinging off the brick walls. He got his hands under her butt and hoisted her. Abby sucked in air. He made her feel so weightless. His cock slid along her wet slit, slotting against her and then in her.

Abby groaned, her sharp intake of breath echoing in the small confined space. She wanted more of him and got it, her weight bearing her down, down upon his eager cock pounding up to meet her.

Her back grazed over the cold bricks. She didn't care. Sex this wild came from beyond her deepest fantasies. His heated body against hers grounded her, made everything real. This wasn't a fantasy, and she reveled in it, tangling her hands in his hair.

Myles pressed her back against the wall, bowing his body to

nuzzle at her breasts, using the space between them to jerk his cock into her again and again.

She grabbed the sides of his face and drew him toward her, capturing his mouth with her own hungry one. "Fuck me," she whispered between kisses. "Fuck me hard."

He stiffened against her with a sharp intake of breath, but her writhings soon overcame his surprise. He held her against the brick wall, powering into her in short, sharp thrusts.

"Oh, oh God," she moaned, clawing the back of his shirt. She hovered on the brink of coming, his each thrust bringing her closer.

She clamped down around him, her climax slamming through her, making her scream. Abby held on, lost in sensation, dimly aware Myles still fucked her.

He groaned, deep inside her still-convulsing cunt. He sagged against her, still holding her against him.

Abby drooped in his arms. She didn't think she'd be able to stand if Myles let her go. She listened to their combined breathing, echoing down from above.

She stirred, and Myles let her slip from his arms and from his cock.

"Myles?"

His sweaty forehead didn't stir from where it rested on the top of her head. "Hmm?"

"You know . . ." she mused, "I have a flashlight in the plane."

"Flashlight?"

"A torch, without flame."

He tried to pin her with a look but she ducked her head. "You are the most unusual woman. You think of the most practical things after a seduction."

Abby chuckled. "Our breathing seems to travel a long way up. Maybe the crumbling bricks aren't hiding places but footholds."

Myles pulled away, bringing a little more light into the room as he craned his neck to look upward. "Possible. You wouldn't want a priest finding it after all."

"Why not?"

"It's pagan."

Abby laughed at his constricted voice. "Kind of funny that it's hidden in the same place as the priests. Your ancestors must have a twisted sense of humor."

"It still runs in the family, or so I'm told." He stepped out into the chapel proper, buttoning up his breeches. His torn shirt hung off his shoulders, baring most of his chest to view.

Hating to stop looking, Abby bent over and pulled on her trousers, feeling their combined come wet her panties. Straightening, she pulled her hair back into a ponytail, but lacking a hair band it fell loose about her face. It was too short to tie back anyway.

"Will you help me hide it?" she asked, stepping past him.

"Help you hide what?" he followed, brushing down her shoulders and back. "Brick dust," he explained at her curious, sharp look.

She nodded. "If any of the locals find the plane—well, I don't know what they'll think it is, but flying doesn't get invented for another hundred years."

"You flew?" Myles circled her. "You don't have wings."

"In a *machine*," Abby corrected him. "Look, are you going to help or not?"

"As your 'plane' holds some wondrous tool that will help me find the, ahh, object, I have no objections to rendering you any assistance you may need."

"So kind of you," Abby replied with drawling sarcasm. "It's not far. We can walk."

Myles watched Abby's bottom, its outlines clear against the tight confines of her trousers. Bent double, she disappeared into the plane, leaving him to wonder at the marvel that had brought her here.

A *plane*, she called it. He had a hard time believing it flew. Nothing resembled wings, everything being hard and inflexible.

He sighed. 'Ms.' Deane may as well have come from another world, let alone another time. Authority rested on her shoulders, and even this setback—and he saw in her eyes that she counted landing in 1807 as such—seemed nothing but a wrinkle in her capability.

No shrinking violet, this one, and a veritable wanton in bed. His cock stirred, and he banished the image of her sprawled on the bed. He grabbed a pitchfork and tossed the first forkful of hay across the plane's shiny body.

Ms. Deane had angled the plane into the haystack, but half the plane still laid bare, with one wing sticking out. Had any of the local villagers or farmers seen it? He kept shoveling. Had Abby not told him, he wasn't sure what he'd think of it. Some kind of experimental locomotive?

The loose flaps of his shirt got in the way and he pulled it off over his head, wiping the sweat off his forehead before tossing it onto the ground. He kept working until all but the outermost edge of what Abby called the wing had been draped in hay.

Abby threw out the last of the cases from the plane and jumped to the ground. She reached up and swung shut the door. "There," she said, dusting off her hands, "it's locked up tight in case anybody . . ."

Abby turned to face him. He leaned on his pitchfork stuck into the earth and regarded her astonished gape.

She licked her lips. "You, ahh, took your shirt off."

He shrugged, knowing his muscles rippled. "Somehow it was ripped."

He enjoyed watching her blush. She might look harder than nails, but she wasn't immune to a man's charms. Indeed, she seemed a mite starved of them.

Abby straightened her jacket. "Covering it with hay isn't going to work."

Myles regarded his handiwork and had to agree. "The farmer isn't going to be happy we ruined one of his stacks."

She gnawed at her lip. Her plane mustn't be discovered. "Is there a barn or outbuilding back at the house we can wheel this to?"

"Wheel it?" Myles regarded the hay-covered plane with misgiving.

"It's a light plane. A cart horse should be able to pull it with little trouble."

"You might have more trouble with the country lanes. Besides, the house isn't mine, remember? What if somebody finds it?"

Her shoulders sagged. "Maybe I'll go back before then."

She sounded pessimistic. Glimpsing her vulnerability drew Myles to her. He slung a companionable arm around her shoulders. "Maybe. I will help wherever I can."

She faced him, patting his sweaty chest awkwardly. "Thank you." She took a deep breath and straightened her shoulders, looking up at him. "Shall we go find your prize?"

He glanced meaningfully at the remains of the haystack. "Are you sure you would not wish to lie with me first?"

"Myles Hardy, you are insatiable." She grinned at him but shook her head, pulling a strand of straw from his hair. "My skin's far too sensitive for a tumble in this stuff." She threw it away.

Myles pulled her into his arms. "You didn't object to brickwork."

She drew his head down to hers. "That was different," she whispered, a breath away from sealing his mouth with a kiss. "I don't know what it is about you, Myles Hardy, but you make it impossible for a girl to think straight."

He threaded a lock of her hair off her upturned face, smiling down at her. She was so deliciously fresh. "And you are quite unlike any woman I have ever known."

Her lips twisted. "I'll bet." She pulled away from him, bending to pick up one of her leather bags. She slung it over her shoulder. "Let's go find this thing."

She strode off in the direction of the house. Myles picked up the other bag and followed, shaking his head at the odd little pang inside of not having this wild girl as his for much longer.

Back at the chapel, Abby pulled out the flashlight and handed it to him. "You turn it on by twisting the bottom."

She watched him eye the flashlight curiously. "Are you sure this isn't one of your toys? Seems it's made in the right shape."

Abby choked. "Don't you think of anything else?"

He twisted the base and backed away from the light beaming into his eyes.

"Face it away from you," she advised, trying not to laugh.

The beam skittered across the chapel walls. Myles shook his head free of the dancing light motes in his vision. Stepping into the priest hole, he directed the light beam upward. He scanned the dark space above.

Abby joined him, peering up. "Well?"

"There isn't much in the way of a foothold. Might be they used a ladder, but I don't see any place where they'd stash it." He handed her the flashlight and tried to haul himself up.

The brick crumbled and he fell back against her. Abby steadied him, the brick wall digging into her back. "Do you know where the ladder is?"

Myles shrugged, still looking up. "No. You are lighter. Maybe you could climb, or if I could lift you." He grinned at her. "Have you ever been an acrobat?"

Abby shook her head, fending him off. "Not even in junior gymnastics."

"I won't let you fall." His smile had the power to soften her resolve.

She eyed him uneasily. "The bricks won't let me either, and they're harder." He gave her a pleading look. She sighed, giving in. "But don't say I didn't warn you."

Abby held out her hand for the flashlight. It found its way into her palm. As it was still on, she directed the beam toward the priest hole's ceiling.

The flashlight's range stopped before the ceiling became visible. She saw how the walls narrowed into an apex. "I won't have to go far," she said, more to herself than to Myles.

"If you brace yourself on the brick wall," he suggested, "I'll support you."

"Yes." Abby got out her leather gloves from her back pocket and put them on. They'd protect her hands from the worst of it, even if they were not made for heavy labor like this. "Give me a boost."

She found a foothold at knee height and wedged her shoe in. Grabbing the bricks, she hauled herself up, Myles's large hands giving her an extra push. Scrabbling to hold her place, she tried to ignore the way he palmed her bottom, holding her without a tremor of effort.

Abby pulled herself up, finding plenty of toeholds in the crumbling mortar but not any actual loose bricks. She tugged on each within reach, finding no give in any of them.

Creeping upward by inches, she searched in vain. Beneath her, Myles shifted, his arms stretched overhead. "Stand on my shoulders," he grunted.

She braced her arms against either side of the narrowing priest hole and let him guide her feet to his shoulders. It seemed awfully precarious, but Myles kept a firm grip on her ankles.

Shaking, she reached above her and found the bricks had closed in. "I'm at the top," she reported, trying not to wriggle too much. "Won't be much longer."

"Take your time," he called up to her, coughing in the face of falling brick dust.

Gripping the flashlight's end with her mouth, she tried each brick, and not one budged. She precariously made a turn, her feet switching places, trying behind her.

"Nothing." Abby looked down between her feet at his brown hair coated with a faint layer of red dust. "Um, how do I get down?"

He twisted his neck to look up at her. She caught the flash of his grin in the faint light. "Same way you went up."

Gnawing at her lip, she flung her arms outward, bracing herself. Tentatively, she lifted one foot from his shoulder, blindly seeking a foothold for it.

Again and again, her foot slipped.

"I can't," she moaned. "I'll fall."

"You won't," he coaxed, his voice sure and strong in the half dark. "I won't let you."

Paralyzed, Abby took deep breaths, her nose filling with the dust she'd stirred up. She coughed, trying not to choke. She got up, surely she could get down again. She reached out with her other foot, glad of the sturdy grip Myles resumed on the first. Nothing.

"I can't find a foothold." She tried to reach out farther, leaning at an angle.

"Steady!" Myles called up. "Try crouching down. If we can get you sitting on my shoulders, you can slide down from there."

It sounded as good a plan as any. "You just want your face in my crotch," she returned, keeping her tone light, even as her voice shook.

He laughed. "Too bad you wear those trousers, otherwise I might enjoy your descent more."

She huffed a laugh in response. "OK, let's try this."

Keeping herself braced between the walls, Abby crouched,

until she sensed she almost sat on his head. With one arm, she reached down, feeling for the edge of his shoulder.

He grabbed her hand. "I've got you."

She let her foot slide out from his shoulder and soon found herself sitting on his shoulders, her thighs tight about his head. Reaching out to the wall to steady herself seemed to be a better idea than ripping out a handful of his hair.

He pried her knees apart and took a deep breath. "What a pity that you are not facing the other way."

"I thought this way would make it less frustrating for you, seeing as I'm in trousers."

"How kind of you," he remarked in a droll, deadpan voice.

Abby stifled a snort. "I'm sliding down you now," she warned.

Leaning forward, she slid her left leg forward, preparing to slide the other down his back. Her body had other ideas. Instead, she swung around and forward. She grabbed him around the neck, her right leg hooking over his left shoulder in an effort to stop from falling. Her left leg hooked around his waist in an effort to stop from doing the splits along his body.

Myles caught her, holding her close. His hand slid up her right thigh, reaching her knee. "Hold on," he warned. He guided her leg until it latched about his waist.

She looked up into his face. His eyes twinkled with the same laughter that caught the corners of his mouth, but it didn't hide the intensity of his awakened desire. If she had any doubts, the sensation of his cock pressing between her parted legs dispelled them.

Abby fought the urge to press herself even closer, her relief at not falling quickly becoming subsumed under her own heated need for him.

"Abigail," he moaned, bringing his mouth down on hers.

The urge to fight her need to surrender to him vanished.

4

Myles carried her out of the priest hole, setting her on the chapel's small altar. He pressed her against the cold stone, granite worn almost smooth with time. "I cannot wait to be inside you again. What is it you do to me?"

She stared up at him, clearly lost for an answer. "Here?"

He leaned over her, his aching cock pushing against the rough fabric of his breeches. He thumbed the buttons free and reached for her futuristic fastener. "Here," he growled.

He nibbled on her lower lip and claimed her mouth before she protested. Her arms twined around his neck, her feet sliding up along his thighs. Myles banished the thought of being in a chapel. Think of it as a table.

Pulling down the fastener, he tugged her trousers down and off. "You're beautiful," he breathed. "So beautiful." He smoothed back her dusty blond curls.

"Flatterer." She tweaked his nose, but he saw the confusion that flitted over her face.

He kissed her, plunging his tongue inside her mouth, possessing her as surely as she possessed him. She wasn't the kind

of woman who usually attracted him. Besides her obvious oddness and her uninhibited soul, she had a broad streak of practi-
cality that none of his past lovers possessed.

But her soft curves moved against him, her wet slit sliding
along his cock. The urge to bury himself inside overpowered
him. He slid into her, his passage smooth and slick. He groaned,
sensation wiping out all else. Nothing else existed for him but
her. This wonderful, crazy, eccentric woman.

Pulsing in and out of her, he lost himself in their joining,
closing his eyes to everything but the fire inside.

He reared back, standing straight and burying his cock even
deeper inside. Abigail cried out, her back arching and driving
him in farther. He marveled at her silent demands. Even whores
waited to discover a client's needs, but Abby took charge.

Opening his eyes, he watched her writhe beneath him. At
some point, she had unbuttoned her top, the sides falling back
to the altar. Her undergarment was gone.

Unable to reach him, her arms stretched over her head, her
breasts jutting upward. Her eyes squeezed shut, her skin blushing from her hairline down to her round breasts.

Her sweet cunt squeezed around him, pulsing hard against
his pounding cock. Her release rippled up and down his shaft,
her cries ringing out in the small room.

He fucked her harder, gripping her hips, bellowing as his
seed mingled with hers. Pulling out, he tucked his still-hard cock
into his breeches. He'd found release and yet he still burned for
her. What was it about her that made him still want her even
after he was done?

She blinked at him, dazed and breathless. "I don't think I
can move." Her lips curved in one of her rare genuine, un-
mocking smiles. "You're amazing." Her mouth twisted, mocking him once more. "If that's not too much of a boost to your
ego."

He chuckled. If nothing else, her teasing derision eased the tension between them, if only for a little while. He hefted her into a sitting position, his breath stilling when she leaned her head against his chest.

For one long moment, he didn't want to let her go.

"We should do something about your manner of dress," he said at last, hating to break the comfortable silence.

"You keep saying that." Her hands slipped from his back. "What's wrong with it? There's nobody here to see I'm not wearing a dress."

He toyed with a lock of her hair, looking down at her through his long eyelashes. That trick usually worked wonders, but not with Ms. Deane. She saw through his more obvious ploys. "There are wardrobes upstairs."

She hesitated.

"It'll be fun." He grinned. "Then we can take another look at those plans."

She rolled her eyes. "Won't skirts get in the way of exploring the house?"

He shrugged, pretending a casual air even though the image presented to his mind of her skirts wrapped around his head made him burn with wanting her. "I would much enjoy having you on my shoulders and looking up."

She swatted him, swinging her leg around him and sliding off the altar. She let the hem of her blouse cover the tops of her legs. Myles found himself riveted by all that bare flesh. She'd covered up before, so he thought she was at least somewhat modest, but she didn't seem to care as she walked across the tile floor.

She looked over her shoulder and caught him staring. "I could just wear this," she purred, putting her hands on her hips. That action revealed the curved rounds of her bottom.

He swallowed. His cock went rock hard. He saw her gaze dip and her cheeks color. Perhaps she wasn't as brazen as she made out.

Attempting the same casual air, Myles shrugged. "If that is what you desire."

She opened her mouth to reply and shut it again, turning away. "Let's find some clothes."

Myles grinned, seeing her desire for him written plain on her face. He didn't need to see her expression to know she wanted him. He'd received evidence enough of that already.

"Follow me."

He took her upstairs to the third floor, flinging open a door to reveal a remarkably feminine boudoir of creams and pinks and ruffles, even though most of the articles of furniture were covered in heavy cream sheets.

He stepped inside and turned to watch Abigail's reaction. Her step slowed, her eyes surveying everything. "This is . . . this is . . ."

"A little too childish for me," Myles interjected, seeing her features slip behind a deceptive, calm mask. "And not at all a measure of the girl who sleeps here."

"You know the family?"

He twitched a cover sheet aside and lounged in a spindly cherry wood chair. "I made a point of it."

"You'd do anything to find that . . . that thing." Abigail ignored the room, folding her arms. "Even woo a bitchy princess?"

His brows rose. "That's an apt summary of somebody you've never met."

She didn't back down, her face lighting up with triumph. "I am right, aren't I."

Myles looked down at his hands loosely clasped before him. "It was not a success." He rose and headed toward a door off to the side. "Her wardrobe should be through here."

Abigail sat in the chair he just vacated. "Why?"

"Excuse me?" He frowned at her. Why did she not dash for the pretty fripperies that could be hers like other women? Was it her mannish dress? Did she prefer being masculine? He looked her over, seeing the straight cut of the blouse and the bare legs.

He had to face facts—Ms. Abigail Deane simply wasn't like other women.

"Why was it not a success? You're handsome, charming . . ."

"She thought I was after her money." He delivered a short, ironic bow. "My ego thanks you. Lady Elaine Winterton cast me aside because I wasn't rich enough for her."

"You mean she didn't see through your machinations?"

He leaned against the door lintel. "Hardly anyone remembers that my family used to own this place, and Lady Elaine Winterton is not a bookish kind."

Myles watched Abigail approach. Her hand rested against his chest, a warm comforting touch. "I'm sorry," she murmured. She looked up at him, and he blinked at her cool gaze. "Do you suppose I'm actually going to *like* any of her dresses?"

She passed him and entered the dressing room, heading for the large trunks and wardrobes.

"There's always her mother's gowns," Myles snapped, angry. Her cold and accusing eyes accused him of seduction for a statue. He cursed himself for an idiot. Why not just come out and say he'd seduced and schemed for the statue?

Her gaze narrowed. "Thank you. I'll bear that in mind." She turned her back on him in clear dismissal.

He stepped back. He'd never known a woman to have the same commanding effect as that of a superior officer. For a brief moment, he wondered what his colonel in his old regiment would think of it and then dismissed the idea. "I'll wait out here until you're ready to try on something." He managed to stretch a smile. "You're going to need some help getting into those gowns."

Abby waited until Myles had gone and slumped onto the nearest trunk. Her head fell into her hands. She'd had her suspicions, even accused him of them, but it was pretty plain it was all true: Myles Hardy wanted her for her knowledge of the house, her plans, and of the future.

Not for her. Even her body was an incidental bonus.

She knew better than to let a man like that get his way. She'd figured out and dumped such types before, even the hot-looking guys. Why was Myles Hardy different?

Gnawing on her fingernail, Abby pondered him. She thought she'd stopped being the type to jump into the sack just for the hell of it. Myles changed that. Despite her suspicions, she'd helped him. Myles changed that too.

Sighing, Abby got to her feet. If she looked deep enough inside her she'd find the answer. She was afraid. She didn't know how to deal in this world, and her only ally was Myles. He might be a lying, conniving, charming son-of-a-bitch, but he was all she got.

She opened one trunk and then another. Folds of soft fabrics greeted her view. Printed muslins, embroidered silk. She picked up one of the muslin gowns, shaking out the paper trapped in its folds.

Holding it up against herself, she looked down, frowning. "Myles!" she called, hating to do so.

He appeared in the doorway. "Yes?" he inquired in a low voice.

"I don't think this is going to fit."

Myles sighed, folding his arms. "I suppose your modern undergarments will not hold you in?"

"I'm not wearing a corset," Abby declared, glaring at him.

He held his hands up in mock surrender. "Then perhaps we should try Her Grace's gowns. I assure you, her gowns are of the latest style."

Grimacing, Abby refolded the gown and replaced it in the trunk. "Lead on!"

She followed him out of the princess's bedroom, down one

hall, and up another. He stepped into another room decorated in an earlier age of dark wooden paneling and bright green walls. A large four-poster bed dominated the room.

They walked into the adjacent dressing room, and Myles threw open a trunk lid. "Try one of these." He pulled out a simple gown of muslin edged with a wide border of black embroidery.

She stripped off her blouse and bra, reaching for the gown. Pulling it over her head, the muslin fabric cloaked her like a voluminous night gown.

She gave Myles a look.

He laughed at her. "There are ties." He stepped forward. "If you will allow me . . ."

Abby stood like a mannequin while Myles walked around her, pulling tight on tapes here and tucking them in there.

Finally, he stood back and surveyed his handiwork. "There," he said, with more than one note of pride.

He drew her toward a mirror. Abby blinked at the utterly feminine image. Her short hair seemed at odds with the outfit.

Myles ruffled her curls. "Short hair is la mode, so I understand. A pretty ribbon will be nice."

Abby looked at his reflection in the mirror. "If I didn't know better, I'd think you were gay."

"Gay?" He frowned at her, his hands coming to rest on her shoulders. Her skin grew heated at his touch. Absurd. The slightest touch made her want him.

She stepped away, turning to face him. "A homosexual."

Myles's features froze, his jaw locked into an open position. He blinked and recovered. "I hardly think so."

Abby shrugged. "Well, you do know your way around a woman's wardrobe."

"That is supposed to speak to my sexual experience, not . . ." He trailed off.

He looked so woebegone Abby took pity on him. "I did say

if I didn't know better," she soothed, letting her hand rest on his arm. "Thank you for your help."

Myles tucked her arm under his and escorted her from the dressing room. "You don't look pleased."

Admit she didn't like herself for caving into his every demand? She didn't think so. "I just can't see myself crawling around in attics in this stuff." She lifted the skirt. "It's so impractical. There's nobody here but you, so why wear it?"

"Because if anybody descends on this house, we will not have time for you to dress."

She had to admit it had taken a lot longer than she expected. "Fine," she snapped, irked at having to give up the last of her modern things. She scanned the room and grabbed a cord that held back the bed curtains. The green velvet material fell forward while she tied the long gold cord about her waist. "If I fold this up, tuck it under here . . ." In moments, she had created a minidress. "All I need to do to change is remove the cord."

Abby demonstrated, grinning.

Myles grinned back. "I have to admit I like the new style."

She snorted. "You would." She took a deep breath and said something she never thought she'd say. "Let's go take another look at those blueprints, shall we? And you can tell me more about this thing we're looking for."

Abby took satisfaction in Myles's stare. "I would have thought . . ."

"What, that you are a manipulative bastard?" She shrugged. "I know that already. However, there's nothing else to do, right?" She paused. "Oh, I suppose we could try and find out how to get me back to my own time."

Myles spread his hands. "I would hardly know where to start."

"Neither do I." Her mood sank, but she rallied. "This is better than doing nothing."

He drew her into a one-armed hug. "I've never known anyone like you."

She pulled away. The compliment stung. "I'm not surprised. Women's liberation hasn't happened yet."

"Liberated from what?" He followed her downstairs to the blueprints lying partially rolled on the gigantic kitchen table.

"Men." She shot him an amused glance over her shoulder. Baiting him was too much fun. "In my time, women have careers of their own, can vote in elections, and hold office. Anything they want to do."

Myles leaned against the kitchen door lintel. "But—"

Abby looked up from the blueprints, grinning. "Don't worry your pretty little head about it. It doesn't happen for another hundred years. I doubt you'll be around to see it."

He pushed off the doorway. "That doesn't make me any easier in my mind." He strode around the kitchen table and pulled her upright. "And it's not pretty, or little. I'll beg you to remember that."

His mouth came down hard upon hers, plundering hers, dominating hers. He held her against the long length of his body. She had two choices: fight him or surrender.

She curled her arms about his neck, drawing him even closer. Her leg hitched around his, bringing their groins together.

He broke off the kiss, breathing heavily.

Abby blinked up at him, dazed. "Male brutality," she purred. "Gotta love it."

His grip tightened on her arms. "I'd never hurt you," he hoarsely declared.

Bringing both her hands down his neck and up to cup his face, she murmured, "You have no problems in dominating me into submission."

"You did not object."

"You didn't hurt me." She reached up on her toes and kissed the tip of his nose. "I don't know what is going on between us, but no matter how much you infuriate me, I find I only want you even more."

"You admit that?" He examined her face.

She met his searching gaze. "I admit it, although I don't understand it, and I'm not at all convinced it'll last." She smirked, retreating into sarcasm. "You have some unpleasant character traits . . ."

His smile matched hers. "Like being a manipulative bastard?" he burred. "Is that any worse than being a woman who does not know her place?"

She drew back, stung. "Excuse me? I know my place, and it is not here." Abby thumped on the table and the blueprints rolled up with a snap. She collected the roll of paper and tucked it under her arm, stalking off.

"Wait." Myles grabbed her arm. At her glare, he released her. "Abigail . . ." he wheedled. "I only meant to tease."

Abby paused by the door, her fingertips drumming on the thick roll of blueprints. She knew he played her, teasing her the same way she provoked him. "Sorry," she said, facing him. "I'm still a little too freaked out by all this."

Myles nodded, although she saw in his expression he didn't fully understand.

Returning to the kitchen table, Abby spread out the blueprints. Unable to meet his gaze, she focused on the blue markings before them. From the corner of her eye, she saw him draw close and yet not close enough to touch her.

For all she knew, she'd put him off her entirely with her little temper tantrum.

"You've searched the attics, I take it." At his confirmation, she flipped the page, revealing the first floor. "Now, I seem to remember the owner saying there was a secret passage somewhere."

"Aside from the priest hole?" Myles leaned forward, his shoulder brushing hers.

"I think so." Abby stepped to the side, putting a little distance between them before she faced him. "What did your granny have to say about it?"

Myles shrugged. "Nothing that made sense."

"Try me."

"I wrote it down before I realized what nonsense it was." He patted his pockets. "Must've left my notebook upstairs." He held out his hand. "Come with me?"

Abby raised an eyebrow. "You're a big boy. You know your way."

He grimaced. "I'm worried you might run off."

"What? Run from the hand that feeds me?" She smiled, saccharine sweet. "Of course, that doesn't stop me from biting it."

"Or licking it," Myles added with a leer.

Abby rolled her eyes. "You're incorrigible."

He grinned. "And you like it." He extended a hand to her.

She crossed to him and took his hand. His grip comforted her. With his other hand, he whipped the curtain cord from around her waist, letting the gown fall to her ankles. "That's better."

She gazed up at him. "Better for who?"

"Even I have limits. If I look at your legs any longer I won't be responsible for my actions."

Abby snorted. "Sure you will."

He drew her into his arms. "You have no idea about the effect you have on me, do you?"

Her fingers walked up his chest to where his shirt gaped. "Oh, I have a fair idea."

He cleared his throat. "I'll go get my notebook."

She backed away. "I'll make us some lunch." She surveyed the kitchen. "Somehow."

"Somehow?" Myles held up a hand, forestalling her reply. "No, I don't think I want to know." He vanished down the hallway.

Abby stood staring after him. How odd that the room felt

much emptier without him in it, and it had nothing to do with his height or broad shoulders. Weird.

A little of the bread and cheese remained, but Abby had grown tired of that. She found some cherries in a bowl. A narrow door stood off to the side that looked like it might be a walk-in pantry. Did they have those back then? Er, now?

She opened the door and fell back, covering her nose and her mouth. She pushed open the back door and took a deep breath. She sucked in the fresh air. How could anyone eat those birds? It stunk like they'd been hanging there for days, months.

Stumbling out a few steps, she found a stone bench and sat on it. How could she live in a time like this when it was so . . . so uncivilized? She vowed to go vegetarian.

She stared across the large dirt patch behind the mansion to a simple green lawn and a greening garden. She perked up. Vegetables. Surely some of them were edible.

She strolled along the rows. Some early lettuce, some herbs. Now, if she could just find the tomatoes . . . although she suspected it was too early in the year for them to be ripe, but maybe an early variety existed.

Unearthing one of the small lettuces, she turned back for the house.

Myles burst through the door, stopping short when he saw her. He sucked in his breath and watched her approach.

"You all right?"

"Thought you'd vanished, back to your own time." He shuttered his desolate expression.

His fake cheer didn't fool her. "No such luck," she replied in bright tones. "Found us some greens though."

"You're dressed appropriately." He beamed down at her, his sudden sunny expression arousing her suspicions. "We could eat at the local inn."

"And waste valuable searching time? I think not."

"It's now or never. The moon isn't full enough to travel at night."

Abby blinked. "Oh. Oh, I see."

"This is *my* mission, Ms. Abigail." He softened his words with one of his charming smiles.

Those didn't fool her for a minute. "You're right. This isn't my project." She managed a smile. "It would be better than stale bread and cheese."

"Agreed. I have a carriage in the stables. It will take me a little time to get ready. Why don't you go find a bonnet?"

She stared at him. "A bonnet?"

He gave her one of the looks she gave her minions. *He learned that one fast.*

"Very well. I'll go find something."

They sat on a bench in the common area of the tiny inn at the end of a long trestle table. Abby sat across from Myles, her elbow jostled by her neighbor.

She gritted her teeth and glared down at her food. The innkeepers had crowded far too many people into the small space, leaving narrow corridors to and from the bar. Surely it was against the fire code. If there *was* a fire code.

"Did you bring the notebook?" She pushed the unidentifiable lumps of stew from one end of her bowl to the other.

Myles patted his coat. "Right here."

"And the riddle?"

Munching, Myles patted his pocket again.

"Well?"

He swallowed. "Too many ears."

Abby huffed in impatience. "Are you for real?"

"I am not familiar with that phrase." Myles frowned, gesturing she lower her voice.

"Is it that secret?" she amended.

"I'd rather not take the risk." He smiled in apology. "I'll explain it all to you later."

Abby returned her attention to her meal. She'd much rather talk about their search rather than . . . well, anything personal. She stuffed a large forkful into her mouth, avoiding his eyes. In the time it would take to chew and swallow this gristle, it'd be time to go home.

"When we have found—" he lowered his voice,—"the item, we will be leaving the house. Is there anything you would prefer to do?"

Delicately, she placed the gristle on her plate. "What are my options?"

"There is not much to choose from," he admitted with a grimace. "I thought this merited discussion because I realize you must need some sort of occupation."

Abby gestured for him to continue, touched by his thoughtfulness.

"Governess and housekeeper are the respectable trades. I think you can guess the less acceptable ones." His gaze slanted away. "There's wife, too, of course."

"I know my Jane Austen. Without a family or fortune, I'm unlikely to find a husband who wouldn't treat me like a serf." She tried to sound calm, quelling her shaking hands in her lap.

"There is that. A governess's life isn't pleasant, and I am not referring to squalling brats but of husbands and older brothers who might take a fancy to you." He *did* sound calm and disaffected. Was he so sure she wouldn't make a scene?

"Ugh." Abby made a face. "And I suppose as vacuums and washing machines don't exist, I'll have to learn to keep house from scratch."

"It would be a challenge," Myles supplied helpfully, frowning over her odd words. "You seem to like those."

Abby examined his face for any hint of teasing. She found none. "You know me pretty well for such a short acquaintance."

He smiled, or more accurately, leered. His voice dropped to a low burr. "One discovers a lot after a bedding."

Choking on her mouthful of wine, Abby swallowed her laughter. "You assume a lot."

Myles smiled. "I've been right so far, haven't I?"

She acknowledged it with a pursing of her lips. "Train me as a housekeeper and I'm sure I'll get by."

He nodded. "Good. I could use one after all."

"Your housekeeper?"

"Why not? Who else would put up with your attitude?"

She wanted to throttle him. "I thought housekeepers were supposed to have attitudes," Abby shot back.

"They still know their place." Myles gentled his words, his features softening.

"Don't sass the bosses. I think I've learned that one already."

Myles's bloom faded. "I wish we knew what brought you here and how to get you back."

Abby shrugged. "I wish I knew too." She glanced sidelong at her unknown dining companion. "I don't want to talk about it here."

"I understand." He tossed the rough beige cloth napkin onto the table. "Have you finished?"

Abby eyed her plate and found it empty. "I guess I had more of an appetite than I thought."

Grinning, Myles rose, extending a hand to her. "Let us go then and speak of private matters."

Their neighbors overheard this last. "Oh ho!" boozed one, his whiskered chin specked with beer froth. "Good luck to you, lad!" He raised his pewter mug to a chorus of sniggers.

Abby's neighbor grabbed at her skirt as she rose. "Give us the leavin's when you're done, guv?"

"How dare you!" Abby swatted his hand away. When it didn't budge, she turned her swat into a hard karate chop. The man yelped, shaking his hand and staring at her in astonishment.

Myles grabbed her arm. "We should leave before you start a fight."

Abby let him guide her outside. "I was handling it."

"Believe me, I saw." He hoisted her up into the little gig and walked around to the other side, unhitching the horses.

A woman hurried out from the inn and handed Abby a package. Bemused, she accepted it, shooting Myles a questioning glance.

"It's dinner and breakfast." He swung up into the tiny seat next to her. "What was that you did in there?"

"Karate, an ancient martial art." Abby massaged her hand. It had been awhile since she'd practiced.

"How did you come by it?"

"I took a self-defense class." The gig lurched forward, and Abby gripped its side.

"To protect yourself?"

"Of course. There isn't always a man handy to fend off an attacker." She shot him a glance. "I'll bet there isn't even always a man handy in this time."

"You needn't worry about that here. I'll protect you." Myles puffed his chest.

For a brief moment, Abby wanted to see him in action, his muscles rippling and the power within him unleashed. She cleared her throat. "You won't always be around."

He said nothing, shaking the reins.

They rode along in silence for a while. Abby sought a topic. "I don't understand how this happened. There is no time travel technology in the twenty-first century. Well," she amended, aware she babbled, "not from my part of the century. So, how then? Some weird genius waving a beam about without knowing? How?"

"I think I have the answer."

5

Abby gaped at Myles's calm response. "You know the answer?"

"If the future does not possess the technology, then there is only one possible solution." He paused for dramatic effect. She wanted to kick him, but her skirts got in the way. "You came here via supernatural design."

Abby gawped. "What? You mean magic?"

His shoulders hunched. "I should have known you are not a believer. Even in this modern world, such things are scoffed at, but there are things that cannot be explained."

She rolled her eyes. "Modern science finds explanations all the time."

"Not for this."

Abby had to admit it. "No, not for this. Not yet."

"But Abigail—"

"Abby," she corrected, and flushed. She only let family and close friends call her Abby. Already she'd invited him to use the name. However, Myles might be the closest thing to a friend for the next two hundred years.

His warm smile diminished her regret at telling him even further. "Abby," he purred.

In the silence that followed, Abby forgot all about their conversation. All she saw was his impassioned brown gaze, and when he rested a hand on her thigh, all she felt was the heat emanating from him, seeping into her skin.

He cleared his throat, looking ahead to the road. "But Abby," he said, his voice charged with a different color. He sounded eager, yet apologetic. "But Abby, if you had not arrived with your house plans, I might still be rambling aimlessly about the house looking for the statue."

"We still haven't found it yet." Abby frowned. "Why would some supernatural thing want me to help you?"

"Maybe it wants to be found."

Abby's eyes narrowed and her dis-ease grew. She remembered her initial impression of Myles Hardy as being a bit simple. "What is it?"

"A statue."

"Of what?" Honestly, it was like pulling teeth.

"A Greek god."

"There are a lot of statues of Greek gods," Abby pointed out. "Why is this one so special?"

Myles cracked his whip over the horse's back and wrestled with the reins before he answered. "Perhaps I'm putting too much stock in my grandmother's ravings. She didn't want me to find it. She said it was hidden for a reason."

"But she suffers from dementia."

"Well, yes, there is that." He shot her a quick smile. "How ever you made it here, I am glad of it."

"Do you really believe in the supernatural?"

He shot her an apologetic look. "You're the first supernatural event I've personally experienced. For a moment, I thought my grandmother was right. But you are likely correct it is some future technology neither you or I have experienced. Maybe you got caught on the tail end of some time traveler's pathway."

Abby shrugged, her bodice constricting the movement. "Anything is possible."

They reached the house, traveling through a curved drive of beech trees. Myles urged the horse into a trot, and Abby grabbed onto her bonnet, the breeze tugging at it.

He drove around to the back of the house, helping her descend from the gig. "I'll take care of this and meet you inside." He gave her a swat on her behind.

Leaping, she shot him a daggered look and headed for the kitchen. Even though Myles had disavowed his speculation on some supernatural effect, the thought of him being so irrational disturbed her. Even the worst charmers had some sense.

Taking off her bonnet, she tossed it onto the kitchen table. Supernatural or not, she was here and that was that. She might as well take Myles's hint and make herself useful.

She unrolled the plans, poring over them until Myles entered the kitchen from the courtyard. "I think I may have found an anomaly in the plans. Take a look and see what you think."

She shuffled aside, holding the place with her forefinger. "Here and here." She pointed to an unusually thick wall. "And if you look at the next level floor plans . . ." Again, she pointed it out.

Myles surveyed the plans in silence, flipping back and forth.

"What do you think? Is it purely structural?" Abby peered over his shoulder. "Part of an exterior wall of an earlier building? That would explain the thickness."

"But it doesn't explain why it isn't consistently so along that wall."

"Maybe the other parts fell down."

"It would take the whole wall down if that were so." Myles pointed just south of the thickened wall. "See how it tapers off? I'll wager there's some concealment along that wall so the regular observer cannot tell."

"What room is it?"

"The study." Myles looked up, and Abby was surprised to see the lack of excitement in his expression. "I've examined that room already. There are no concealed doors or passages; I looked. There's a story about a secret passage in my family—but that was before the Civil War. Maybe it was found and destroyed or filled in."

"It's possible," Abby allowed. "Why don't we take another look?"

Myles looked out the window. "The light is going. Let's delay it until the morning."

Abby frowned. "The morning? Why wait?"

He fished his small notebook from his coat pocket. "You wanted to look at my notebook, remember? My grandmother's riddle?"

Abby looked at the brown leather cover of his notebook and her plans. She leaned against the kitchen table, giving him her full attention. "All right. Whatcha got?"

His brows rose at her slangy words but he made no remark about them. Abby imagined he must be getting used to her strange talk. "Well, here's what my grandmother had to say."

Flipping open the notebook, he thumbed through the pages. "Found it," he said at last. His cheeks flushed. "It doesn't make a lot of sense."

Abby folded her arms. "I'm listening."

Myles cleared his throat. He took on a faraway expression. Abby wondered what he saw.

The cottage stank of urine and musty dirt. His grandmother lay in a narrow cot, her flat chest rising and falling with difficulty.

"You came," she croaked.

He hunkered down beside her, his boots scuffing dust from the dirt floor. "I am sorry it took me so long. I was told you were dead."

"Your father never thought so," his grandmother wheezed, her dark eyes clouded.

"He died years ago." She gave out a sob, and he winced. He should have known she hadn't heard the news. He patted her hand. "He went quick," he mumbled.

The old lady sighed. "You are here about the statue."

His eyes widened. How did she know? "Yes."

"It is at the old family estate."

"Yes, I know. But it was hidden, many years ago. Do you know where?"

"So long, so long ago." His grandmother sighed. "You should let it rest. Let it be."

He frowned. "Why?"

"It has great power."

He winced, hating to hear her utter such nonsense. "It's made of stone. Whatever power it had died with the god's believers years ago," he snapped. "I need to find it."

Her cloudy gaze grew sharp. "What need have you—?" A rattling sigh escaped her lungs. "Ah, I see. You seek to become Chosen . . ."

"The Dilettanti Society, yes—"

"No!" She gave a dismissive wave, and her hand fell hard on the rough blanket. "It is a twisted way, my child, a dark and twisted way."

Myles gritted his teeth. "Where is it?"

"Seek it not in the sunlight, nor by the light of the moon. Seek it in the hardiest of ancestral stead." His grandmother shivered. "It is lost, lost."

"In the old family home, of course!" Myles smacked his fist into his palm. "But where in the house? You promised to tell me when I was old enough."

"It did your father no good, no good at all."

"I *will* succeed." Myles gripped her hand so tight she squeaked in pain. He released her, giving her hand a soothing pat. "Please, grandmother."

"From earth's base lusts, to earth's base lusts he returns. Descend into hell and forever burn."

Myles scribbled down her words, his heart sinking. She spoke nothing but riddles. Had he come too late to find her mind intact?

She bolted upright, gripping his arm. "Do not seek it, do not seek it. We Hardys have forsaken the lore. It will bring disaster upon your head."

"Nonsense." Myles gently pried her clawed grip from his arm. "I will be careful, I promise."

His grandmother only shook her head, lying back on her pillow and closing her eyes.

Myles waited for a few minutes, wondering if she would speak again, but the old woman's lips pursed shut and she turned her face to the wall.

He kissed the withered cheek and took his leave. He arranged with a local villager to look in on her.

Abby frowned. "That's not particularly helpful."

"No," Myles agreed, taking back his notebook. "That's why I've been methodically searching this building. It has to be here, somewhere."

Abby patted his arm. "We'll find it."

"We must."

Catching the tension in his voice, Abby tilted her head. "Must?"

His lips twisted and he shrugged. He pushed away from the kitchen table, heading for the door. "You will think it's foolish."

Abby made to follow him. "Perhaps," she allowed. "But we have nothing better to do."

Stopping in the doorway, he faced her. The bitterness fled his features, replaced by a crooked smile amidst the glow of desire. "I tend to disagree with that statement."

Striding toward her, he scooped her into his arms, his arm supporting the back of her knees. Startled, Abby grabbed at his neck. He juggled her until she settled more securely in his arms. "You're not so heavy."

Abby glared at him through slitted eyes, trying to ignore the sudden surges of heat washing through her. The mildest touch made her vibrantly aware of him, and this intimate hold was hardly mild. "Put me down."

"Not on your life." Myles chuckled, heading for the stairs. "You really don't like being out of control, do you?"

She let her voice grow cool, even though she burned for him. Two could play his game. "If you mean, do I prefer being asked before being fucked, then the answer is yes." Through slitted eyes, Abby saw him start.

"Where's the fun in that?"

Abby ducked the kiss he aimed at her forehead.

He heaved a sigh, stopping on the landing. The joking faded from his face, replaced by civility. "Very well. Ms. Deane, will you please show me more of your toys?"

Twining a finger around a lock of his hair, Abby fluttered her eyelashes. "If you like."

He shook his head at her, dislodging her loose grip on his hair. "You are a strange woman, Ms. Deane."

"If I were not, you wouldn't be able to take advantage of me the way you have been. I know karate, remember."

It didn't faze him. This time she didn't duck when he bent to kiss her. The slow, sensuous kiss lasted longer than she first thought it might. Its gentle heat seeped through her, calming her fiery need for him but making her clit throb harder for him.

He broke off the kiss, his eyes unfocused, his lips parted. "Take advantage? You seem pretty willing to me."

She smiled up at him, her lips parting for another kiss. She didn't care what he said so long as he got her into bed. What was the point of fighting it? He wanted her and she wanted him. Simple.

Myles took the last of the stairs in a long, loping stride, kicking open the bedroom door. He deposited Abby onto the bed, covering her with his body in almost the same motion.

The long skirts trapped her legs and Abby squirmed against him, reveling in the feel of his weight upon her. Capturing her mouth with his, he ground against her, his trapped erection pressing hard against her soft flesh.

Abby wrapped her arms around him. She returned his kiss, holding the back of his neck as she returned his kiss, hard and deep, their tongues slipping past each other.

Breaking off the kiss, Myles rested on his elbows, gazing down at her with an awed gaze. "You are a wonder," he breathed. In a sweet, curious gesture, his lips brushed the tip of her nose.

Abby sucked in her breath, not prepared for such tenderness. *This is just sex, nothing else, didn't he know that?* Why not just enjoy the fiery chemistry for what it was? She slowly let out her breath. Surely it had something to do with his being a gentleman, being polite rather than sincere.

"Shall I choose the toy?" she whispered.

"So long as I get to choose next time," he returned, rolling off her and propping himself on one elbow.

Abby scrambled out of bed, heading for her suitcase. He'd seen the dildo and been little impressed with it. The vibrator had been a success, but that wasn't the end of her toys.

"I like a little variety," she murmured, kneeling before the suitcase. She unzipped it, lifting her shirts aside, crinkled now, and surveying her array of toys.

OK, so maybe it was overkill to bring so many, but the same old, same old night after night soon lost its spark. Variety spiced up her nights. At least he hadn't discovered her reading material.

She bit down on her lower lip. Sharing that could be fun.

Making her selection, she retrieved her choice from the suitcase, concealing it in the palm of her hand.

Myles eyed her from the bed. "Did you forget something?"

She didn't reply, delivering her most mysterious smile. Reaching the bed, Abby held out her hand. A small cylinder nestled within her palm.

Squinting, Myles retrieved it from the palm of her hand and held it up to the afternoon light. "It looks like an oversized bullet."

Abby snapped her fingers and held out her hand for its return. "It's a vibrator, travel sized. Do you want to see how it works?"

He nodded, settling back onto the piled pillows. "Are you a little overdressed for that?"

Abby restrained a sigh. The damned dress. It would take her forever to get out of it, even if she could figure out which bit of cord went where. With a shrug, she hoisted her skirts, holding them bunched at her waist.

"You're wrinkling it."

"So?" Abby challenged. "Who else is here to see it but you?"

He delivered a begrudging nod, his lower lip in a delicious pout Abby wanted to kiss. He waved. "Do continue."

Abby lifted one leg, letting the foot rest on the mattress. She twisted the dial, and a soft buzzing filled the air. Holding the small vibrator like a pencil, she let it trace a path over her pubic mound, avoiding the lips and her clit already peeking out between them.

She rolled the small vibrator over her inner thighs, first one and then the other, drawing the toy closer to her center. All the time, she watched his face, the way his eyes tracked the path of her vibrator, and her hips swaying forward, the nearer she got to reaching her clit.

Licking her lips, she held the tiny vibrator between her fingertips. She slid it down over her mons to where her clit's tip brushed against her pubic hair.

The rounded buzzing tip touched her clit. Vibrations sent echoes of pleasure through her. Her eyelids fluttered shut, but she forced them open, forced herself to watch Myles watching her.

She slid the tiny vibrator along her outer labia, feeling her nerve endings tingle. She wanted to press the buzzer against her clit until an orgasm catapulted her over the edge, but she held back, toying with the vibrator, sliding it up and down but not penetrating any deeper.

The faint buzzing swooping past her clit demolished her good intentions in delaying her orgasm. She bent her knees, parting her damp folds, the little vibrator slipping against her slick flesh.

She swirled the tiny vibrator around her quivering hole and along her soaking pussy to her clit. Circling the small buzzer around and around, Abby at last lost herself in the building wash of approaching orgasm.

A hand covered hers and her eyes flew open. Myles knelt on the bed, deftly plucking the small vibrator from her hand.

"Enough," he murmured, his voice hoarse. "This little toy is getting more of you than I."

She fell forward, letting her slight weight bear them back onto the bed. Myles rolled, trapping her beneath him. Abby wrapped her legs around him, drawing him in close.

He kissed her hard, his teeth nibbling, one hand holding her arm to the bed. He made a small space between them. The return of his weight brought the welcome stab of his cock.

Losing little time, he slid inside her, his mass stretching her in a way her little vibrator never could. She moaned, squeezing her cunt muscles around him. *Oh God, when had sex ever been this good?*

Awed, she stared up at him, finding his gaze mirroring her thoughts. *Did she look like that?* she wondered. *Impassioned and awed, eager and confused, all at the same time?*

He withdrew and thrust in, and she cried out in pleasure.

Her heels battered against his muscular buttocks, urging him in again and again.

Something tumbled across the pillow, catching her eyes, and she turned to see. The mini-vibrator, still buzzing. Myles drew her into an even closer embrace, his hands cupping her shoulders.

The intimacy disturbed her, although they'd had sex often enough. Having him that close was wondrous but a little scary. Abby let go of him long enough to retrieve the item, still vibrating. She thumbed it off, planning to drop it, but a better use came to mind.

Switching it back on, she palmed it, sliding her fist between their two bodies. Myles paused in his steady thrusting, curiosity written in his expression.

She smirked at him, slipping the vibe at the apex of her vee, over her engorged clit. Biting her lip at the sudden added sensation, she used her heels to urge him deeper inside her.

He buried himself to the hilt. Abby watched his concentrated frown dissipate into surprised pleasure. Myles ground his groin against hers, the tiny vibrator trapped between them, buzzing the base of his cock and her clit at the same time.

"Dear God," Myles gasped, his eyes closing. He bucked against her, each plunge pressing the little vibrator against her clit. Her pulse surged with each connection, the faint background buzzing in between keeping her on that delicious edge.

Abby clung to him, lost in the heady sensations. More than the action of his cock, or the vibrator's buzzing, she reveled in the burning warmth of his embrace.

With his eyes closed, she was spared his regard, spared the knowledge that this joining left him in bewildered wonder too. It freed her to enjoy the exhilaration of being fucked by him.

Abby's moans escalated in volume, release upon release breaking over her, driving her on to want an even more explosive climax.

His face twisted into a rictus of delight. "Abby," he grunted, and his heat filled her, his come pulsing and spurting inside her.

Myles sagged, resting his sweaty forehead on the pillow next to hers.

At last, he untangled himself, ending on his back beside her. She rolled onto her side, watching him tuck a hand behind his head. His chest heaved.

Abby had difficulty catching her breath herself. A delicious ache filled her body, giving her no incentive to move. After having sex three times in one day, she thought she might start feeling a bit sore, but pleasant satiation denied any pain.

The next morning, with the plans in hand, Abby followed Myles into the study. Shelves upon shelves lined the room, leaving space for only a few tall windows to share the morning sunlight.

Dust covers hid tables and chairs from view. Abby guessed at them from their form, although one drape-covered item defied either simple description.

She dropped the plans on the largest flat surface and unrolled them, orientating them so that the walls lay in parallel with the diagrams.

She anchored one end with the end of a heavy dust cover, her nose wrinkling at the rising dust. "Where do you think this is?" She pointed at the thickened wall marked on the blueprints.

Myles examined the diagram and then the room itself, returning to the blueprints to check his bearings. "It's along the outer wall, which is odd, because the entire exterior is all built with the same stone."

"And we think this might be an earlier part of the house."

"Yes."

His abstracted reply didn't disturb her at all. He worked much the same way she did, completely absorbed in his task, mind racing to solve the conundrum before them.

"By my estimation," he said at last, "it should be by that corner." He pointed in front of them and to the right.

Abby followed the direction of his finger and started examining the bookshelves. Nothing seemed out of the ordinary. She retraced her steps, stopping when she came to the first window. She leaned on a shelf. "I don't see anything."

"Any catch will be hidden," Myles told her. "Although I've been over this room already."

Her elbow slipped. Startled, she shot upright, looking at once to where her elbow had been. The books slid in a couple of inches.

"Weird."

"What?" Myles headed toward her and the suspect wall.

Abby gave more of the books a shove. "The shelves here are deeper than—" She moved to the shelf under the wall and pushed on the book spines. The books didn't move. "Than these shelves here."

"They've made the room look square—"

"Even when it's not."

"So that means . . ." Myles headed for the room's corner— "that the entrance is here somewhere. But I searched here before."

Abby joined him. "Maybe you missed it." He shot her a glowering look. "What? It happens." She pointed. "You take that side, and I'll take this, and we'll meet in the middle."

They scoured the bookcase, pulling and pushing on every book within reach in the hope it might be a lever. They met in the middle, Abby checking the lower level, while Myles took care of the upper shelves.

Myles stood back with a disappointed sigh. "I told you."

She ignored him, feeling under the shelves themselves for a lever or button. She joined him, echoing his sigh. "There's definitely a space back there, but how do we get in?"

Myles had strolled away, examining a portrait hanging over the fireplace, the only book-free part of the room, except for the space under the windows. "I never noticed this before," he said, gazing up at the portrait.

"What?" Abby joined him. She saw a portrait of a young woman set in an ornate gilt frame. The likeness mirrored those of Holbein and Tudor monarch portraits she'd seen in books. The oils gleamed but the subject looked flat. Clouds of auburn hair floated about her face, outshining the jewels gracing her ears, bosom, and waist. In her slender white hands she held a small stack of tiny books.

"There's a copy of it that belongs to the family." Myles stepped closer to the portrait. "It's a miniature, but I recognize that face anywhere."

"Who was she?"

"She was the mistress of one of my ancestors," he replied, not looking at her, leaning in to examine the edges of the painting. Abby left him to it, surveying the room in greater detail.

His knuckles grazed the frame. "That's odd."

"What is?" Abby turned from her examination of the bookcase on the far wall.

"The painting is stuck to the wall." He nudged the frame harder. "As in permanently affixed."

"I have a copy of the hotel brochure in my bag. I know it has a picture of this room in it. Should I get it?" At his absentminded nod, Abby picked up her skirts and made an unladylike dash for their room. On the way, she wondered what Myles's ancestors would think if they saw her baring her legs. She shrugged. Myles alone would pitch a fit if they weren't by themselves.

Brochure in hand, she ran back to the book room, skidding to a stop a few feet from the doorway.

The room was empty.

"Myles?"

Had the mysterious time-traveling beam that sent her here captured Myles and sent him sometime else?

She raised her voice. "Myles?"

6

"**M**yles?" Abby called, her voice scooping in pitch at his freakish disappearance. "Where the hell are you?"

A ponderous creaking presaged the moving of the bookshelf. Myles's brown head, dusted now with spiderwebs, poked around the corner. "Did you call?" he chirped, grinning.

Abby's fears vanished in an instant. She returned his grin with one of her own. "You found it!"

Myles pushed open the secret door farther. "Yes, ma'am." He extended a hand. "Come and see."

Abby tossed her brochure onto the dustcloth-covered desk and hurried over. "How did you work it out?"

He tapped the side of his nose, "It's a secret." His grin grew wider at Abby's irritation. He guided her around the door.

Abby blinked, her eyes adjusting to the sudden darkness. In her absence, Myles not only found the secret passage but had lit a candle to guide their first few steps. The candle sat embedded in its own wax on an outcrop of milled stone.

Narrow walls sandwiched irregular stone steps. Gaping

holes billowing with ancient spiderwebs showed the path Myles had taken before she called him back.

"Everyone must have known about this when it was built," she whispered. "How secret can it be?"

"You paid the masons well, maybe even pensioned them, and eventually they died, taking the secret with them." Myles bent and picked up a taper from a small basket resting on the bottom step. Draped in more web, they'd been sitting there for many years undisturbed.

He lit the taper from the candle. "Shall we see where this goes?"

Abby stepped closer, grabbing the back of his coat. "Just keep the spiders off," she muttered.

He shot her an amused glance over his shoulder and ascended, Abby close behind. The step height changed from shallow to steep, making her stumble and fall against Myles.

He didn't seem to mind, using the taper to light each successive candle during their ascent.

"Somebody had this very well planned," Abby muttered.

Myles agreed. "I'll wager that the differences in step are to keep track of how many more steps there are to go—or perhaps where to move more silently. I believe we're heading for the servants' quarters, which makes a lot of sense."

"How so?" Abby asked, stubbing her toe yet again. She didn't know how Myles moved like a cat in the dark. He hadn't taken a single wrong step. Of course, he had more light than she.

"My ancestor kept his mistress on hand. That portrait, remember. She had a room in the servants' quarters, available to tend his every need whenever he wanted, presumably by this secret staircase."

Abby sniffed. "Didn't his wife ever figure out she fed one extra mouth?"

"If she did, there's no record of her complaint. Perhaps she was relieved. They did have ten children after all."

Her laughter echoed in the narrow space. "In that case, I can see the benefits of a mistress. Ten children! The poor woman! How many did he have by the mistress?"

"None, so far as I know, but that doesn't mean there weren't any."

"Do you suppose the statue's hidden in her room?"

Myles paused, causing Abby to run into him. He caught her around the waist. "It's possible, but if so, surely it's in common use now and some curious servant . . ."

She heard the worry in his voice. "Then you'd know about it, wouldn't you? Wouldn't it be in the papers, or on display downstairs?"

He nodded. "True." His lips brushed her forehead. "But it means it's not in her room."

Abby would not be discouraged. "Then it's here in the passage, or somewhere else in the house."

He squeezed her. "Of course," he replied, good humor restored. "Let's see where this leads first before we search it."

They ascended the last remaining stairs, the space narrowing. A simple wall of wood blocked any further passage.

Abby craned over his shoulder to see. The wall fell open, and they stepped into the servants' quarters. The roof slanted, the pitch steep.

"We're in the attics," Abby said, wincing at her obvious statement.

They stood inside a dilapidated room. The beige wall colors ran with faint intricate patterns. A simple narrow bed, a chest of drawers, and a rocking chair. A threadbare rug graced the space between bed and chair. A small table with an inkwell stood nearest the narrow window, a thick book closed on it.

Myles crossed to it, and opened the book. "It's the housekeeper's room now," he announced, shutting it again. He turned and surveyed the room.

Abby did likewise. "You can hardly see where the door to the passage is," she remarked, examining the way they came.

They spent an hour searching, coming up with nothing of note. No hollow walls where the statue might be secreted, nothing.

"It must have been too risky to hide up here." Myles dusted off his hands, his shoulders slumping.

"Maybe in the stairwell itself?" Abby suggested, prying open the hidden door.

His shoulders hunched. "When it could be exposed at any time from the outside? So many homes were cannonaded during the Civil War, it wouldn't have been safe for such a valuable piece."

"Let's look anyway," Abby declared, stepping onto the first of the stairs and switching on her flashlight.

"We will not find anything," he grumped.

Not facing him, Abby rolled her eyes in some safety. "Why don't you tell me about this mistress of your ancestor." Schooling her face into a flirtatious smirk, she glanced over her shoulder and batted her eyes. "I like erotic stories."

Pretense dissolved into a sudden, real need. She really wanted to have his dirty words fill her ears. Clearing her throat, surprised at the sudden tension strung in her groin, she stepped down. She swept her flashlight over the stone walls and low ceiling for some sign of a hiding place.

Myles snorted. "That sort of thing wasn't passed down."

"Well, then make one up," Abby snapped, annoyed that he ruined her fantasy.

His large hands landed on her shoulders. "A demanding woman, aren't you?" he purred.

Her insides turned molten, Abby managed a sputter of indignation. "There's nothing wrong with knowing what you want and asking for it."

"Nothing at all." His lips pressed against the top of her head. "Found anything yet?"

She shook her head. "I'm not even sure what I'm looking for."

"Something that doesn't look quite correct, or perhaps something that looks too perfect."

That wasn't much help. They made slow progress down the stairs. "The story?"

"Ah yes." His hands tightened on her shoulders. "After dinner, my ancestor retired to his study, presumably to drink liquor. No woman was permitted to enter this masculine den and so he was free to stay in solitude, or ascend the secret stairs to his mistress.

"His mistress was a rare character: of good breeding, but rendered impoverished by the Wars of the Roses. She had delicate features and the palest skin, for her contract kept her sequestered in doors. Yet she was no meek miss, being naturally wild and passionate."

"Oh, do tell." Abby paused and shoved on a rock jutting out from the rest. It didn't budge, nor did it move when she pulled on it.

"One night, my ancestor prepared to go upstairs to his mistress. He'd not gone halfway, his path lit like ours is now—or would be if you didn't have that modern gadget—and out of the shadows, he saw his mistress descend.

"She wore nothing but a translucent gown, her white skin glowing through the thin fabric. My ancestor felt a rush of unmitigated lust rush through him. He met her on the stairs, unfastening his breeches with one hand while he pulled her to him with the other."

Myles whirled Abby around, shifting to stand on the lower step. She gasped, flicking off the flashlight. Her nipples pressed in hard nubs against the soft fabric of her gown.

He undid his breeches, his large cock springing up, hard and erect. Abby sucked in her breath. "You know, I've been trying to restrain myself from taking you ever since we stepped into this secret place," he murmured, his lips just a breath away from hers.

Was that why he had been so tetchy? She had no time to voice the question. His mouth came down upon hers, kissing her hard. He hauled her against him, making his purpose very clear.

As if she'd had any doubts.

His hungry kiss ended at last, and their breaths sounded loud in the narrow space.

"What happened next?" Abby whispered, knowing he'd do the same to her. "What did your ancestor do next?"

Myles rested his forehead against her shoulder, his muscles tensed. "He took her, right here on the stairs. He laid her out on all fours and penetrated her from behind."

"Yes," Abby breathed, excited beyond words. "I want that, Myles. Do that to me."

He captured her mouth in another hot kiss, searing her senses. She rubbed against him, his cock finding its way into the folds of her gown and against her cunt.

"Turn," he commanded, his voice a groan. She did so, reaching behind her to stroke the backs of his thighs and over to his buttocks peeking out from his loosened breeches.

He humped her, his cock cleaving a way along the cleft of her bottom. He captured her breasts with his hands, loosening the ties of her gown, baring them to the cool air, no doubt glad she had not worn her bra.

Tweaking her nipples, he tugged on them harder, sending rapturous lightning through her. She writhed against him and his large cock, feeling the back of her gown dampen with the exertion.

"On your knees, wench," Myles growled, "before I explode over your nice gown."

"My only gown," Abby reminded him, sinking to her knees. She hitched up her skirts, protecting them from the rough stone steps that bit into her knees.

She bent forward, her breasts hanging free from the confines of her bodice.

Myles didn't waste any time, on his knees behind her. He bared her rump, pushing her skirts to one side. His heat warming her bared thighs, he didn't plunge right in her as she expected, but delayed.

Using his cock, he toyed with her slit, sliding back and forth along her nether lips, his thighs a whisper away from hers. She spread her legs farther, wanting him inside her.

The pressure from his teasing cock vanished, replaced by his fingers, teasing her lips apart, driving in toward her wet cunt. Her slick flesh gave him easy access. When he reached her clit, brushing over it, she gasped in pleasure.

She braced herself against the steps. "Myles," she begged, "just give it to me. I want it hard and dirty."

"Do you?" Myles toyed with her clit until she started humping his hand. Her soft cries echoed up the narrow way.

"Please, please," she begged.

He rubbed over her wet clit. Sheer pleasure thrummed through her, her racing heartbeat sounding loud in her ears. She ground against his hand, hearing the sucking sound of her wet sex making contact.

A new thickness probed her cunt. Abby let loose a rush of delighted air. His cock pressed against her, seeking entry. For a moment, she had the ridiculous thought he might be too large for her in this position, but he slid inside without a hitch.

Their groans mingled, initial satisfaction achieved. She arched her back, wanting him inside her all the way. He gave her another inch.

And another. Planting his hands on her hips, his fingers dug into her soft skin. With a jerk of his hips, he buried himself deep inside, grinding against her bottom.

He held her steady, pounding in and out of her. Her head spinning, Abby wailed her pleasure. Her hands slipping, she braced against the step rise above her. Her body shook with each one of his thrusts. Her head lowered, eyes closed, she lost herself in the wild rush of wanting he aroused in her.

Every part of her seemed on fire and tingling, even the bottoms of her feet, all straining and reaching toward the anticipated mind-blowing release.

Myles grabbed a handful of her short hair and hauled her head up. She cried out, her back bending into a deeper bow. Myles's cock slid in even deeper.

He filled and stretched her, his cock dominating her flesh. He pulled out and plunged in again, the sharp contact rending a scream from her lips. Her senses seared and blinded by his assault, she yearned for a cataclysmic release. More, she wanted more.

Nothing existed but him: his hand twisted in her hair, his cock inside her, his muscled thighs between hers. She overflowed with the sweet golden tension, her breath rasping in the damp air.

The orgasmic explosion grew within, building and building until her universe consisted of nothing but her awed screams.

Myles bent over her, drawing her into a more intimate embrace, his cool palms covering her hot pinpricks of nipples. He tugged at them, keeping her in an orgasmic state. Her cunt convulsively squeezed around him, but he rode it out, and she didn't feel the hot splash of his cum inside her.

Opening her eyes, Abby stared at the blurred steps before her. Myles still fucked her with a merciless pounding. Her vision blurred and jogged with each thrust until Myles roared, his hips jerking, uncontrolled, and she was awash in his come.

He slid out of her, and a sticky trail beaded itself along her inner thigh.

Her vision cleared and she gasped.

On the step, someone had carved letters. *HYPOGAEUM LIBIDO.*

Myles kissed her shoulder. Part of Abby hardly noticed, while another part of her rejoiced in his tenderness.

"Myles," she whispered, her voice hoarse.

He made a tired "Mmm?"

"Myles, I think I found something."

He came alert at that.

Making room for him at her side, Abby directed her flashlight at the carved words. Squished together, one hip pressed against rough rock, Abby found it hard to focus. "That's Latin, isn't it?"

Myles grunted, tracing the carved letters with a fingertip. "Do you know the language?" he whispered.

Abby shook her head, and then remembered that Myles might not be able to see her in the dark. "No. I know little bits of graveyard Latin, but that's about it."

"Hmm." His response wasn't derisive or dismissive. "'Libido' means 'lust'."

"I thought it might," Abby replied, nudging him.

He ignored her, looking at the other word. "This one I'm not so familiar with." He straightened up, getting to his feet and helping Abby to hers. "We are right next to a library, so let's see if the old fellow has a Latin dictionary handy."

Abby held back. "You don't think it might be under this step?" She tapped the inscribed step with her big toe.

Myles paused. "It's possible." He knelt again, bending over the stone stair. Abby restrained the urge to ruffle his hair. "It's well mortared in."

"We'd need tools then," Abby suggested.

Myles rose again and gave her a swift hug. "Indeed. I think you shall have to don your modern attire for such a dirty task."

"Perhaps you should have thought of that before you took me here on the—"

"Shh!" Myles clamped a hand over her mouth.

Eyes wide, Abby listened for what had startled Myles. She heard nothing out of the ordinary.

Until she heard the sound of a door closing. And closing again.

Twisting in his grasp, Abby looked sideways at Myles. "I think the owners have come home." He released her. "It'll be the servants first, to prepare the house, but we must make our appearance."

"Can't we make a run for it?"

"Do you mean to escape?" Myles gave a defiant headshake and descended the last few steps to the study. "Not a chance. Not while the statue is still in this house. I told you, I know the family. We'll make up some little story." He took her hand and drew her out into the daylight. "Come, we must tidy ourselves and hide your things before the servants find them. Thank heavens I picked a guest chamber."

They crossed to the study door and Myles peeked out, looking in one direction and then the other. He grabbed her hand. "Let's make a run for it."

7

They dashed up the stairs, giving up silence for speed. Myles's boots clomped on the wooden floorboards, even those overlaid with rugs. Abby ran behind, her boots clunking on the floor.

Abby didn't notice if anyone saw them. She hoped not.

In the bedroom, Myles shoved Abby's suitcases under the bed, making sure the counterpane hid them from view. Abby stood in front of the mirror, trying to brush the creases out of her gown.

"Take off your dress," Myles instructed. He watched her struggle out of her boots. "We need to find you some decent footwear. Something flat and not—" He waved his hand in the air, lost for words.

"Chunky?" Abby supplied, "I have some ballet flats." She pointed. "In the suitcase under the bed."

Sighing, Myles heaved them out while Abby kicked off her boots. Abby retrieved her flats, slipping them on her feet.

"Now, a ribbon for your hair." Myles rummaged through the dressing table in hope of a stray ribbon. He held up a faded green one, the threads coming loose at the ends. "This will have to do."

Abby fashioned it into a sort of hairband and stood back from the mirror to survey her handiwork. "Will I pass?"

"I hope so." Myles gnawed on his lip, surveying her with a more critical expression than Abby's gay best friend. She sighed. She might never see Richard again.

Finally, Myles nodded. "Now, we need to come up with a story."

"I thought you said they knew you."

"They know me," Myles confirmed with a long-suffering air. He sank into the chair by the window. "They do not know you. In this time, you have no family, no connections."

Dread settled in her stomach. "I have you," she whispered, her voice hoarse. She hated to admit her dependency on him but he'd given her little other choice but to remind him of his promise.

"So you have." His warm, genuine smile, unfettered, sent her heart skipping. "But I'm afraid I will not add very much consequence."

"I don't need much," Abby pointed out, glancing at him via the mirror. "Just enough not to get tossed out on my arse."

His lips twitched in an otherwise stern visage. He hadn't been successful in preserving a serious expression for the brief time she'd known him. "Try not to use language like that, my dear, or they'll think I found you in the gutter."

Abby blew him a raspberry, grinning at his quickly masked smile.

He pursed his lips. "We have a few hours yet before the family arrives. We shall come up with something."

"What about the servants? Won't they ask questions?"

"Oh, they might ask who we are and why we're here, but I shall assure them that we came ahead of the owners. It just remains to see what we'll say to the Wintertons."

Abby frowned. "Won't they check with their servants and catch us in the lie?"

"Oh, hardly." Myles waved off the concern. "They will be too pleased I spared them from their master's wrath that they will not share any discrepancy."

"You're so sure." Abby gnawed her lip. "He's the type to lose his temper?"

"Fearsome fellow," Myles said, his good nature unaffected. "Cold as ice. Freezes you with a look."

Abby blinked. "And you think you can charm him into letting us stay?"

"Why not?" His wide grin made her heart skip. It became clear Myles was an adrenaline junkie. His mood was contagious.

She folded her arms and gave him a look, trying not to let it show that his ebullient mood affected her.

"I didn't marry his daughter. He should be happy about that."

"That all depends. Is she married now?"

"Er . . ."

"So we need to come up with a *really* compelling story."

He looked abashed for all of ten seconds. "Ah yes." Myles rose from where he sat on the edge of the bed and started pacing. "Let me think . . . What would stop the duke thinking I'm still after his daughter?"

Abby gaped. "You chased a duke's daughter?"

"For access to the statue, my dear. Like you so astutely observed earlier, she's a touch high and mighty."

"More than a touch, I'll bet," she muttered, ignoring the jealous twinge. Why should she be jealous?

He grinned at her, the grin growing wider when she scowled at him.

"Solving your problem may solve mine," Abby remarked. Her spread arms took in the entire room. "We are sharing a bed, after all."

Myles stopped before her, gazing down at her with a lazy,

sensual expression. "Would you mind if we posed as a married couple?"

"We don't actually have to get married, do we?" The last thing Abby wanted was to be tied to a man technically two hundred years dead.

"Not unless we are found out." Myles swung open the wardrobe where a large rucksack slumped at the bottom. He crouched, rifling through the pack. At length, he rose, something clenched in his fist. He held his fist out to her. "Here, wear this. It was my mother's."

His fingers uncurled to reveal a red gold band, leaves engraved around it.

Biting her lip, Abby took it, her fingertips grazing his palm. "I hope it fits." She slipped it onto her left ring finger. It went over the knuckle with some difficulty. She held it up to the light. "It fits." She shot him a shy glance. "I promise I will give it back when all this is done."

He bent forward and kissed her forehead. "You can be sweet, Abby."

Abby blushed, discomfited. "Yes, well, don't expect it to happen too often."

He chuckled. "Do not be ashamed of having a heart, Ms. Deane."

He knew just how to prickle her, but this time she refused to bite. "We still have time to kill, don't we?"

Myles nodded. "We need to work out the details of your life."

"I cannot come from an obscure family?"

"Not with a duke."

Abby pouted.

Myles laughed and drew her into an embrace. "It was a good thought, Abby."

She frowned. "It has to be that way, Myles. Anything other than an obscure family and he'd know about them, surely."

"You overestimate the duke in matters of recall." Myles twisted his lower lip between finger and thumb.

"You know I'm right," Abby persisted, sensing a chink in Myles's armor. "I might not be an authority on the rules of this time, but how likely are you to marry someone from a well-known family?"

Myles gave her a long, long look. "I'd marry somebody from a respectable family. My ancestry is ancient and respected, even if it's but a shade of its former glory."

"So you'd marry into other old, poor nobility then?"

Myles gave a reluctant shrug. "It would be too crass to suggest I would marry for money."

Abby snorted. "You just did."

He let the remark pass unchallenged, not even stooping to make a face. "However, the old duke would agree I am an unreliable sort. To have made an equally unreliable marriage—"

"Excuse me?" Abby interrupted. "I am not unreliable. I am punctual, practical, and anything else you care to name that fits the word reliable. Exactly the sort of person an unreliable sort would need to keep him on the straight and narrow."

His grin seemed so self-satisfied, Abby started to wonder if she'd been played. She glared at him, suspicious. Why did he let her come up with all the obvious answers?

"So, we have explained my presence," Abby said, her brows still lowered. "But what excuse do we have for being here in the first place?"

"Depends upon which of the family makes an appearance," came Myles's blithe reply. "If young Winterton is there, he'll allow us to cotton onto his tails. The fellow has a taste for adventure."

"And if he's not?"

"Then we'll say we expected to meet him here. And before you ask, if he's not expected here, then I'll suggest that our letters must have crossed in the mail."

"But then we'll have to leave," Abby pointed out.

Myles shrugged. "There will be other chances at the statue. Next Season, if need be."

"Next season? You mean in the winter?"

He regarded her as if she'd just grown another head. "Those kind of questions will reveal you as a fraud. The Season is the time the gentry spend in London attending Parliament and eyeing potential brides."

"Ah." Abby made a mental note not to ask questions of anyone outside of Myles, who knew her secret. "When is the next Season?"

"Spring. They should still be in London however." He frowned. "The weather hasn't turned cold yet. I wonder what has happened?"

"Do you think someone alerted him to you being here?"

"Then the servants would have turfed us out long since, on the points of pitchforks." Myles shook his head. "No, there must be some other reason. We'll need to find it out. It might become useful to us."

"I had no idea you were such a schemer."

"Didn't you?" His charming smile had a sweet yet mischievous quality to it. "I take my opportunities where I can, Abby. Best for you to remember that."

Abby nodded. She rose and crossed to the window. It overlooked the extreme left of the rolling lawns in front of the house. The carriage drive, the gravel glowing golden in the late morning sun, curved into view on her far right.

"So we wait."

She glanced over her shoulder to see Myles slumped into the sofa chair, his eyes closed. Abby turned back to the window, fingering the heavy gold ring on her finger.

Hard to imagine she'd been cast back in time. Harder still to find herself lost in the most exciting sexual relationship she'd ever experienced. Even harder yet, the very notion he'd agreed to pretend to marry her.

Although there hadn't been much in the way of alternatives. "Hello, meet my floozy Abby Deane?"

Somehow, she didn't think that'd go over well.

Movement outside caught her eye and broke her ruminations. Two carriages, one following the other, hove into view. Dust seemed not to mar their glistening black paint, nor the shining hides of the four matched black horses that drew them.

"Someone's coming," Abby called in a low voice without looking away from the window.

She sensed Myles join her, his hand resting on her shoulder. "It's the Wintertons," he confirmed. "That explains why the servants have been too frenetic to pay any heed to us. They've arrived much sooner than I expected."

His hand slid down her arm to nestle in the crook of her elbow. "Shall we go greet them, my dear?"

Abby swallowed, stemming the sudden fluttery quiver in her stomach. She turned with him from the window. They left their room and headed for the main stairwell. "Any last words of advice?"

He squeezed her arm in reassurance, smiling down at her. "You will not disappoint," he said. His sunny expression darkened for a moment. "Do not mention the statue under any circumstances. If the duke got wind of it—"

They descended the grand staircase, watching a collection of servants scramble to line up on either side of the tall double doors that would reveal their lord and master.

Myles swallowed. "Courage."

On some unseen signal, two footmen stepped forward and opened the doors, letting in the last of the afternoon sunlight. It streamed golden across the marble floor, marred only by the shadows of the Wintertons.

With a nudge from Myles, Abby remembered to continue descending the staircase. She gathered her skirts in one hand, keeping them pulled to one side as opposed to lifting them up. She figured this made for a more decorous descent.

As it turned out, she needn't have bothered about being careful because nobody noticed them, including the Wintertons, until they'd reached the bottom.

She'd had plenty of opportunity to observe them beforehand. A thin, white-haired man, dressed impeccably, she'd immediately labeled as the duke. Nobody else had his presence, a way of expecting attention and finding it.

A young blond woman dressed in gorgeous velvet greeted the servants with a friendly smile, clinging to the duke's arm. His daughter, she guessed. Behind her, another young woman, red-haired, imperiously ignored the bows and curtsies of the staff.

Myles hadn't given her a complete family tree, so she supposed he'd neglected to mention there'd been more than one daughter. She wondered which one of them had been Myles's target.

Abby caught the moment the redhead spotted Myles. The girl's lips pursed even tighter and she glared at Myles, slaying him with her daggered look. *That one.*

A young redheaded man standing at the redhead's side paid attention to nothing else but his shoes.

"Where's the old dragon of a duchess?" Abby whispered to Myles.

Despite the fact she'd scarcely breathed the words, the duke's head shot up out of a low conversation with what looked like one of the senior servants.

"Hardy," he snapped, his voice strong and clear despite his age. "What the devil are you doing here? Who is that baggage?"

So much for looking respectable.

Myles released her, sinking into a deep bow. Abby attempted

to mimic the depth in her awkward curtsey. "Your Grace," he intoned. "I was beginning to wonder whether you were coming."

"I beg your pardon?" The duke closed the distance between them, his blond daughter still on his arm.

"Your son—" Myles paused to flutter his fingers at the red-headed young man who only now paid attention to the proceedings. The young man grinned, his face turning redder than his hair.

"Your son"—Myles picked up the thread of his conversation, "was kind enough to invite us on our way home from the North."

The young man frowned but neither protested nor affirmed Myles's words. When his father turned to look at him, his expression smoothed out into a bland, polite smile.

"My son should learn to consider the wishes of his father before sending out invitations."

"I'm sure he meant to tell you of it. After all, he thought it might be quite the thing for you to meet my new bride."

"Did he now?" The duke's piercing blue gaze examined Abby. "Her?"

Abby let her expression grow cool and bobbed a curtsey. "Your Grace."

"If you had known we were coming, I would have expected you to have dressed more suitably. You look"—and the duke's gaze scoured Abby—"distinctly disheveled."

"That gown looks like Mama's," the redheaded girl put in.

"It does rather," the duke agreed. His white brows beetled together. "Explain."

"I lost all my clothes," Abby blurted, twisting her loaned wedding ring. "We had a terrible accident on the way here—"

"Not far from here at all," Myles put in, shooting her an encouraging smile.

"All my clothes were ruined, absolutely ruined. My wedding trousseau, everything. My dear Myles fared a little better. I

was all set to turn tail and go home, but he insisted we stay."
Abby rolled her eyes in mock exasperation. "He thought you
wouldn't mind if I borrowed a gown. I could hardly be presented to you in rags." Finishing her story, Abby took a steadying breath.

"As opposed to borrowed weeds." The duke's pale cheeks
colored.

"Oh, how tragic!" exclaimed the blond woman, either un-
aware of her father's wrath or seeking to avert it. She turned to
the duke, leaning into him. "My dear, you will allow me to give
her some of my wardrobe?"

The duke's annoyed expression transformed into indulgence.
"My darling, you may do anything you wish. You are the duchess
now." He shot Abby a sharp glance. "The old dragon died."

Abby flushed, astonished at the acuity of the old man's hearing. "I'm sorry."

Myles bobbed a bow. "I fear my new bride is far too sensible
to read the lady's magazines. Of course, she doesn't read the
newspapers."

"Sensible?" The angry color in the duke's cheeks faded. "I
see now why my son thought it a good idea for us to meet. I'd
have never believed that a sensible woman would have given
you the time of day, Hardy."

"It was a surprise to me too, Your Grace." Myles shot her a
fond look. Abby's cheeks grew warm and she stared at the
floor. "I hope she will curb the worst of my habits."

Abby shot him an annoyed look. "I wasn't aware you'd
married me because you needed a nursemaid."

The duke burst out in laughter. "You married a shrew!" His
eyes sparkled. "I think I may like your company, Mrs. Hardy."

His acceptance seemed to release the new duchess. She slipped
from her husband's side and took Abby's arm. "Let us go upstairs and we'll see what we can find you that will suit."

"You are too generous," Myles said for Abby, giving her an encouraging nod.

She didn't need it. If it took her out of the eye of the duke, she was happy. She accepted the duchess's arm and they ascended the stairs together. Abby copied the manner in which the duchess held the skirt of her gown.

They paused on the landing. The duchess glanced down. "Elaine, will you not join us?"

The redhead's lip curled.

"It looks like she'd rather die first," Abby dared to whisper the confidence to the duchess. The woman was very likable and sympathetic.

The redhead turned red and looked fit to explode.

Abby stared in amazement. "She can't have heard that!"

The duchess laughed. "The hall was originally built so that even the quietest of whispers could be heard anywhere else in the space. The original owners didn't believe in secrets."

Abby managed an embarrassed smile and shot an apologetic look at Elaine. The redhead flounced off in the other direction. "Myles didn't say," Abby said when they resumed their ascent.

"You must be on very intimate terms with Mr. Hardy to speak of him with his Christian name so easily."

Abby gave her a look. "Well, he is my husband!"

"Quite so, but did your mother tell you not to allow intimacy outside your bedroom?"

Abby flushed. "Myles—er, Mr. Hardy—makes it easy to forget."

The duchess chuckled. Abby might've been mistaken but she thought she heard an envious note in her amusement. Abby might've dared to ask a friend about it, but this woman was a stranger, both in fact and due to her alien mindset. Not refer to a lover/husband by his first name? How weird was that?

They reached the duchess's door. Abby paused, expecting

the duchess to lead the way inside, but she kept walking. Abby pointed to the door. "Isn't this . . . ?"

The duchess eyed the door with a weary expression. "That is the former duchess's room."

Abby bit her tongue. She wanted to take this woman to task for letting her dead predecessor maintain such a presence, but she reminded herself she didn't know the whole story yet.

"How long have you been married?" she asked instead, catching up to her.

"Not quite a year." The duchess opened a door. "Here we are."

Abby stepped in. The room was as spacious as the other, befitting someone of the duchess's rank. The thrown open curtains. let in fresh air and the last of the light. Hung with sumptuous velvet, simple white lacy linen sheets decked the bed, one end folded back, ready for the duchess's slumber.

The duchess walked to another door and opened it. "Let us see what I have. My husband has insisted on far too many gowns for me."

"He encouraged you to shop?" Abby laughed. "Usually it's the other way around."

The duchess smiled. "You might not have heard that my marriage was quite an increase in station for me. My husband is eager to show that I am equal to task."

"Ah." Abby turned from surveying the closet space that housed the duchess's incredible wardrobe. "Are you happy?"

"That's a forward question, Mrs. Hardy." The duchess frowned.

Abby sighed. She should stick to simple subjects. "I'm sorry. I'm sometimes too curious for my own good."

The duchess brushed away her apology. "Let us see what I have. I suspect my old simple gowns might work for you. I kept them."

She knelt, tugging a small chest out from its place under row upon row of boots and slippers. She opened it and pulled back a layer of protective paper. She held up a gown, a simple plain gray with a high neck. "What about this?"

Abby took it from her and held it up. "I like it. It's simple, no nonsense. Myl—Mr. Hardy will miss the cleavage view."

The duchess smiled up at her. "He has plenty of opportunity for that in the evening." She turned back to the trunk, her head dipping. "Here, let's see if I can find one of my evening gowns. Without a scarf, it might please your husband."

"Thank you." Abby received an armful of gowns for day and evening.

"Would you—" The duchess looked at her feet. "Would you like to try them on now? I can summon my maid to make any adjustments."

"I would like that." Carefully, Abby laid the gowns over a trunk. She tried to reach behind her back for the first of the buttons and gave up. She looked over her shoulder at the duchess. "I'm sorry, but could you help?"

Abby expected her to summon a maid, but instead she unfastened the buttons down the back of her gown herself. The duchess's fingers skimmed over Abby's skin, peeling the gown back.

"Mrs. Hardy!" the duchess gasped. "You are not wearing any stays!"

Unseen by the duchess, Abby winced. "Myl—Mr. Hardy grew impatient with getting the thing on and off and forbade it while we're on our honeymoon." She manufactured a sigh. "It was packed with everything else I lost."

The duchess patted her bare shoulder. "You have had a most eventful honeymoon."

Abby snorted a laugh. "Life with Myles will always be an adventure." She touched the borrowed gold band about her finger. It was the truth. She might not ever be able to ascend to the skies for her taste of freewheeling fun, but she might find it living with Myles. If he honored his promise to help her out.

Abby let the loose gown fall to the floor. Keeping her back turned, she reached for the first gown. The last time she'd been even close to naked in front of another woman had been in the gym changing rooms during high school.

She hurried out of her borrowed gown and into the new one.

"Here, let me help." The duchess caught the neck of her gown, pulling it up and fastening the buttons.

Abby faced her, tugging at her bodice. "How do I look, Your Grace?" She wanted to reach in and adjust the position of her breasts but didn't feel comfortable doing so. Far too common to do before a duchess, even a newly raised one.

The duchess surveyed her. "I think if you are to wear my clothes then we can dispense with titles." She flushed. "I'm not fully comfortable with them, and you seem to prefer the use of Christian names anyway. Call me Lucy, please." Her voice dropped. "Just between us, you understand."

"Got it. Call me Abby." She swirled her skirts. "What do you think of the dress? Is it that bad?"

"Abby, you really need stays." Lucy cleared her throat. "May I?"

Abby had no idea what Lucy asked. "Sure," she said, bracing herself.

Lucy reached out, cupping Abby's breasts. "Excuse me," she murmured. She reached into the neck of Abby's gown and hefted one breast and then the other into the bodice proper.

"Ahh, I could have done that." Abby tried to think of the duchess like her OB/GYN. Surely the woman didn't just feel her up. She imagined it. Right?

"Of course." Lucy withdrew a few steps. "But as your husband insists on you not wearing the stays . . ."

Abby reached out and took Lucy's hands. "You were helping. I'm sorry. With my husband's attentions, I'm a little sensitive." That had to be it.

Lucy smiled, squeezing Abby's hands. "I can see we're going to be intimates quite soon. We seem to talk about the most personal things."

Abby blushed. She'd put her foot in it again. "I'm sorry."

Lucy squeezed her hands again. "Do not be. I would like to have a friend."

"Don't you have any?" Abby frowned. Was the life of a duchess so lonely?

"My childhood friends write to me when they can," she said, turning to smooth the gowns on the trunk. "But they are quite busy with their own lives, and now that I'm a duchess . . ."

"They're afraid to write?"

"In case they appear to be hangers-on." Lucy sighed. "I do have a particular friend, but she's traveling around the Mediterranean and her letters come rarely."

"Then I'd be happy to be your friend." She and Myles had a greater chance of not being asked to leave.

Lucy hugged her tight. "I'm glad." The hug went on for a long time. Abby tried not to squirm. At last, Lucy pulled away, ducking her head. "I'm afraid it will be a cold supper tonight. We did not give the staff enough notice to prepare a hot meal."

"That's fine," Abby replied, gazing into Lucy's face. She gave the duchess a one-armed hug. The title didn't matter at all. "And if you need to talk, Lucy, I'm here to listen."

Lucy smiled. "Thank you. Now if you'll help me change, we can go down to dinner."

8

It hadn't been easy to help Lucy, the duchess, change without a maid's help. Abby hoped that Lucy hadn't noticed or at least chalked it up to nerves at attending a duchess. Lucy didn't pass any remark or look suspicious at her mistakes. They descended to dine.

They entered a room gorgeously decked out in gold. Myles rose and crossed to her at once. "My dear, you look absolutely enchanting."

The duke glowered. "I thought I told you to dispose of those old gowns."

Lucy blanched for a moment, settling beside him. "I must have had a premonition I would need to give them to a soul in need."

"Her Grace has been very generous," Abby put in, her enjoyment in being close to Myles diminished by witnessing the duke's public rebuke. "I imagine they are good for mucking about in the garden."

Lucy smiled at her, her face strained. "I do keep one old gown for that, although I've had little chance to use it."

"There's nothing like coaxing the earth to produce beautiful things," Abby enthused. She decided not to mention her green thumb experience was limited to pots of African violets.

"And was that what you were doing when we arrived?" drawled Lucy's stepdaughter, her lip curled in disdain.

Abby faced her, masking her annoyance. She'd dealt with plenty of rude people before, who were in powerful positions over her. This one she couldn't walk away from. "I didn't feel I ought to use your mother's entire wardrobe."

"Thief," Elaine snarled in a mutter.

"Elaine!" Lucy gently reproved, not a note of anger in her voice. "You must have a care for people less fortunate than you."

"Like you were, I suppose," her stepdaughter mocked.

"Elaine!" The duke snapped. "You will apologize to your stepmother and to our guests for your ill-behavior."

Elaine pouted, mulish. "My apologies," she said to the room in general.

The duke managed a thin smile for his guests. "It has been a long journey for us, most tiring. Forgive our bad manners."

"We shall not presume too much upon you tonight," Myles acknowledged with a brief bow.

"You are too kind, Mr. Hardy. Eat with us, and we shall not intrude on your honeymoon any longer."

The young viscount spoke up. "I hope you'll spare me a few moments of your time after dinner. Port?"

The duke coughed. "My boy, when you are wed and on your honeymoon, you will realize you ought not disturb the newlyweds." He turned to his wife, patting her knee.

Abby relaxed a little. The duke's unmistakable fondness for his new wife put her at ease.

"In the morning." Myles didn't dare to contradict the duke. "I'm sure my wife will spare me for a few hours."

Abby opened her mouth for a sassy retort and shut it again at his warning look. She managed a thin smile. "Of course."

Dinner remained a strained affair. At the end, the duke excused himself to look over estate business in his study. Myles begged their excuses soon after.

In their room, Myles paced, storming to the window to look out and back to her. Abby slumped into the sofa chair and watched him. "What's the matter?"

"His Grace doesn't want us to stay. He made that pretty plain while you were upstairs with the duchess. I had to do some quick thinking to bring the viscount onto my side. He's at least intrigued enough to hear me out tomorrow."

"Then you'll be happy to hear that I've made fast friends with the duchess," Abby told him with a nonchalant air. "She really is nice."

Myles paused. "Then we might have a chance. The duke's study holds the Latin/English dictionary we need and he's ensconced in there tonight."

"But he spoke of being tired. He'll go to bed soon and then we can go down—"

"He was making excuses. He'll be up for hours yet. I suggest we get some rest. While I coax the viscount into letting us stay, you find out what that Latin word means. Meanwhile—" His worried expression transformed into a leer. "I believe it behooves us to satisfy our hosts that we are a newlywed couple."

Abby rose, crossing to him and enveloping herself in his embrace. It was so easy to fall into his arms, so natural. "Sounds like a good idea to me. Should I squawk 'Lawks, a'mercy, sir! You do not expect me to do that!'?"

Myles laughed. "This is not a restoration comedy, wench. Just give me sounds of satisfaction."

Abby echoed his laughter. "You will have to work to get that result."

"Not too hard, I'll wager." He bent his head, pressing his lips against her neck.

Unbidden, a sigh escaped her lips. His teeth nipped her in a silent "I told you so". Abby's eyes fluttered shut, reveling in the heated sensations wrought by Myles's mouth. She never knew her neck could be so sensitive.

His head dipped lower to nuzzle the hollow between neck and shoulder. "You're going to leave marks," she whispered.

"Then they'll know you've been thoroughly bedded." He glanced at her, making her aware of the length of his boyish and seductive eyelashes.

"They already know—well, the duchess does. I told her that I don't wear any stays because you've forbidden them. They take too long to take off, you complained."

Myles laughed, swinging her around. "You are a worthy accomplice, m'dear."

She grinned at him, delighted at his pleasure. When had a man actually lifted her like that? It was like a scene out of a movie, but he was real. Her hands slid down his flexed arms.

Very real.

He lowered her, spinning her around to face away from him. "Now let's get you out of this wretched gown."

"It's not wretched. It's very nice. The duchess gave it to me." Abby reached behind her, pushing back against his groin and his prominent bulge.

He ground against her, cool air wafting across her back while he unfastened the tiny buttons of her gown. She shivered, shaking her shoulders and shimmying out of the gown's bodice.

He pushed her away, letting the gown slide to the floor before turning her to face him. They came together in a clash of mouths, hungrily seeking their mutual pleasure. His warm hands slid down her back, cupping her buttocks and drawing her hard against him.

She rubbed against him, her hardening nipples sparking against the rough weave of his coat. "You are far too overdressed," she breathed, breaking their kiss. She forced space between them, tugging at the buttons on his coat, on his breeches, pulling at the white shirt underneath.

"Patience, patience!" Myles chuckled. He stepped back and stripped down, no unessential movement wasted.

Naked, he posed for her, hands on hips, his cock bouncing to rigid attention.

"Very nice," Abby remarked with a leer of her own. "Now, what are you gonna do with it?"

"Woman, you are provoking." He grinned to belie the irritation of his words. He charged her, capturing her in his arms, barreling her backward against the wall. "We shall have to fix that."

Abby gazed up at him. "Really? I thought you loved it."

His face softened for an instant. "I do." He chucked her chin. "Yet it does not mean I will not respond to it. Like this."

With his body, he pressed her against the wall. His mouth came down on hers hard and unyielding. Abby surrendered to him, opening her mouth to his. He strafed her body with his hands, teasing and tugging until her body sang for him.

His hands settled under her bottom and he hefted her upward. She wrapped her legs around his waist, feeling his cock press against her wet slit. She moaned, writhing against him, until the head of his cock pressed against her slick hole.

What was it about this nineteenth-century man that transformed her into a wanton? She knew the answer before the question even fully formed. He satisfied her.

She wanted him in her, filling her. She hoisted her hips, hoping he'd slip in, but with a flex of his buttocks, he held her at bay.

She whimpered, clawing at his bottom and lower back. How could he deny her?

The head inched in, moans expelling from both of them. She rocked against him, wanting him in deeper, but he denied her again.

With a grin, he denied her, supporting her thighs and holding back from sticking his entire cock into her.

Abby groaned. "Now who's being provoking! Myles, please!"

Inch by inch, he slid inside her, filling her and stretching her in a way she had come to relish.

"Yes, ohh, yes."

He withdrew, grunting, and thrust into her hard.

She screamed and he paused. "Don't stop," she begged him. "It's heaven."

His brow furrowed. "It didn't hurt?"

She had enough of her sense left to give him one of her looks. "You've never worried about that before. Besides, didn't you want sounds of satisfaction?"

He huffed. "Please do not sound like I'm killing you."

"Oh, I won't," she promised, cupping his cheek. "Don't you worry about that."

He kissed her, a kiss unlike his usual demands, soft and gentle. "Ready?" he whispered.

"Are you kidding? Quit talking and fuck me."

They exchanged grins. Myles firmed his grip on her thighs and plunged into her again.

She let out a little sobbing moan. Again he thrust, and again she cried out. Harder and harder, forcing sweet cries of delight from her throat until her keening cries blurred together into one.

He cried out, pumping into her in a sharp jerking motion before subsiding against her.

Pressed between Myles and the wall, Abby gasped for breath. She rested her head against Myles's shoulder, slipping into a delicious exhaustion.

Myles pulled out, scooping her up before she sank to the floor and staggered to the bed. He collapsed on it, taking her with him, wrapping her into an even-tighter embrace.

He kissed her hair. "Abby." He groaned her name.

She snuggled in closer, but Myles shifted, rising over her. He looked down at her, his brow quizzical. "What is it about you, Ms. Deane?"

A mite discomfited by his question and startled out of her postsex haze, Abby blinked up at him. "What?"

His finger curled along her cheek. "I worry. You find me a solution, and then you proceed to make me feel very, very good indeed."

Abby smiled. "That took two, you know."

His gaze grew heated, his eyelids lowering. "Indeed." He captured her lips into one last, hot and searing kiss before lying beside her and spooning behind her.

They breakfasted early, missing the Winterton family. Abby sighed in appreciation for her first hot meal.

Myles watched her pile her plate from the sideboard, a smirk growing on his face. "That's a most unladylike appetite."

Abby gave him a look. "And whose fault is that?"

He laughed, smirking with pride.

The younger Wintertons entered. "I found Elaine lurking in the hall." Viscount Winterton headed straight for the buffet.

"I was doing no such thing," his sister huffed. She poured herself some tea and collected some toast.

Abby caught her disdainful expression and raised her own eyebrow in turn, tucking into the rich food on her plate. "Oh, this is too good," she said between mouthfuls.

Viscount Winterton turned to Myles. "I heard some strange noises last night. Wailing . . ."

Abby choked, covering her mouth with a napkin. She exchanged an amused look with Myles.

"I cannot think what that might have been." Myles buttered his toast, scooping a forkful of scrambled egg on top.

Abby remained silent, watching the viscount over the rim of her teacup.

"It was disgusting!" Elaine burst out. She looked down her nose. "So common!"

The viscount's smile twisted. "That is jealousy speaking, sister dear. You turned down Mr. Hardy, remember?"

Elaine scowled.

"Do not tease her," Myles said, shooting a sympathetic look at the flushing Elaine. "It is not nice."

Elaine put her cup down with a clatter. "I do not need you to defend me."

Myles raised his hand in surrender and returned his attention to his breakfast. He pointed a knife in the viscount's direction. "When you are finished, let us go for a walk and discuss matters."

"Manly business, I suppose," Abby remarked, swallowing.

He shot her a warning glare.

Elaine rose. "I'm going for a ride." She flounced out before Abby dared to invite herself.

"My apologies," the viscount said. "I fear I baited her too much."

Abby shrugged. "That's what brothers are for."

"You are quite understanding." The viscount bowed from his chair.

In a short while, the two men rose and left together, the viscount following easily on Myles's heels.

Left alone, Abby finished eating and headed for the library. She browsed the shelves, searching for the Latin/English dictionary that ought to be there.

"May I help you, Mrs. Hardy?" The voice came from behind her.

Abby spun. "Your Grace, you startled me."

"My apologies. What are you looking for?"

Abby tucked her hands behind her back, feeling like a caught naughty schoolgirl. "A dictionary. I need to look up the meaning of a Latin word."

The duke rose, stretching his stiff back as he walked around the side of the desk. "Perhaps I can help." He leaned against the desk, folding his arms. "Although what interest a woman would have in such a language boggles the mind."

Restraining the urge to rip the duke a new one, Abby managed a sweet smile. She mentally ran through all the replies she wanted to say.

"Mrs. Hardy?" the duke prompted, his features expressionless.

Abby decided to ignore his comment and forge ahead. "If you will just point me in the way of the book I need, I won't disturb you any longer."

"I'm not disturbed." The duke's eyes narrowed. "What is the word? Mayhap I can spare you the strain of looking it up."

Abby's hands twisted behind her back, swirling with indecision. If she told him the word, he'd want to know why. "I can read," she reminded him, retreating to defensiveness.

"I am sure you can," he smoothly returned, "else there wouldn't be a word you'd need to translate. I spent years of school learning Latin. It was a long time ago, but I am not all that rusty."

"Myles learned Latin at school too, and he didn't know the meaning of it."

The duke waved toward the bookcases nearest her. "You'll find it on the second column of bookshelves, third shelf from the bottom."

Abby dropped an abbreviated curtsey. "Thank you." Pulling out the book, she laid it across a sofa chair back. Flipping the pages, she scanned down the page until she found the word.

"Hypogaeum. Basement." The duke's voice at her ear made her jump. She slammed the dictionary closed and spun to face him. He retreated a step. "What an unusual word to seek."

"Maybe I got the word wrong." Abby chewed on her lower lip. "It doesn't make sense."

"I believe the word is very straightforward." The duke's lips quirked. "Is it the context of the sentence?"

"Yes, yes. That must be it," Abby agreed hastily. "I shall have to find out that word again and come back." She twisted to pick up the heavy dictionary and handed it to him. "Thank you."

"You're welcome," the duke purred, drawing closer. "You're more than welcome."

Abby had never run from a fight, but in this time with so little influence and so many unknown rules, she didn't know how far she could push the duke and still win. From the leer on the duke's face, he had other payment in mind.

She fled.

Abby headed for the outdoors. It didn't make any sense. Why would *basement* be inscribed on a stair?

"Mrs. Hardy!" a feminine voice called. The duchess hurried over to her at a trot, a paper parasol bobbing over her head. "You forgot your bonnet," she said on reaching her. She held the parasol over the two of them. "Although I suppose you lost that in the accident as well."

Abby smiled. They stood in the house's shade. "Actually, I do have a bonnet. I left it upstairs. I, ahh, ran into your husband. It was a bit disconcerting."

"He does have that effect on people," Lucy admitted. "But he really is warm and tender underneath—although perhaps I shouldn't be giving away his secrets. What happened?"

"I went looking for a dictionary."

"And he teased you for needing to use one," Lucy finished, guiding her along the graveled walk toward an old-fashioned knot garden.

"Why, yes!" Abby turned to her. "How did you guess?"

The corners of Lucy's lips turned upward. "I am married to him, my dear."

Abby flushed. "Yes, of course. I'm sorry. I shouldn't have been so surprised."

Lucy tucked her arm in Abby's. "I know you were not ex-pected by my husband, but I told him last night that I am glad you came."

"And?" Abby prompted. Did the duke care of his wife's feelings?

"He is glad also. Although I am sure you do not wish to stay once your husband has completed his business with my step-son."

"I have no idea what it is, but it does seem to me that it might take awhile," Abby hedged, not knowing when they might find the statue or the young viscount got fed up with Myles's tales.

"How rude for it to occur in the middle of your honey-moon. I, ah . . ." Lucy flushed. "I heard you last night."

It was Abby's turn to blush. "It seems the entire household heard us. I'm sorry. We're used to being alone. I will ask Myles if he will be a little more considerate tonight."

Lucy laughed. "Do you really want that?"

Abby grinned. "Not really. Last night was . . . I'm not going to embarrass you, am I?"

"My dear Abby, you will find me very difficult to shock." Her cool words belied her pink face.

It didn't mesh with Lucy's quiet demeanor, but Abby fig-ured you always had to watch for the quiet ones. Like herself. "Well, last night was incredible. The best yet."

The thrill of being overheard was only half the reason. Myles's skills as a lover were undeniable, but a deeper bond had formed. She inhaled the soft scent of the lavender beds, turning the no-tion over and over in her mind, Myles's wedding band twisting about her finger.

She had to be careful, very careful, not to fall for Myles Hardy. In her vulnerable position, the results might be embar-rassing. Plus, she had no Cosmos in which to drown her sorrows.

The young viscount hailed them, startling Abby from her

reverie. She shot Lucy an apologetic glance for being noncommunicative.

"We're going riding! Don't wait up!" the viscount hollered. Myles gave them a last wave and disappeared around the corner of the house with the younger man.

"Don't wait up?" Abby echoed, disbelieving. "This better be good."

Lucy tucked Abby's arm a little tighter into hers. "I hope I will be able to distract you from your absent husband. Surely after last night, you cannot complain."

Abby's lips pursed. "No, I suppose not. I just wish I were a little more involved. I don't like that he's keeping this from me."

"Men's business." Lucy dismissed with a wave. "Come, I will show you the gardens and then we'll sit and talk."

Abby swallowed, dreading making more than light conversation. She'd give herself away half a dozen times, and even a new friendship couldn't prevent possible eviction. She straightened her shoulders. She could do this.

Lucy loaned Abby a maid in order that she be presentable for dinner. Abby listened to the maid's chatter, trying to keep the characters in her stories straight. How large was the Winterton family anyway? And just how many estates did they possess besides this one? Stacks, by the sounds of it.

"You look beautiful." Myles lounged against the doorway.

The maid chittered. "She's not dressed."

The gown hung off her shoulders. "Finish buttoning me, Mary. We won't let Mr. Hardy undo all your good work."

The maid dashed to comply, fumbling her duties under Myles's watchful eye. She hurried out.

"You do look beautiful," Myles repeated, strolling into the room. "I see you've found some stays."

"Yes, they're more comfortable than I thought."

"Seeing your bare back was incredibly erotic," Myles drawled. His lips brushed her bared shoulder. "This isn't one of Lucy's old gowns?"

"No, it's not. Belonged to the former duchess." Abby pulled away. "I assume you need to change."

"I do." Closing the door, Myles made short work of changing, leaving Abby little time to admire the view. "I found out something very interesting. It seems the new duchess caused a bit of a scandal in London. That's why they are home so soon."

"And what are you plotting with the viscount?"

"Just keeping us out of trouble." He looked in the mirror and tapped his nose. "No need to worry." He curled fresh linen around his throat.

She let the mystery go. For now. "I like it better when your throat is bare."

He arched an eyebrow. "It's not proper."

Abby sighed. "I should have guessed."

"There is one thing missing from your ensemble." Myles fished something out of his pocket. "I want you to wear this tonight."

Her eyes narrowed. "Have you been going through my things?" She plucked the miniature vibrator from his open palm. In the shape of a butterfly, it hung from a belt. "This doesn't go around my neck."

Myles grinned. "So I surmised. I also figured it out." His hand slipped into his coat pocket and the butterfly came to life in her hand. "Wear it tonight."

Abby held it by the belt between her fingertips. "This is definitely not proper."

"The sound it makes is so soft, nobody will hear it." He drew his arms around her, kissing her forehead and dipping lower.

She ducked. "I'm not worried about the sounds it's going to make. I'm worried about the sounds I'm going to make."

He released her, his lower lip threatening to pout. "I will not get carried away, I promise." He switched it off.

Abby shook her head. "You have no idea . . ."

He got down on his knees before her. "Please, Abby. Why else would you have it if you didn't plan to wear it in public?"

"It gets me out of a bad mood."

He grinned. "You seem to be in one now." He held out his hand. "Allow me."

Sighing, Abby gave him the remote vibrator. He slipped the belts around both her legs. Abby lifted her skirts, allowing Myles to slide the belts up until they held in place.

She held her breath as his fingertips skimmed over her pubes. She swore she felt his breath across her slit. He parted her cunt lips and positioned the little butterfly over her clit.

He sealed it with a kiss.

Abby gave a soft moan, reaching down to his head through her gown. He kissed her again, his tongue flicking out and between her cunt lips. He gave her a long lick, tasting her swiftly rising arousal.

"Myles," Abby moaned. "I think I am officially out of my bad mood."

He ducked away, straightening her skirts for her. "None of that unusual underwear, I see."

"The maid didn't think it was proper." Abby sighed in disappointment that he'd stopped. "I'm getting heartily sick of the word."

Myles stood up and kissed her. Abby tasted herself on his lips. "That's why I like you so much." He kissed her again. "Come, we will be late."

The family awaited them in the drawing room. The duke greeted them, rising. "I am reminded of the reason why one never invites newlyweds to stay. Dinner gets cold."

Myles's hand slipped into his pocket. The remote vibrator came to life, pulsing against her clit, waking it. The heat rose on her cheeks. She shot Myles a look. The vibrator stilled, and Myles's hand left his pocket.

"Our apologies," Myles said, deadpan. He bowed. "I was so overcome with my wife's beauty that we lingered overlong. I do hope dinner isn't ruined."

Lucy rose, tucking her arm into her husband's. "Shall we go see?"

Abby and Myles trailed behind the family, taking their seats last. A welter of plates heaped with all manner of rich food lay along the center of the table. Abby eyed the roasted pig's face and her stomach rumbled. Next to it lay a platter of heaped vegetables, carrots, and greens. After that a pair of chickens, a huge tureen of something bubbling and brown that looked like some sort of onion soup, and beyond that . . . well, Abby couldn't see without craning her neck, and she guessed that to do so wouldn't be proper.

As Myles sat across from her, she followed his every lead, including drinking the wine. On her third glass, she caught an almost imperceptible shake of Myles's head. She set the glass aside, concentrating on her food: first the soup, then the meat and vegetables, then trifle for dessert.

Thoroughly stuffed, Abby followed the other women out of the room. "Have you ever thought what they do in there?" Abby asked, settling beside the duchess on a sofa in the drawing room.

"Drink port, smoke, and discuss politics," Elaine piped up from a sofa across the way.

"Tea?" Lucy proffered, looking concerned at her stepdaughter. "Elaine, when did you—"

"I was bored at a party, and I always wanted to know." She pouted.

"I think it's strength of character that you dared to find out," Abby put in, patting Lucy's knee to console her. Her hand froze in place, the remote vibrator coming to life between her closed thighs.

"Really?" Elaine looked so hopeful, Abby started to wonder how much attention anyone had given her before.

"You didn't get caught, did you?" Abby asked. The girl shook her head. "Smart, too."

Elaine beamed. "I didn't like you at first because you stole Mr. Hardy from me, but you are quite understanding."

Abby gritted her teeth, the vibrations increasing in her crotch. She clutched Lucy's knee, who didn't seem to mind. "With a man like Myles Hardy. You need to be."

Lucy covered her hand with her own. "Mrs. Hardy, are you quite all right? You look quite pink. Elaine didn't embarrass you, did she?"

"Of course not." Abby clasped her hands together. "I'm a little warm. I think I might go stand by the window and get some air."

She rose, her legs wobbling. She bit down on her lips, heat shooting throughout her. The remote vibrator set her clit on delicious fire. She wanted to hump something, anything.

Reaching the window, she gripped the curtain, closing her eyes. With her other hand, she covered her breast, pinching the nipple through the thin silk material and the stays that lay underneath.

Why didn't he turn it off? She was going to come right here in front of the duchess and ruin everything for them.

9

"Are you sure you are not ill?" Lucy joined her by the window. "You look quite flushed."

Abby darted her hand away from her bosom. What could she tell Lucy? She bit down hard on her lip, gathering strength to reply. "Do not mind me. It will soon pass."

A moan escaped her lips at that.

Lucy's brows lowered. "Abby?"

Almost rendered blind by the pulsing sensations of climaxing, Abby patted Lucy's arm, her fingers brushing air. "Please, I will be fine in a moment."

Lucy glanced over her shoulder at her stepdaughter, who scowled at the pianoforte keys. "That wasn't a cry of pain, Mrs. Hardy."

Abby's breath came fast and shallow between parted lips. "Lucy, I—"

The duchess waved off her incipient protests. "I have never seen the like before."

"I don't . . . know . . . what you mean," Abby gasped out,

determined to keep up the pretense to the very last. What did Lucy speak of? Her tiny remote control device didn't exist in the nineteenth century.

"I have known a sensual woman before." Lucy's voice dropped to a whisper, softer even than Abby's panting. "She introduced me, showed me what was missing in my life . . . and then my duke came. But Abby, I have never before seen a woman be so affected just by being in the presence of another woman."

The vibrator blessedly stopped. Abby sagged, grabbing the curtain to make sure she didn't fall. "Lucy—" Her voice sounded husky from unvoiced screams. She cleared her throat. "That isn't it. I wasn't like this when in your rooms, remember?"

Lucy's frown deepened. "Is it Elaine who overwhelms you then?"

Abby gave her a look. "Hardly."

Lucy took Abby's still-trembling hand between her own. "Your moans were not cries of pain but of desire, of lust. I know the sound . . ."

Biting her lip, Abby sought a way out. "Lucy—"

The drawing room's door flung open and the men joined them. Abby shot Myles a filthy look, but his grin only grew wider.

Lucy caught her expression. "It is a pity we cannot tell the men when we wish them to enter." She released Abby's hand. "We will speak of this later, yes? I would wish you to be frank."

Lucy glided away to join her husband, folding her arm into his.

Myles crossed to her, still smirking. She thumped him in the arm. "What's wrong with you?"

"What's wrong?" Abby hissed. "What's wrong is that I climaxed in the presence of the duchess. She *knew* I was aroused! Do you want to get us thrown out before we've found—" She rolled a wave, rendered wordless in her anger.

"We have not been asked to leave," Myles pointed out with unflappable calm, although a faint furrow formed between his brows. "I thought you would enjoy it."

She gave him *that* look. "You know I did," she admitted. "But I didn't enjoy sharing quite that much enjoyment with the Winterton women." Abby held out her hand. "Give me the remote." Myles didn't reach into his pocket. "Myles, the remote, the dial."

He shook his head. "Where will you put it? You have no pockets."

Abby glowered. She hated to admit he was right, but such a device couldn't go unexplained if seen. She glanced beyond him, seeing their heated, whispered conversation observed by the others. "Please don't tell me we cannot whisper in this room either."

Myles glanced over his shoulder and then drew her into his arms. "Let them think we're arguing over my arrangements with the viscount."

Abby gazed into his eyes, her own narrowing. "What arrangements?"

"All you need to know is that it enables us to stay until our task is complete."

Abby practically squinted her fury at him. "Please do not treat me as a child," she snapped. "I have every right to know."

"Do you? This is my project, not yours."

She pushed out of his arms. "I think I'm going to bed. And don't think of trying anything either."

"Like this?" His hand slipped into his pocket. Her too sensitive clit flared into life with the vibrations of the tiny butterfly between her legs.

She clamped her thighs together, trying to catch her breath. "That's exactly what I mean." She steeled herself to move. "Good night, and don't hurry up after me."

Myles's lips tweaked. "We'll see about that."

Abby left him and went to curtsey before the duke and duchess. "If you will excuse me, I find myself quite tired." She caught the meaningful look exchanged between husband and wife and groaned inwardly. Lucy had obviously shared her observations with her husband.

Why had Lucy betrayed that confidence? What would the duke do with that information? He'd already made one pass at her.

She hurried from the room, gasping when Myles increased the intensity of the vibrations against her clit. It was so unfair.

Before she even reached the stairs, her desire burned from deep within her gut, a line of white-hot heat running from her clit to her cunt and into her belly. She hurried up the stairs, wanting to reach her room before she came again.

The pulsing of her clit pounded in her ears, in her harsh breathing. Her sight fogged and she grabbed the banister. Pressing her hand against her mound, she let the first orgasmic wave wash over her.

It hit her sooner than she expected, far swifter than before, a climax less intense but offering some form of relief.

All too briefly, however. The remote vibrator continued to buzz mercilessly against her clit and the tension within rose again, rising to a greater height than before.

With each step, her juices smeared across her inner thighs. Each step was a sweet torture, pressing the vibrator even closer against her tender flesh. Her cunt hole pulsed with need, grasping for thick, hot cock. God, that was what she wanted, something to fill her, to pound into her until she screamed for mercy.

On the carpet runner near the door, she collapsed onto all fours. She wanted him, she wanted him now. She curled around the tortuous delight, feeling the crest of her climax rise higher and higher. She cried out, moaning her desperate need. Her cunt pulsed and convulsed, yet denying her her release.

Oh God, she wanted it, she wanted it so badly.

Someone drew her to her feet. Myles. Without opening her eyes, she knew it was him, knew he would claim her, ending the evening's exquisite torture.

Dazed, she leaned against him, her feet dragging, too uncoordinated. She wanted him right now on the floor, right there writhing beneath him. Why did he delay in taking her? She groaned. Of course, it was improper.

And still the vibrator taunted her clit. Why didn't he stop? Did he want her to come again without him? She mewled an incoherent protest. He swung her onto the bed.

His weight settled beside her and his hands lifted her petticoat and skirt to her waist, folding them back with some delicacy.

Parting her legs, she felt his weight move between them. Her eyelids seemed too heavy to open and so she enjoyed the light trailing of his fingertips over her wet curls, tracing the curvature of the narrow black belts fastened around her thighs.

He touched the vibrating butterfly, pulled back, and after a pause touched it again.

"Please, please," Abby begged. Why did he tease her so? "I want you inside me. Please!" She squirmed on the bed, lifting her hips to prove her need.

After a long moment, something hard pressed against her hole. It didn't feel right. She couldn't sense him hovering over her, couldn't feel his heat.

The hard thing pressed inside. Abby moaned, recognizing by the texture that he used a dildo. Not one of hers though: the head of this one seemed shaped a little differently. It pushed inside, the bulbous head causing her great pleasure.

It slid in smoothly, easily, her soaking cunt eagerly drawing it in. The dildo rocked in and out of her in short, sharp staccato bursts. She heard her soft gasps fill the room until it sounded like there were multitudes of her all dying with unassuaged lust.

The dildo plunged in deep, deep and hard, pressing up against her, massaging her clit from inside. The two-pronged attack undid her. Too much, too much sensation. She soared, sobbing, begging for that final thrust to send her over the edge.

Abby screamed, writhing wildly on the bed. She was there, she was there, she was going to come. She screamed again, her hips lifting high from the bed, the dildo plunged deep inside.

The remote vibrator went still at last. Her cries echoed throughout their room.

With a start, Abby realized those cries were not her own.

In a swift, whispered conversation, Lucy related her encounter with the highly sexed Mrs. Hardy. "Will you arrange something?" she begged him. "I want her."

"I would like to see this for myself," the duke concurred.

When Mrs. Hardy begged to be excused, Lucy's grasp tightened on her husband's arm. He took her silent cue and bade them all a good night.

They paused in the hall, watching Mrs. Hardy freeze on the stairs, rocking her hand against her quim. They followed her upstairs at a distance.

Finding her collapsed into a rocking, moaning ball, the duke took charge, gathering her up and helping her to Lucy's room. He laid her out on the bed and sat on the bed's broad expanse next to her, his eyes avidly upon his wife's face.

Lucy acknowledged his attention. The very thought of him watching her and Mrs. Hardy made her wet and eager. It brought back exciting memories of another encounter, one that her duke had also witnessed.

Delicately, Lucy peeled back Mrs. Hardy's skirt and petticoats, revealing her naked groin. Her thighs gleamed with her wetness. Seeing the contraption balanced on top of Mrs. Hardy's mound, Lucy exchanged a surprised, silent query with her husband.

Was this what Abigail meant that it was unnatural? What had her husband afflicted her with? Lucy hesitated.

He nodded at her to continue. She brushed her fingertips over the narrow black belts about Mrs. Hardy's hips, moving in toward the center, touching the odd butterfly shape.

She jerked her hand away. The miniature butterfly trembled violently. Lucy gestured to the duke to try it. He did so, pressing down a little harder than she and making Mrs. Hardy moan.

More than anything, Lucy wanted to taste her newfound friend, but her friend's soft cries made her change tack.

"Please, I want you inside me," Mrs. Hardy moaned, her flushed head tossing on the pillow.

Lucy obliged. She quietly opened a drawer from a table by her bed and drew out her own dildo. Well-polished wood, it gleamed in her hand, and she pushed it in between Mrs. Hardy's parted legs.

Mrs. Hardy went wild, bucking and fucking the dildo, her cries growing ever louder, almost forcing the dildo into her cunt, overflowing with juices.

Lucy, her gaze fastened upon the delectable sight of Mrs. Hardy's heaving form, sensed more than saw her husband shift position.

His hand slipped under her own skirts, reaching up between her already-parted legs, reaching her own juicy quim. He rubbed along her moist slit, and Lucy bit back a moan.

He dipped his fingertip into her hole, coaxing forth further moisture and using it to make her slit slick and hot. He teased her little nub of pleasure, drawing closer behind her.

He covered one of her breasts with one hand, furiously frotting her clitoris below. Lucy imagined Mrs. Hardy who teased her, Mrs. Hardy who squeezed her bosom, Mrs. Hardy whose cries mingled with her own.

Lucy plunged the dildo deep inside her friend, felt her grip it, seizing up as her release washed over her, writhing upon the bed.

The sight of it took her breath away. The sight of it delivered her own release and she cried out, rocking hard against her husband's hand.

She raised her sagging head at Mrs. Hardy's gasp.

"You're not . . . you're not Myles!" Mrs. Hardy colored in embarrassment. "I—I had no idea!"

Winterton slid away from behind Lucy, sitting at Mrs. Hardy's side. "We had no idea you did not want this. Our pardon."

Lucy ducked her head, pleased at the insincerity in her husband's voice. He'd enjoyed it as much as she.

"Tell me," he continued. "What is this contraption you have strapped to yourself? How does something so tiny vibrate by invisible means?"

Mrs. Hardy swallowed, her throat constricting and her gaze darting between Lucy and her husband. "It's run by miniature clockwork. It's—it's a toy meant to arouse."

"And you've been wearing that all night?" Lucy asked, hoping she didn't appear too eager.

Mrs. Hardy nodded. "That was why I . . . I was not myself."

"I have never seen the like," the duke said. "Where did you find it?"

Lucy tried not to squirm with delight. She knew her husband wanted it for her.

"Ahh," Mrs. Hardy dithered. "My husband gave it to me."

"Your husband?" the duke mused. "Part of his overseas travels, I suppose."

Mrs. Hardy didn't reply, pushing down her skirts. "If you will excuse me . . ."

The duke leaned over and clamped down upon her thigh. "I hardly think so, my dear."

Mrs. Hardy raised an eyebrow at him. The sudden wash of confidence in her expression made Lucy bite her own lip in sudden doubt. Had she misread Mrs. Hardy?

"You have been pleasured by my wife and have pleasured my wife. Now it is my turn."

Mrs. Hardy scooted back against the headboard, the duke's one-handed grip keeping her to the bed. "You will do no such thing."

The duke mildly raised his white eyebrows. "But of course not, my dear. It is clear that your affections do not lie in my direction and I have learned not to force any woman's hand. But you will watch my wife and me. It will afford us both great pleasure."

"Watch?"

"If you will not abide by my simple request, I will expect you to return to your rooms, pack your baggage, and leave at first light tomorrow."

"Leave?" Mrs. Hardy straightened her back. "Do what you will, Your Grace. I will watch."

Lucy's duke released Mrs. Hardy and turned to her. "On your knees, wife."

Lucy scuttled past him, getting on all fours alongside Mrs. Hardy. Through the loosened falls of her blond hair, she saw Mrs. Hardy sit, her face and body stiff and emotionless.

Behind her, Lucy felt her husband position himself.

"Ahh," he moaned, rubbing his cock against her slit. "How sweet and wet you are!"

He plunged into her, making her jerk and cry out. He grabbed a handful of her hair, holding her at the shoulder, another hand grasping her hip and he pounded into her, again and again.

Through her swaying locks of hair, Lucy watched Mrs. Hardy. The woman's chest rose and fell with increasing swiftness, the color of skin becoming rosy once more.

Lucy sighed. That their sex act aroused her friend gladdened her. Mrs. Hardy might indeed be persuaded to make a proper arrangement as her new personal friend. She reached down between her own legs, finding the soaking, swollen softness of her clit and rubbed at it, her arm buckling under both her weight and her increasing desire.

"Yes," groaned the duke. "Yes! Hold me tighter, wife, tighter!"

Lucy obliged, squeezing her already-convulsing cunt muscles around his plowing cock. She loved his demands. They gave an edge to their intercourse, just the edge she needed to find a deeply satisfying release. She cried out, the delicious tension spilling over, blinding all her senses.

She tried to catch her breath, her husband still furiously fucking away at her. She heard him grunt and grunt again before he sagged against her back.

He pulled out, slapping his softening cock against her bared rear. "That was most satisfactory," he said, the coolness of his voice belied by his panting breath.

Mrs. Hardy folded her arms. "May I go now?"

Lucy didn't see or hear her husband's response, but Mrs. Hardy slid from the bed and made her escape.

Lucy sprawled across the rumpled counterpane. "Do you think it would work with her?"

"She has the same fire as your first friend," her husband mused, stretching out alongside her and taking her hand in his. "It is a possibility, but you must remember she is a newlywed. She may not be interested, or her husband may choose not to make her available to us. Men can be quite possessive in the early days of wedlock as you well know."

Although his words saddened her a little, she beamed at him, the memories of their honeymooning making her warm all over again. "Indeed, I do."

Abby hurried along the hallway and dashed into her room. There might be a chance she'd reach it before Myles did, and then he never need know—

She rocketed to a stop. Myles stood by the bed, and next to him her black suitcases stood in neat order.

"I have taken the liberty of packing your bags for you," he told her in a flat voice. "You will take them, find somewhere else to sleep tonight, and be on your way tomorrow."

Abby wanted to scream at him, wanted to rail at him that this was all his fault for driving her mad with the remote controlled vibrator, but she wouldn't give him the satisfaction yet.

"I don't see my blueprints," she said, controlling her voice into calm. She gripped onto her wedding ring. She'd give it back if she had to.

He sent her a sharp look, quickly veiled by nonchalance. "You cannot have them."

"They are mine," Abby insisted.

"It's not my fault you broke our deal."

"Deal? What deal?" Abby sneered. "That in exchange for sharing your bed I give you the house plans you need? What sort of deal is that?" She stalked up to him, shoving him in the shoulder. "Our deal was that you would protect me from the unfamiliarities of this world, not merely make me your bedmate. I have not reneged on that deal."

"Oh no?" Myles fists closed tight, but he didn't hit or shove her. "Would you care to explain what you were doing in the duke's bed just now? A charming little threesome you'll make, I'm sure."

Her jaw dropped. "You saw?"

"When you weren't in our—this room, I came looking for you. I know what you sound like when you're about to climax." His nostrils flared, his lips forming a tight white line. "I peeked through the keyhole. I saw you with him, with her. With *them*."

Abby stared at him, unable to believe his violent reaction. Hadn't they agreed that they'd share the pleasure but not make any sort of commitment? She growled. *Damn double standards.* "And I suppose you could sleep with any slut who happened to take your fancy, like Elaine, and I would have to be happy with that?" she challenged.

He shrugged, his skin darkening. "I had assumed you were exchanging my protection for his. If you do not wish to end our arrangement, then you better explain yourself."

He gave her a chance. "You won't believe me," she murmured, sinking onto the bed.

He remained silent, condemning. She had nothing to lose but give it a shot. As much as it galled her, she wasn't ready to part with him yet. She enjoyed being with him, a simple pleasure heightened by the amazing sex they had. And certainly not in exchange for the ducal Wintertons.

Abby looked him in the eye, tilting her head to see his face. "I thought it was you." She gripped her hands tight in her lap. Her low and angry voice betrayed her. "I was out of my mind with lust, with desire, from that damned vibrator—" Her voice grew sharp. "I fell onto the floor. It felt like I was in one long, sustained orgasm. Someone picked me up." Her voice choked. "I thought it was you."

To her surprise, a sob escaped her throat. "I thought it was you touching me, fucking me with that dildo. I couldn't understand why you'd choose that instead of—"

She blinked away incipient tears. "When I opened my eyes and saw it wasn't you, I—" She took a deep, calming, strengthening breath. "The duke demanded I stay longer, to watch him and his wife or he'd throw us both out."

Myles sat beside her, his features much paler than before. "You stayed for me, for a mission that means nothing to you?"

"It means something to you," Abby whispered. "That was enough for me."

He covered his face with his hands, rubbing it. "You really thought it was me in there?"

Abby flushed. "I wanted it to be you."

Myles slung an awkward arm around her shoulder. "I must apologize, Ms. Deane—"

"Not Abby?" she prompted in a small voice.

"The depth of the apology requires a formal expression," he said, lifting his head out of his hands. He looked at her with large, woebegone eyes. "Abby, I apologize for overreacting."

She leaned in against him, relishing his warmth. "I'm sorry too."

He kissed the top of her head. "So I am forgiven?"

She looked up at him, finding his lips close to hers. She wet her own. "Absolutely."

Their mouths met. It reminded her of a first kiss, tentative, seeking a happy resolution between them.

Her lips parted, letting him into her mouth. Wrapping her arms about his neck, she wanted to let him know that she still wanted to be with him.

He drew her down onto the bed, imprinting her body with his. He leisurely explored her mouth, letting her do the same to him.

She still wanted him, the fire of it burned deep within her belly. Her clit burned too—at least she still had sensation there, but her parts had been well satisfied. Could she rise to the cause again?

Twisting her head away from his, she gasped out, "Myles!"

He propped himself up over her. "What is it?"

"I never got a chance to tell you. I found out the meaning of *hypogaeum.*"

New life danced in his eyes, the heated desire showing his true passion. It wasn't her. "Will you tell me?"

"Of course." How could she not? "It means *basement.*"

"Basement?"

"You've looked there already?" Abby tried not to sound too disappointed.

"How could I?" he retorted, frowning. "There is no basement."

10

———————

"What do you mean . . . ?" Abby shoved at his shoulders. "Of course there is. Where are the blueprints?"

He rolled off her, heading for the small closet that contained his belongings. "I hid them in here." He pulled them out and returned to the bed.

Abby stood, her legs wobbly, giving him room to lay the plans open on the bed.

"Show me." Myles indicated the plans. "Where is this basement? This house has never had one."

Abby bent over the bed, smoothing out the roll of paper. She flicked over the pages until she came to the one she wanted. "Right here." She pointed to the subterranean level of the home.

"And what is in there in the future?"

"Nothing. It's blank walls, a completely empty space. If I remember the report correctly, there were charcoal marks from fires."

"It does not sound promising."

"Considering you didn't even know it existed and it was written on the secret stairway . . ." She trailed off, giving him an impatient look. "It's worth a shot, isn't it?" Abby frowned. "It's not like you to lose heart."

He leaned against the bed's backboard. "I've been disappointed too many times, Abby." He pointed at the blueprints. "How do we get into it?"

"The entrance must be hidden in this time, otherwise you would've found it by now."

He smiled at her confidence in him. "And in your time?"

"There's no saying that the entry to it isn't some later addition," Abby warned him. "But it's a place to start."

She pored over the plans, flipping one page back and forth, looking for the way in from the floor above. "These things are so complicated . . ."

Aware of Myles's tapping boot, she kept her eagerness in check. If she skimmed too quickly, she might miss it. "Here." She tapped the paper. "That's where the entrance is now."

Myles examined the location on both pages. "That doesn't make sense. That's the footmen's quarters now. You can't hide an entry there."

"Maybe it's behind the plasterwork," Abby suggested. "Would there be a hammer out in the stables or somewhere?"

"Or that could be the modern entryway and the old one is walled off in some other location." Myles frowned. "Isn't there anything else? Any other possible way in?"

"It's below ground." Abby sighed. "We could dig our way in."

"A little hard to hide, let alone explain," Myles remarked. He tugged on the end of the blueprints. "It's late. Let us look at them again in daylight with fresh eyes."

He laid the rolled-up blueprints to one side. "Right now, I want to hold you, Ms. Abby Deane, and have you sleep in my arms."

Sleep sounded incredibly good to her. "You got quite formal there, Mr. Hardy. I guess you must be quite serious about getting some rest."

He grinned, his concern and worry gone in a flash. "Absolutely." He flung back the covers and started to undress.

Watching him, Abby kicked off her slippers and slipped off her stockings. Unfastening the front flap of her gown, she was forced to wait for Myles to come to her assistance.

He turned her around, peeling the garment from her form, undoing the ties that kept her gown gathered and together.

She looked down over his bare back, the muscles rippling. His loose brown hair brushed over his broad shoulders as he worked. "I have to say," Abby mused, "that nothing beats being undressed by a handsome naked man."

He chuckled. "I'll wager I can think of a few things." He rose, pulling her chemise off over her head, leaving her naked. "But not tonight." His eyes glinted, dark with emotion. "Tonight, I want to hold you."

She stepped into his arms. His warm embrace filled her with an erotic security. She doubted they'd sleep much that night. Abby thought it a shame she'd had to travel back two hundred years in order to find a decent man.

Abby woke to find Myles standing by the window, utterly naked except for a strategically draped set of blueprints. Fortunately, he held them up to the light, and that gave her a full view of his assets.

She half wished she was American so she could say, "Nice ass . . . ets." Instead, she propped up her head and feasted on his taut, round buttocks. His pale, smooth skin might be innocent, if it weren't for the way his muscles clenched and the clear evidence of last night's lovemaking: red half moons from where her fingernails dug into his backside.

The rattle of paper drew her attention upward.

Myles grinned over his shoulder. "Enjoying the view?"

"Immensely." A self-satisfied smirk tweaked her lips. "And did you give a good showing to the folk outside?"

"Alas," he sighed, "the windowsill is too high."

"What a pity," Abby commiserated. She sat up. "Did you find anything?"

Myles nodded, his amusement fading. "I found your basement. I worked it out." He brought the plans over and lay them down across her lap. Abby avoided looking at his groin and focused on the blueprints.

"Your basement is here." He outlined the space with his finger. "The plans show the kitchen." His finger drew across the page. "Here's the pantry, but the rest of this space is empty, unidentified, except for some supporting walls and columns."

He sat beside her, releasing the blueprints and letting them roll up. "There are rooms that currently exist in this building that are not shown here. Here's my theory: at some point between now and your time, modifications took place."

Abby frowned. "What's there now?"

"A still room, storage space, and servants' quarters. I've been all over this place, Abby. There's no statue to be found. No place to hide it."

Pushing the blueprints onto the floor, Abby kicked the roll of paper. "Then why was that Latin word carved on the secret stairway?"

Myles shrugged. "A false lead? Some bored person waiting on the stairs?"

"*Basement* is hardly the word I'd use if I were bored on the stairs." Abby grimaced.

"Oh?" Myles took her chin between his fingers and turned it toward him. "And what would you carve?"

She jerked out of his grasp. "Not that," she snapped, glad her mouth didn't run off and say what she thought. *Myles 4 me 4 ever* was hardly a mature answer. Nor a commitment-free one.

"Abby," Myles crooned, "disappointments happen in this business. It's here in this house somewhere. We'll find it."

Abby managed a twisted smile. She wanted to share his hope, his optimism, but memories of last night came rushing back. Memories of a horny duke and duchess, both wanting her.

She let the worry out in a long sigh. "I wanted to find it today. After last night with the duke . . ."

He drew her into a one-armed embrace, kissing the top of her sleep-mussed hair. "Do not concern yourself about them. We shall be inseparable from here on out, and they'll never get another chance to—"

He left unspoken exactly what they would do.

Abby hugged him. "You would do that?"

"Of course." He kissed her hair again. His mouth trailed over her temple, down her cheek to her neck. He murmured against her skin. "I promised to keep you safe. I meant it."

Abby relaxed into his embrace, baring her neck to his further kisses.

He pulled away, clearing his throat. "It is late. We should go down to breakfast before someone comes looking for us."

"But we're a honeymooning couple." Abby returned the favor, kissing along the bared column of his throat. "Why would they want to do that?"

Myles drew up her face even with his. "Truth be told, I'm hungry. I thought I'd give a polite excuse before my stomach started rumbling."

Hunger definitely figured into the equation: hunger of both kinds. "I guess we need the energy from the food."

He grinned, kissing the tip of his nose. "And we have that statue to find." He drew her to his feet and smacked her bare rump. "Now get dressed, wench."

"Wench?" Abby shrieked. She reached for a towel from the nightstand and snapped it across his behind. "Watch it, mister."

He jumped. The look of outrage on his face made her laugh out loud. She darted out of reach, scooping up her chemise.

She dressed as far as she was able, waiting for Myles to finish tying his cravat before he took care of the loose tapes of her gown.

Once done, he gathered her in his arms, tapping her on her bottom. "I forgive you for that swat," he told her, his voice low and hoarse.

His mouth came down on hers, and it looked like breakfast had been forgotten.

Not for the first time, Abby cursed the Regency-era mode of dress. Just the thought of the time-consuming undressing put them off consummating their desire until later. She pointed out her lack of underwear, but Myles had decided not to muss his cravat.

Abby stabbed a slice of ham with more force than required and transferred it to her plate. Myles had loaded his plate already and ate at the dining table behind her.

What had got into him? One minute he couldn't keep his hands—and mouth—off her and the next his cool distance reduced her importance. Geeky distraction about that damned statue wasn't the cause, Abby was almost sure.

The Duchess of Winterton entered, sidling alongside her. "My apologies for last night. We should have asked . . ."

Abby dashed her a frowning look. "Yes, you should have."

The duchess flushed, laying a gentle hand on her forearm. Abby stilled. A jerk might send her plate of food all over the duchess's stylish gown.

"Mrs. Hardy, I would not like to lose your friendship," the duchess pleaded in a low murmur.

"Your Grace . . ." Abby didn't know how to reply. The wrong answer could find her and her husband out on the streets.

"Please, give me another chance," the duchess begged in a whisper. "Please, show me by calling me Lucy."

Struck with the sudden insight that the duchess was a lonely woman, Abby smiled at her. "Lucy, it is my turn to say I'm sorry. I will be your friend."

Lucy beamed, transforming her woebegone face into a joyful, angelic one. "Thank you! Would you like to come for a walk with me after breakfast?" She said this last question loud enough to be overheard.

Abby shot a look at Myles, who dabbed his lips with a napkin. "That sounds like an excellent idea, doesn't it, husband?"

"I'll leave you ladies to your privacy." At Abby's daggered expression, he continued, "But if you don't mind I would like to join you. I haven't seen anything of what must be a gorgeous estate."

Lucy, her equilibrium apparently restored, gazed at him down the line of her nose. "I am sure we will not be attacked by ravening wolves, Mr. Hardy."

"Oh please," Abby begged. "I hardly saw him at all yesterday. He can walk in front of us, out of hearing range."

Lucy smiled. "Very well. I cannot keep two newlyweds apart."

The conversation remained light and inconsequential until they parted to change for the walk. Lucy had a maid deliver a pelisse for Abby and a pair of boots.

Abby met her in the downstairs hall, the boots already pinching her feet. Myles idled by the front door.

Lucy smiled at her as she descended the stairs, taking her arm the moment she reached her. "Shall we go?"

Fifteen minutes into the walk and Abby knew she'd made a mistake. Lucy remained arm in arm, their bodies touching. Myles strode ahead, switching the long grass on either side of the path with a stick he found.

"Your husband is a handsome man," Lucy observed, her arm a constant pressure on Abby's.

"Yes, he is." Even at a distance, Myles was easy on the eyes.

Abby considered herself fortunate he found her, rather than the duke.

"I can see why you married him," Lucy continued, "although I am surprised you need to resort to marital aids so early in the marriage. Forgive me for asking, but is all well between you? He seemed distant this morning."

"He has much on his mind," Abby said. "As for the marital aids, as you call them, they're mine, not his. It's not that we need them, it's just fun."

Lucy leaned closer. "You are skilled in the arts of self-pleasure?"

Abby's cheeks burned. "You could say that."

"As am I," Lucy assured her. "There is nothing to be ashamed of."

"This talk is a little more frank than I'm used to," Abby admitted, wishing Myles could read minds. She needed him with her.

"Such things are not usually spoken of, I know." Lucy squeezed Abby's arm in reassurance. "I wanted you to know we are of like mind."

"Why?"

"I have something to show you." Lucy branched off the path.

Abby drew breath to call to Myles.

"Wait," Lucy said, pinching Abby's arm. "This is for you alone."

"But—" Abby dithered. Call Myles, risk ending the friendship and getting turfed out, or go with Lucy and risk—well, whatever that had been last night.

She sighed. Would her new relationship survive another erotic encounter with the Wintertons? Was it worth it to find this statue? She expelled another breath of air. Myles would find her. They weren't about to disappear into the woods.

"All right," Abby conceded.

Lucy beamed. "I'm glad. It's right across the way, through those woods."

Abby almost groaned aloud. *So much for not disappearing into the woods.* She pasted a smile on her face and followed Lucy along the narrow path. She glanced over her shoulder to see if Myles had noticed they'd deviated from their ambling course.

He had. The twisting of her pelisse must have caught the corner of his eye, for she spotted him turn toward them before the branches eclipsed her view.

He made to run, but Abby stayed him with a hand. He nodded and walked slower, more purposeful. Without being too far behind her, he'd catch up before anything, well, happened.

She hoped.

The trail narrowed the farther into the woods they went. Daylight turned green, filtered through the leaves of ancient trees.

Abby frowned. She'd expected the trees to be a lot younger, but these looked like they'd been here since forever. "These trees are pretty old," she remarked.

"They've been here since before Queen Elizabeth's time," Lucy told her, turning to walk crablike along the narrow path in order to speak to Abby at the same time. "The records don't go back further than that."

"The Winterton family lost their records from before then?"

"The Wintertons didn't own it then. Not until the Civil War, after Elizabeth." She faced forward to watch her step. "My duke is underplanting this old grove. See?" She pointed out young trees with fresh black loam piled around their base. "If you look up, you'll see he's laced the trees to bring in a little more light for them. Trees don't last forever."

"It feels like they do," Abby replied, wondering for the first time if this wood even existed in the twenty-first century.

Lucy laughed, a bright unfettered sound that seemed quite unlike the quiet, kind duchess. "Come on. I did not bring you here to look at trees."

Abby glanced over her shoulder, but there was no sign of Myles. She followed Lucy along a winding and sometimes almost nonexistent trail. Bushes caught at her skirts and her pelisse, and she heard the sound of material tearing.

She grimaced. She didn't have a lot of clothing to wear instead. She kept walking, easily keeping up with the duchess.

Lucy abruptly halted. "Close your eyes."

Abby frowned. "But I'll trip!"

"Take my hand." Her gloved fingers closed around Abby's bared ones. "I'll take care of you."

Abby got the feeling she meant for more than just the short trip to her surprise. Closing her eyes, she let Lucy lead her, stumbling but managing to maintain her balance.

Lucy stopped and Abby fell against her. Lucy caught her, holding her upright in an embrace that was a little too long, a little too intimate.

"Can I open my eyes now?" Abby wanted to escape Lucy's close proximity.

"Yes," Lucy whispered, her breath brushing Abby's cheek.

Definitely too close. Abby opened her eyes, automatically stepping back. Her gaze swept across the small glade they stood in. Trees pressed in all around, some of them so covered in ivy she couldn't even see their trunks.

"It's pretty," Abby observed, turning around to make sure she hadn't missed the surprise.

"Over here." Lucy set out across the glade toward the stand of trees where the ivy was the thickest. Abby followed, unease twisting in her belly.

A curtain of ivy hung between two trees. Lucy pushed the ivy back, stepping into the gloom beyond. She held it back for Abby.

Abby stepped through and her jaw dropped. The gloom had misled. Another layer of ivy pushed back to reveal glorious white marble.

It stole her breath. She stepped into the round space. It was some sort of folly, some sort of temple. What she'd thought were tree trunks were columns, supporting a rounded roof with a circle cut in the center, opening onto blue sky. Streams of light came down through it, the light doubling in strength from the white marble.

"What is this?" she breathed.

"It's a folly," Lucy told her, stepping across the leaf-littered floor and turning in a circle, her arms wide open. Well, as far apart as the constricting sleeves allowed.

"It might be folly to be here," Abby muttered under her breath. If she didn't recognize it as a building, would Myles?

"Did you say something?" Lucy called to her, her bliss not diminished in the slightest.

Abby shook her head, moving toward her.

"This—" Lucy's outspread arms took in the entire folly, "this is Diana's temple."

"How do you figure that?"

Lucy frowned. "I would have thought you'd have a slightly more romantic mind."

Abby shrugged. "I've been accused of worse."

"Look up." Lucy pointed to the ceiling. "Look at the dancing women. They have to be Diana's."

Abby squinted against the glare, shifting position better to see. What looked like the natural striations of marble at first glance transformed into a relief of women dancing and playing music, their ancient Greek clothing falling off their forms.

"I thought they would be hunting," Abby remarked. "Belonging to Diana and all."

"But there's this statue . . ." Lucy strode across to the far side of the folly temple.

Abby stilled. A statue? Myles's statue?

Lucy pushed back another veil of ivy. "Right here."

Abby stepped forward for a closer look. A female statue

stood in the small alcove. A bow and quiver, along with a hound at her feet. "That's Diana," Abby agreed.

"Isn't it wonderful? My duke showed it to me when he brought me here on our first visit to this estate. At the time, I was quite disconsolate and it cheered me up."

"Why were you sad?" She didn't seem much happier now, truth be told.

"A close friend refused our hospitality. I so wanted her to come at once, but my husband thought if we waited a little longer she would be more amenable, but alas, she's far too stubborn. Maybe one day . . ." Lucy sighed wistfully.

"Amenable to what?" Abby asked.

Lucy flushed. "Before we were even married, my husband knew I held a certain, ahh, fascination for other women. My friend, I believed, felt the same way. But she refused . . ."

Abby felt sorry for her. "Sometimes it is hard to tell . . ."

"It was she who awoke me to these desires, so I know she had the capacity for it."

"But what happened? Why did she refuse you then?"

"She fell in love with a man." Lucy sighed. "Much like you, I suppose." She chewed her lower lip. "I made a mistake, didn't I, thinking that you—"

Abby cut her off. "Yes, I'm afraid you did. I'm sorry. Even if I did fancy both men and women, being in the honeymoon phase, I'd not be easily distracted, even by one as beautiful as you."

Lucy turned away, head down. "It is nice of you to say so, Mrs. Hardy."

Abby touched her shoulder. "I would still like us to be friends. Myles—Mr. Hardy—and I practically eloped. You can guess how well that went down." In silence, Abby thanked her high school English teacher for making her read *Pride and Prejudice.*

"Went down?" Lucy turned, frowning at her. "What an unusual turn of phrase."

Abby flushed, her silent praise turning to silent cursing. "I meant that my family and friends do not approve of the match."

"And no small wonder," Lucy agreed. "Forgive me, but your husband has quite the reputation. You know he pursued my stepdaughter?"

Abby nodded. "The idea of it didn't thrill me, but men—what can you do? Of course they shoot for the highest honors. Myles didn't reckon on falling in love." She smirked. Her lips twisted further. If only it were so.

"Nor did you, I'll wager."

Shrugging, Abby didn't dare reply.

"You seem a sensible female, one not likely to fall for an adventurer like Hardy. Especially given your strong opinions on the foibles of men."

Abby grinned. "I think I'll thank you for that compliment." She held out her hand. "So are we friends?"

Lucy's thin but genuine smile gave her hope. "Friends." She didn't take her hand but surveyed the temple standing around them. "I wish it were otherwise though. This may have been the perfect place for a romantic rendezvous."

She had to agree. "A few blankets to make that floor more comfortable. Some pillows. This place definitely has potential."

"Now I just need to find someone to share it with."

"Not your husband?" The male voice made them both jump. Myles leaned against an ivy-covered column with a warm smile. "You ladies were hard to find."

"You did not think that was our intention?" Lucy demanded, her voice icy cool.

With a glance, Abby saw Lucy didn't want another man in her sanctuary. "This is girls only, Myles. A temple to Diana, Artemis. Boys are definitely not allowed."

He smiled. "My apologies, Your Grace." He bowed to Lucy. "Sometimes I think my wife is more girl than woman."

Abby sniffed, wanting to make some retort but at a loss for

words. She'd get him later. She shot a sympathetic smile to Lucy instead. "Why don't we go back to the house? I've ripped a great big hole in my pelisse. Perhaps you could help me mend it?"

Lucy came to life. "We shall have a maid take care of that. I should have thought to assign you one from my staff. There's a girl who has the aptitude, just not the opportunity, to come into her own as a ladies' maid."

Abby smiled, crossing to join Myles. "Anything to give a girl a chance."

"Good girl." Myles tucked her arm into his. He held out his hand to Lucy. "It would be my honor to escort you, Your Grace."

Lucy accepted his hand, but Abby slipped out of his grasp and put her arm around Lucy. "Mr. Hardy, I think we shall walk ahead this time."

Feeling Lucy lean into her, she stepped out of the temple, brushing the ivy out of the way. They returned to the house.

When they got back, Myles took her to one side. "We have to go back," he whispered.

Abby shot him a curious look. "Go back where?"

He drew her out of the hall and into one of the salons. After checking to see that nobody else was with them, Myles continued to whisper. "To the temple."

Abby's eyes widened. "The statue of Diana? But it's huge! How do you propose getting it out of there?"

Myles shook his head. "No, that statue is a fake. That's no temple to Diana, but to Dionysus. That's where we'll find the statue."

"And the basement?"

"In the temple. It has to be." His grin widened maniacally. "We shall go back tonight."

11

That night, a wary Abby eyed the flickering torchlights. "Won't they see those from the house?"

Myles shook his head. "If anyone's still awake, they won't see us from this angle. There's that nice row of trees blocking their view. You should be pleased. Now you won't fall over quite so often."

"Sorry." Abby lacked good night vision. Perhaps she should have obeyed her mother and eaten more carrots in her childhood.

She sucked in her breath. Her mother. Her mother must be freaking out.

"What's wrong?" Myles's arm fell about her shoulder.

She shook her head, drawing away. "Nothing. Let's go."

With each of them bearing a torch, they set off through the woods, retracing the path they'd followed earlier that afternoon. They walked in silence, reaching the ivy-covered temple in record time.

"How do you know this is it?" Abby whispered.

He shrugged, pulling out more pitch-soaked torches from

his pack, lighting them, and placing them about the temple floor. "I do not know, not for sure. But the statue is newer, I could see that at a glance. The marble is not as fine, the sculpture not as detailed as an original piece from B.C. Greece might be."

"You saw all that from the other side of the temple?"

Myles nodded, crossing to the hidden statue and revealing it to the orange torchlight. "Yes. I have lived my life learning about these ancient arts. I know a fake when I see one. This is even made of the wrong kind of marble."

He let the ivy curtain fall and held his torch up high. The light didn't reach the sculptural relief on the ceiling. "And you were right about these not being Diana's followers."

"You were there, listening that long?" Abby interrupted, glad the dark hid her blushing cheeks. "You heard—"

"The two of you discussing the possibility of sexual intercourse with each other." Myles's cool voice did little to soothe Abby's discomfort. "For the record, I am not that madly in love with you."

Abby snorted. "Thanks, I know that, but we're supposed to be playing newlyweds, remember?"

"My apologies." Myles sounded genuine. "I just had to be sure."

"Yeah, yeah," Abby cut him off, sounding all business while her heart faltered. "You were talking about the ceiling."

He cleared his throat. "Right, the ceiling. Those aren't Diana's followers but are bacchante, female followers of Dionysus, the god of lusts. Lust for good food, good wine, good sex. There were men up there also, half goat, half human. Satyrs who danced to Dionysus' tune."

"Like Pan."

"Yes, he was one of them." Myles lowered the torch, sweeping it before him. "There has to be an entry here somewhere."

"To the basement?"

Myles's grin shone in the torchlight. "To the basement."

Abby lowered her torch also, searching for some sign of an entrance on the marble floor. A loose stone, an uneven surface, a grate, anything. She focused on the marble before her, part of her aware of Myles's every movement on the far side of the temple.

Between them, they quartered the temple in their search, coming together in the middle.

Myles tossed his torch to one side. "It's not here."

Abby followed suit. "Maybe it's outside, around the base somewhere?" She shuddered at the thought. Ivy concealed the exterior and a mass of debris lay around the base—dead leaves and god knows what else.

"We need picks and shovels to clear the base and find that entry. The entry might lie a hundred feet or more away from the temple." His eyes gleamed with the challenge. "I don't suppose the folly was among your blueprints."

Abby shook her head. They'd wasted their time.

He cupped her face in his hands. "Abby," he crooned. "Abby, I'm sorry. I've led you on a fool's errand."

She reached up on tiptoe and brushed his lips with hers. "It isn't a fool's errand."

Without either of them meaning to, the kiss deepened. She drew him closer, feeling his hands skim down her neck and down her back. He leaned into her and she into him. His kisses grew hungry, drawing out her lower lip between his teeth.

"What is it about you, Mrs. Hardy?" he breathed in wonder, breaking the kiss and brushing the fringes of her hair.

"I hope that's a rhetorical question," she replied, trying not to think of his lips so close to hers. She'd never had such an intoxicating kiss. If only there were a few blankets, a couple of pillows . . .

"Hmm," came his noncommittal reply. He looked over her shoulder. "Abby . . ." He sounded distant, musing.

"Yes?" Abby replied, knowing his brain was at work again.

"That alcove is most definitely original to the temple. I'll bet that my ancestor brought it all the way from Greece many generations ago to hide his treasure."

"The statue of Dionysus?"

His sharp gaze chilled her. "I never told you that."

Abby huffed in impatience. "You didn't have to. You've been explaining why you were so sure and Dionysus' name kept coming up again and again." She gestured behind her. "So you think the entrance might be in the alcove?"

As one, they headed in that direction. Abby held back the ivy, allowing Myles to ferry the torches into the small alcove. With the flames flickering around the base of Diana's statue, the two of them set to scanning the walls.

Myles's voice echoed in the small space. "How did you learn to do this?"

Glancing over her shoulder, Abby saw that Myles spoke to the wall. She turned back to her work. "To search efficiently for something?" She shrugged, even though she knew he wouldn't see it. "My best friend lost a ring once, playing football, and we spent the afternoon quartering the field, trying to find it. Good, basic principles that worked elsewhere."

"Is she still your best friend?" Myles's voice sounded odd, and Abby didn't think she could entirely blame it on the echoing chamber.

"She's not born yet," Abby snapped, burying her loss. She'd lost so much. She'd hardly had a chance to miss home, but now? She swallowed. "Sorry. I'm trying not to think about it."

"I understand."

He didn't, Abby knew. How could he? She said nothing, continuing her search.

A heavy thwock and a curse broke her concentration. She turned to see Myles hopping about. He must have kicked a column.

"It's not here," he grumbled.

"It has to be," Abby replied, folding her arms. "It's a temple to Dionysus. Everything but that Diana statue points to it."

"I feel compelled to point out that it's not the Roman Diana but the Greek Artemis. A much nicer name." Myles surveyed the statue. "You are right. It doesn't belong here at all."

He shoved the statue. It rocked on its base for a moment and then toppled, falling through the ivy curtain and smashing into pieces.

"Myles!" Abby gasped, shocked.

"It was a forgery," he snapped, brushing dirt from the statue's base. "It doesn't matter."

Abby joined him. Somehow, a great deal of dirt had piled under the statue. "That's a lot of dirt," she remarked, feeling a bit useless.

"The statue was hollow, a plaster cast." Sweeping the dirt with his foot, Myles revealed an inset brass ring, slightly green with age.

Restraining the urge to clap her hands in childish excitement, Abby reached for the ring instead. She pulled it toward her, and the marble base grated as it shifted. A tiny ring of dust edged the base, falling through the opening cracks.

She grunted. "Ugh, this is heavy."

Myles's hand closed over hers, replacing her grasp on the ring with his, and hauled. With a creaking groan, the circular stone door opened. Myles let go, letting it fall away, leaving a dark hole.

Myles grabbed a torch and looked down, his head almost colliding with Abby's. He made to drop it but she stopped him.

"What if there's something flammable down there? Besides, I brought this." She pulled a small flashlight out of her reticule. Shining the light down, she made out a ladder disappearing into the darkness. Leaning forward, the shaft of light shed revealed a leaf-strewn floor.

She squinted. "It seems to open out at the very bottom. Do you see?"

"Yes, I see. It opens out under the temple proper, I believe." He held out his hand for the flashlight and she handed it to him. "Shall we?"

"After you." She waved the way clear.

Grinning, he swung into the opening and descended the ladder. Reaching the bottom, he called up to her. "Toss down the torches. It's too dark down here."

Abby hurried to obey. Gathering up her skirts in one hand, she paid no heed to the height of her hemline and descended.

"Careful!" Myles's voice echoed. "Those rungs are old. Take care coming down."

At the bottom, she shook out her skirts. "Myles?"

Torches lay strewn around the circular chamber. Myles stood in the center of the room, a golden glow about his body.

He seemed focused on something right before him, the statue Abby guessed, but she found the walls fascinating. In rich colors of gold, red, and blue, painted men and women cavorted together in a variety of pictures. Loose white cloth draped casually about their bodies, easily pushed aside to reveal a breast or a penis.

Women chased men. Men, with the brown hairy legs of goats and horned heads, chased women, their cocks erect and eager. Others ate grapes, the purple juice staining their skin and their skimpy clothing.

"Myles," Abby breathed, breaking the silence. "This is amazing."

He turned. He looked more than a little wild-eyed, and Abby saw why. For the first time she saw what he had been feasting his eyes upon.

"Oh my." The life-size statue's gold plating set the whole room aglow, thanks to the scattered torches. It depicted Dionysus as a man in his prime. Youth had given way to muscle. He held grapes in one hand, and in the other he gestured to the largest cock Abby had ever seen.

She stepped closer. The amount of detail in the sculpture was incredible. So perhaps she shouldn't look so closely at the statue's cock: the rounded head, the thick veins running down its shaft, the ridges of flesh. She dragged her gaze farther up to the six-pack abs. Its broad chest even had the fine detailing of curls of hair.

"Wow," she said, turning to Myles, who looked as starstruck as she. "How do we get it out of here? It won't fit back up the trap door."

"Never mind that." Myles drew her close. "This is the culmination of all my dreams, Abby love. I've been working toward this for years. Once I bring this to the Dilettanti Society, they have to give me membership."

"The what Society?" Abby blinked.

"The Dilettanti Society is a club. The only way to join them is to provide some amazing work of ancient art. My father tried to get in with some beautiful pieces, but they denied him." His lip curled in anger.

Abby leaned against him. "Myles," she purred, enjoying the faint feeling of arousal. Who wouldn't with all this erotic artwork around them? "Who cares about those men? They aren't worth your time." Her fingers crept into the opening of his shirt. "You're better than they are."

"That's why I want to best them." The angry light went out of his eyes. His arms curled around her, bringing her close. "I couldn't have done this without you." His lips brushed over hers.

"Sure you could." Abby smirked up at him. "It just wouldn't have been as much fun."

"Speaking of fun, let's celebrate." Myles set to work unfastening the front flap of her bodice.

"Here?"

"Why not?" His progress of undressing her didn't slow.

Why not indeed? Her heart pounding, Abby untied his cravat, pulling the linen folds free of his neck, followed by the ties to his shirt. She pulled him to her by his lapels. "Myles," she said, desire choking her voice, "I want you."

He groaned, kissing her hard. They tore at each other's clothes, her dress tapes tearing under the stress. Their clothing made for a makeshift mattress on the hard floor.

He lowered her to the ground, covering her body with his, sliding in between her already-parted legs.

"Myles," she groaned between kisses. "I'm so hot for you."

"I can feel it." His cock nudged into her wet slit, penetrating her inch by slow, delicious inch. She moaned, long and soft, her breath tickling his ear.

He set up an easy rhythm, the sounds of their joining echoing in the marble chamber. Abby met each thrust, her entire body trembling with longing, longing for that more which climax brought her.

"Roll over," he grunted, pulling out.

She did so, coming up on all fours, presenting her rear and parted legs to him. He rubbed his cock up and down her soaking slit, the head poking against her clit. She arched her back, enjoying the sensation too much to let it end. She wanted him inside her, but she enjoyed his teasing almost as much.

He pulled back, his cock settling against the entrance to her eager cunt. Abby held her breath, clawing at him in encouragement. She wanted to feel his cock from this fresh angle.

Instead, he drew back farther, his cock probing her rear.

"Myles?" she asked, worried.

"Just relax." His hands smoothed over her buttocks and lower back.

Abby let her breath escape. "It's not that I haven't done it before, but the last time I did was with protection."

Myles's hands continued to soothe her back. "You mean a cundum?"

"Mmm." Abby wished for a less seductive touch. Then she might be able to think.

He gave her buttocks a slap. "Given that I want to be inside you so badly, I'll take the conventional route. But maybe later . . ."

Abby squirmed against him. His promises made her hotter than ever. "I'll look forward to later."

He choked out a laugh. His cock slipped down, probing her wet slit, pushing into her tight cunt. Abby groaned, feeling the pressure of Myles's cock against some very sensitive spots inside her.

With this man, in his arms, all her inhibitions about involvement with the opposite sex vanished. In his arms, her excitement was all that mattered. She wanted him, wanted his sexual skills exerted on her, and only her, until she was a boneless lump of ecstasy.

Myles delivered. He withdrew, not all the way, and pushed back in. He reached around her hips, his fingertips brushing across her clit. Abby bucked against him, squeezing him.

He let out a cry, holding still within her, while he rubbed at her clit, letting her muscles stroke his embedded cock. Her cries joined his. She slumped forward, her arms giving out, pushing even harder against him, until he pressed into her so deep his balls brushed her wet slit.

Her fist pounded on the floor. "Oh God, Myles! Myles, please!"

He paused, remaining still against her impatient wriggling. "I have an idea."

"To move the statue? Can't it wait?" Abby constricted her cunt muscles around his cock, reminding him of the greater importance.

"Oh, that can wait," Myles agreed, "but I saw how you looked upon it. I saw you stare at that cock."

Abby pushed up onto her elbows, looking over her shoulder

at him. "It was hard to miss. Myles, please, I am so close," she begged. "Don't stop now."

He grabbed a handful of her hair, tugging lightly. "Abby, have you ever seen such a large sex toy?"

Abby snorted, twisting her head in his grasp. He didn't let go. "They're called blow-up dolls."

"Are they? Did you bring one?"

"They're not my thing." Abby squeezed his cock, rotating her hips.

"You're not even tempted to try him?"

"Won't I damage it?"

"Ah." Myles's voice held a note of triumph. "You are tempted, aren't you?" He slid out of her, getting up.

She shook her hair free of his grasp and looked up at him. "I'd much rather have you in me."

Myles's lips twitched. "Let me put it this way. It is a fantasy of mine to watch the woman I—care for—fuck another man. This is only way I'd ever let it happen. He's not flesh and blood."

Abby flopped onto her back, sitting up. Her desire surged, mixed in with an emotion she feared she knew only too well. "You mean that?"

He flushed, brushing free a lock of hair that had stuck to her lips. "Of course," he said with a dismissive shrug.

Sensing she had him dangling, she grinned. "I meant, do you mean you're sure I won't damage the statue?"

Myles scowled. "You won't."

Abby rose, her legs wobbling a little, and crossed to the statue. The statue's design gave her a lap to sit on, its cock jutting up at a slight angle. The hand that gestured to its cock would also support her, Abby realized.

She stepped onto the statue's base, her bare foot knocking against its big toe. Swinging her leg over the statue's, she inched forward.

Myles closed in, supporting her. "Let me help," he murmured

into her ear, giving her lobe a lick. He lifted her, his broad hands spanning her waist.

Abby braced herself against the statue's chest, the gilded stone resisting her touch. With Myles's help, she sank down onto the statue. The chilled bulge pressed against her wet slit.

Taking a breath, Abby tried to relax. Myles nuzzled her neck, distracting her. Before she knew it, the cold head of the statue's cock sunk inside.

Abby tensed and groaned.

Myles's grip on her hips tightened. "Does it hurt?" He seemed ready to lift her right off it.

"No, no." Abby patted his hand at her waist. "It's just . . . big."

Myles pressed his lips against her shoulder blade. "Take it nice and slow."

Down and down she slid. The statue's cock stretched her and chilled her insides. It subdued the heat Myles had created in her. Subdued it, but not silenced it. Abby grew aware of a pleasant, deepening ache, a need that Myles had started and that she now wanted to finish.

Before she enveloped all of the statue's length, she raised herself up until just the head remained inside. So much thicker than the rest of it, it stretched her pleasurably right at her entrance.

Moaning, she sank down upon it again, filling herself with its implacable cold. Myles pressed himself up behind her, his cock rubbing against her lower back, his hands shimmying up her waist to cup and tease her breasts.

Already swollen and erect, the blazing of her nipples spread through her body. Myles bent her farther forward, a steady pressure against her back. He pressed a wet digit against her anus, and Abby shivered with anticipation. She hoped he fit, what with one massive cock already inside her.

She made a soft mewling noise of concern. Myles kissed her shoulder blade, his lips pressing warm against her skin.

He inched his finger inside. Abby stilled her humping of the statue, feeling him push past the tight muscle, invading her.

She whimpered, wanting more than anything to resume humping the statue. He penetrated her farther, his finger swirling around her anus.

He withdrew, leaving a stinging slap on her arse. "No room for me," he whispered, nipping the back of her neck.

Abby admitted to a moment of relief before the delightful stretching by the statue's cock reminded her of new satisfaction. Myles resumed teasing her breasts.

She pulsed up and down the statue's cock. It grew warm and slick with her human heat. Her whole body was aflame with need, with the statue's cock inside her and Myles at her back, his warmth keeping the cool of the underground chamber from her.

Gasping and crying out, Abby reached the point of arousal where she had been just a few moments ago with Myles fucking her from behind. The climax built and built until she teetered on the brink of raw, seared sensation.

Her vision swam. The wall paintings danced before her eyes, merging into a swirl of riotous color. It looked like they were melting off the walls, like a child's crayon picture melted by the sun.

Abby blinked, trying to clear her vision, but the urge to reach a higher climax made all else unimportant. Her body, one molten mass of willingness, strove for satisfaction lying just out of reach.

Heat, overwhelming heat, greeted her senses. The cool underground chamber had become a furnace, making it difficult to confirm if Myles spooned about her back. Her head fell back, seeking more air, while she rocked against the statue's cock.

Nails grazed her backside. She gasped. The gold fingertips of the statue flexed, scratching her. Not Myles. Even that didn't rouse her out of her fog of desire.

With effort, she looked down at the statue's chest. The mat of golden hair across his pecs seemed alive, rising and falling.

The statue *breathed*.

In the same moment, the long-awaited climax hit her. She screamed out her pleasure, bearing down on the statue's suddenly alive and pulsing cock. She ground against his groin, milking every last part of her release.

Sagging, she remembered the hallucination that she'd thought the statue actually lived. Its cock remained hard and massive inside her, no longer pulsing, no longer alive.

A groan—an ancient, creaking groan and yet roaring with life—shook the little chamber.

A large hand caressed her cheek, a hand larger than Myles's, the palm cupping her chin, the forefinger stroking her temple.

Abby opened her eyes.

Eyes, alive and sparkling, green as rain-washed ivy and flecked with gold, stared back at her.

Too astonished to scream in fear, Abby gave the full lower lip a tentative touch. Breath gushed over her trembling fingertips, and the lips pouted to kiss them.

The statue lived.

What had been cold gold rendered to real, tanned flesh, still golden in hue. The statue no longer reclined in leisure, but leaned forward gathering her closer to him. Beneath her his broad thighs flexed.

Abby stared and stared. How did this happen? Sex toys weren't meant to become alive. Real flesh and blood. The last thing Myles wanted.

She struggled to disentangle herself from the living statue's grip.

Inside her, his cock thrust into fresh life, burying deeper. Abby cried out, clutching his shoulders, her cunt so sensitive she didn't think she'd be able to handle more sex, and certainly not from a supernatural being.

His large mouth closed over hers, breathing fresh energy

into her. The sensitivity vanished and she opened, accepting his huge cock. She moaned into his mouth. His kiss banished her terror, replacing it with unremitting desire. She wanted more of him, more of this god, nothing else.

She grew aware of being lifted and laid upon the dais, the statue's former base. His cock remained inside her, sliding out a little ways as he moved her. Her bent over her, still holding her secure in his arms. His cock slid into her, pushing past her still-convulsing muscles until she felt his balls brush her bottom.

It dizzied her. Abby no longer thought, lost in the golden statue's needs and desires. She wanted nothing more than to please him. *He* had become paramount in her mind.

She canted her hips, hooking her ankles around his waist, giving as much of him as possible.

"More," the god's voice rumbled, young and alive and very much aware.

He grabbed her legs, hauling them higher, over his shoulders, bending her in two.

It squeezed her clit between her legs, leaving her open and completely vulnerable to him. He thrust into her—hard, violent thrusts.

The sensations spiraled, each thrust pitching her higher and higher until even breathing became a secondary need. Endless moans fled her lips, wailing and twitching within his secure grasp.

The god grunted above her, sweat beading his brow in droplets of gold. He pulsed into her faster and faster, rocking her body with the immense power of each thrust.

Her screams of overwhelmed delight redoubled and tripled until it felt like there were a hundred Abbys and a hundred gods all crying out their pleasure.

The god pulled out of her, rolled over her unresisting body and drew up her haunches. He slid into her dripping cunt from behind, exploding into a frenzied pounding.

Abby's cheek slid along the smooth marble, not even aware

of the missing strength in her limbs. Her eyelids fluttered, lost on the cusp of unconsciousness. She'd lost count of the orgasms she'd had, one after the other, until they all blurred into one.

She had to be dreaming. Her jolted, blurred gaze saw the room had come to life. The bare walls held no images but the painted background of hills and trees. The paintings lived, cavorting before her dais, fucking each other with wild animal abandon, tearing at each other in order to reach climax.

She saw Myles surrounded by three women. He seemed as lost as she, his face buried in the abundant breasts of one, getting a blow job from another, the third working on the clits of the other two.

The cold wash of betrayal startled her from her blissed-out, erotic doze. "No," she whispered.

Lifting herself from the floor, Abby crouched on all fours. Her breasts jerked and swayed beneath her, the god still pounding away into her.

"No," she said a little louder, anguish making her voice break.

The god grabbed her hair, hauling her up onto her knees alone, pinning his cock deep inside her. "Yes," he hissed, reaching around to finger her clit.

He twisted the wet, swollen flesh between his broad fingertips. Abby stiffened, her mind blanking. Her orgasm blinded her: nothing existed but bright particles of light racing and colliding throughout her jerking body.

He released her, and she slumped forward, bent into two. Her cunt still clutched and squeezed the god's cock. This climax demanded more. More than release.

She got her wish. The god roared and her body filled with fresh liquid gold spurting from his spasming cock.

Pulling out of her, he let her collapse onto the dais, her limbs resting wherever they landed.

"You are mine," she heard him say. "Mine."

Oblivion claimed her.

12

Red haze covered Myles's eyes. Against him, Abby burned, her pale skin flushed with desire. Her nipples under his palms condensed the heat, transmitting it to him. He rubbed his cock against her back, content to satisfy himself that way. He *could* take her from behind, but the statue didn't seem to leave enough space to share.

Oh God, rubbing against Abby like a teenaged boy drove him right to the edge. Any minute now and he'd coat her back with his cream.

A woman's hands smoothed down his back. He arched into the touch like a cat. More hands found his cock, squeezing and stroking it, drawing him away from Abby. Another hand snaked up his inner thigh, teasing his balls.

The hands guided him away. He called out to Abby, danger filtering through his befuddled senses at last.

She ignored him and he soon saw why, the red haze clearing his vision long enough to see the statue lived.

Lived. And Abby ignored him for this living statue's embraces.

Still, as much as he disliked this new obsession of hers, he wanted to believe she'd been ensorcelled, that this was not by choice. Even though her sexual eagerness, so fresh and frank, had occupied all his thoughts. Even when he coaxed the young viscount into helping let them stay, his mind filled with her.

Countless women, bacchante, he supposed—satisfied him sexually, no fewer than three at a time plying him with their avid attentions, passing him around like one of Abby's sex toys.

All at once, all activity ceased. Myles slumped to his knees, sucking in precious air in great heaving breaths.

"It is done!" A booming voice reverberated throughout the underground chamber.

Shaking his heavy head, Myles raised it. He needed air, fresh air, to clear away the fog in his mind.

Around him, men and women lay prostrate, arms out-stretched on the floor toward the statue. Where had they all come from? He gave his head another shake and caught sight of the walls.

His mouth opened. The walls were bare of all the painted people. People, he realized, that now were real flesh and blood around him, even the goat-legged satyrs.

He looked toward the center of the room where all those around him pointed in their prostration. Pointing to where the statue had stood on its tall base.

Abby lay sprawled across the base. Unconscious, he hoped, and not dead. The statue stood over her, transformed into a large golden man. He kept all the perfection of the Greek sculptor's chisel, the gold leaf transformed into a deep golden tan. He looked powerful and robust.

"It is done!" The living statue punched his arms into the air in triumph, fists clenched. "We have been freed from our prison, imprisoned by that deceitful Athenian."

His supplicants booed and hissed. Myles wondered how the creature knew to speak English rather than some ancient Greek dialect. It couldn't have been for his ears alone. He knew most of the old Greek.

"Now we live! Once more the world will know the true depths of human desires: the sweet nectar of ambrosia, finer than any wine, will unfetter them from this gross distortion known as civilization. It is *we* who will be worshipped, *we* who will be adored, and none will say us nay. I, Dionysus, proclaim this to be so."

"*Merde,*" Myles cursed under his breath.

At Dionysus's feet, Abby stirred, raising her head from its marble pillow. Myles's heart surged. She lived. She blinked in confusion and then he saw her vision clear, finding him amidst ancient Dionysus's followers.

He held her gaze with a pleading expression. Would she forgive him for what he had done?

"You!" Dionysus's finger stabbed at him.

The power of his command reeled around Myles. If he hadn't been on his knees, he would have fallen on them. He swayed with the unseen blow.

"Bow down to me, mortal. Bow down or suffer the consequences!"

He first thought to defy the god, but he saw Abby's stricken features and caved. Better to fight that battle later, when at least dressed and armed.

He bowed, hiding his face from Abby and the god.

Dionysus reached out to the crowd. "Go forth! Go forth!" he boomed. "And spread my word through all the land!"

Abby groaned at his feet. She sat up, wincing. "We're screwed."

Elaine wandered through the herb garden. The moon tipped full over each delicate leaf. She brushed her fingers over the leaves, releasing rich scents into the clean night air.

It wasn't fair. Why had Myles come back now, bringing that harridan of a wife in tow? How could he choose that common creature after having pursued her?

A daughter of the Wintertons was the highest prize the marriage mart had to offer: refined, delicate, and beautiful. He'd had the brazen idea to pursue her, and abruptly, he gave up the chase.

She'd suspected her father had had a part in that, but now she had to wonder if the new Mrs. Hardy might have had something to do with it.

"Cow," she muttered.

From the hedge encircling the herb garden, she heard rustling. Elaine paused, listening and watching for any sign of movement. It was probably a rabbit, she decided. She'd do the gardener a favor and scare off the creature.

A shadow stepped onto the narrow graveled path. Man-sized, concealed with a cloak.

Had Myles come to his senses and come for her? If he dared, he'd find a short welcome. She'd not be so easy to pluck as his new wife must have been.

She decided against running away. Getting the confrontation over with might bring some peace to her soul. She folded her arms, pushing up her breasts to better advantage. *Let him see what he's missing.*

The figure approached, the cloak's hood hiding his face.

Elaine frowned. He didn't seem quite tall enough . . . "Myles?"

His hands raised to the hood, pushing it back enough to reveal the dark oval of his face.

Elaine gasped. "Who are you?"

His sensual-lipped smile sent her heart pounding. Dark curly hair peeked out from beneath the hood. Thick eyebrows hovered over sparkling eyes of indeterminate color in the moonlight.

"I'm lost," he said. His voice sounded ordinary, but his accent sounded odd.

"You're on private property," Elaine supplied. "Walk around this side of the house, and you'll see a graveled drive. That will take you to the road."

"You are too kind." However, the stranger showed no inclination to move. "Where—where am I?"

"You are on the Winterton estate."

"This is your villa?"

"Hardly a villa," Elaine scoffed. "It belongs to my father."

"And in what country?"

She blinked. "You *are* lost. What happened to you?"

He shrugged. "I fell asleep, and the next moment I woke up, not far from here."

"Oh dear," she said, without much sympathy. "I fear you might have been ambushed. But surely if that had happened, your captors would not have let you escape."

"But I have escaped." He paused, a frown furrowing his brow. "I think."

He seemed well educated, despite the odd accent. Elaine stepped closer, reaching out to his forehead. "Did you take a knock to the head?"

He jerked away and she froze. "No. No, I don't feel the least bit woozy."

"Oh." She didn't know what to do. Her etiquette training never covered this. She stood there, twisting her fingers.

He inched closer. "What country am I in? You didn't say."

"England. Where are you from?" She wondered if he came from a good family.

"Greece."

Elaine relaxed. "That explains the accent. You speak English awfully well."

"Languages are a gift," he muttered. He edged closer, the cloak swirling about his ankles. "You look beautiful in the moonlight."

"Uhh, thank you." Elaine tucked a loose curl behind her ear. "I should go back inside."

"Wait." He grabbed her forearm.

Elaine looked pointedly at where he held her, lifting the same narrow gaze to his face.

"Forgive me." He released her, his fingertips dragging down the inside of her arm and across her palm.

She sucked in her breath. Nobody had touched her like that before. "Who are you?"

"I am called Demetri." Before she realized it, he stepped even closer. His fingertips skimmed her forehead. His voice dropped lower. "You are truly beautiful."

She met his gaze, her heart pounding despite her outward reserved attitude. "I know."

"And do you know this?" he murmured. He dipped in close, sealing his lips over hers. She froze, remaining still under his tender touch. He caressed her face, slipping down to her neck, her shoulder, her breast.

The very tip of his tongue teased along her closed mouth, and without even knowing what she did, she opened her mouth to him.

His kiss grew hungry, and he hauled her against him. She slipped her hands beneath his cloak, finding a bare chest covered in a mass of wiry hair. Exploring, she discovered a leather belt lay diagonally across his chest, but nothing else: no vest, no shirt, no jacket. His captors must have stolen almost everything he wore.

He kept kissing her, never ceasing, wearing down her slim resolve. She wrapped her arms around his chest's muscular barrel, caressing the cords of his back. She traced the muscular lines down, down to his furry breeches.

Furry? It must be traditional Greek attire.

She moaned into his mouth. He didn't stop the kiss for her to cry out her growing satisfaction. At last, someone had slipped past her father's guard. At last, she had someone to love.

Demetri jerked back. His wild-eyed gaze astonished her.

His actions surprised him as much as it had her. He blinked, his lips twisting into an upturned leer. "I want you," he breathed.

She tried to pull away, but he held her firm. "You cannot. Do you know who I am?"

"All I know is that you are beautiful and I want you." He grabbed a flailing hand and pressed it between his legs. "Feel how much I want you."

Poking out from his furry breeches, a pulsing cylinder of hot flesh came into contact with Elaine's hand.

She tried to pull away, her hand sliding up the shaft, but he held her in place. With a gasp, she realized what she held. She'd seen horses in the act, caught the odd servant, although a maid's skirt hid much. He wanted . . . he wanted to do that?

"Can you feel how much I want you?"

"Y-yes," she stuttered, "but it's not proper!"

"Proper? What is proper when you feel this?" He made her hand slide back down the shaft. "Tell me you don't feel the same inside. Hard and needy."

She bit on her lower lip. She didn't know what she felt: an excited fluttering in her stomach and the flowering of something warm beneath that, an urge previously taken care of by her own hand. "I—"

"Trust me," he growled. "It's better with two."

Better? Had he read her mind?

"Yes." He kissed the tip of her nose, relaxing his grip on her trapped hand.

A sob rose and choked in her throat.

He smoothed her cheek. "Do not be afraid. I will not hurt you. I will never hurt you. I will simply give you what you need."

He spun her about, pulling her against him. His cloak parted to envelop her as well, the woolen sides folding over in front. She heard a slight snap and realized that he'd fastened the cloak closed partway down with some sort of clasp.

Before she even thought to investigate, one of his hands slinked down to rest over her mound. The intimacy of his touch, the heat of it seeped through her gown and petticoat. He knew how to touch a woman, knew how to please her.

Leaning against him, she lifted her skirts, scrunching them up until she reached his caressing hand. At her gentle touch, he ceased his efforts. She pushed up her skirts, granting him open access to her private self. His hand descended on her mound once more and she shivered with delight.

"Part your legs." The rough edge of his voice sparked something more than a warm flowering in her belly. Something hotter.

She obeyed, her buttocks slipping against his hard shaft. It excited her more than she thought possible.

His fingers explored her mound, parting her curls along each side of her slit. Her parted legs gave him ready access to the further depths of her slit, but he dallied, tracing the outline of her nether lips.

At last, his lingering exploration reached the upper join. His fingertip brushed over her . . . her . . .

"Your clitoris is so eager. It wants me." He teased it into fuller life, skimming over it, making her want to arch into his hand, even if that meant leaving the excited rubbing of his shaft along her bottom.

She went with the stronger urge, moving against his hand. He teased her into a fever. Her head pressed against his shoulder, the delicious feeling growing near.

He abandoned her clitoris, slipping down between her nether lips, into the slick wetness within. "Oh yes," he hissed, his finger plunging deeper. He slid down to her wet hole and delved inside.

She cried out in surprise and delight. "Oh, more, please." She didn't know what she wanted, only that it had to be something. Something more wonderful than satisfying herself by her own hand.

His knees bent, his shaft dipping beneath her and then up, pressing against her wet slit. "Now, feel my cock fill you. You will be mine."

Elaine thought she might already be his.

He bent her forward. In danger of losing her balance, Elaine reached out and found the low garden wall. The brick chafed her palms, but she didn't care.

Demetri's cock slid into her. The deeper he went and the more he stretched her, the more certain she became of it. He fitted her like destiny.

She was his. It was destined.

His furry breeches warmed the backs of her legs.

"Hold on," Demetri groaned.

Elaine gripped the brick. He pulled out and she cried out at the loss. He grasped her hips, thrusting into her. She rocked forward with each thrust, bowing her back to bring him in even deeper.

He felt good, so good. Each time he withdrew, she pushed back, not wanting him to escape her. He bent over her, nipping at her neck, spurring her on to a wilder bucking.

He took her beyond her wildest imagining. She never knew sex was this good, this wild, and lasted this long. She panted and sobbed, tears of joy streaking down her face.

The release she expected came, and her hips twisted and shook. She subsided, waiting for the pleasure to fade.

But it didn't. Demetri didn't stop and neither did the heady sensations of finding release, intensifying with each thrust. She whimpered, resisting at first, but she gave in. No wonder fathers didn't tell their daughters about this. She never wanted to give it up.

Elaine lost all track of time. Nothing existed but Demetri and the night's darkness. Even the moon seemed to have faded. Her reality shrank further. Nothing existed but Demetri's pounding cock and her wet, never-ending release.

He roared, digging into her hips during his last spasms into her. He stilled, his cock still hard in her wet slit, his breath hot against her neck.

Elaine wanted to collapse, to sink to the ground, but he held her up, so she leaned against the low brick wall, head buried in folded arms.

At last, he pulled out.

Elaine fell to the ground in a boneless heap, twisting to face him. "No, don't leave."

The moon came out from behind a cloud, casting cold light across the small garden. Elaine looked up. A scream choked in her throat.

In his lust, Demetri's hood had fallen back. Two small horns protruded from his scalp. Tiny ridges made them bumpy looking, like a goat's. With the cloak hanging open, Elaine saw his furred legs, instead of the unusual breeches. Not only furred legs, but misshapen, the knees twisted backward and ending in hooves instead of feet.

She covered her mouth. "Oh my God! What are you?"

He skittered backward. "What do you think I am?" His head darted from side to side, looking for an escape.

"The—the devil?" The horns, the animal legs, what else could he be? Elaine stuffed her fist partway into her mouth.

Demetri huffed out a nervous chuckle. "I am a satyr, follower of Dionysus and Bacchus. I am no devil."

"But you—you tempted me into having intercourse with you!"

"Did I?" He edged nearer, no longer appearing skittish. "Did I really force you against your will?"

"N-n-no." What had she done? What had she done it with?

"I merely fulfilled your most secret wish: to succumb to your desires and be wholly satisfied." He extended his hand. "And I will do it again, for I see despite your fear you remain in need and attracted to me."

"Attracted?" Her lip curled in scorn. "To a monster?"

"No more monstrous than the darkness in your own heart."

Elaine staggered to her feet, shaking her head. "No, no." She turned and fled.

Dionysus pointed to Myles. "Take this man from here and pleasure him until he can stand no more."

Abby watched four women, naked but for long, tangled hair falling to their ankles, gather around Myles and coax him to his feet. They led him away. Myles stumbled, looking over his shoulder to where she lay at the god's feet.

When he had gone, Dionysus knelt beside her. "Come," he said, extending a hand. "Let me show you such pleasures that you will not weep for your mate."

Abby brushed her wet cheeks with the back of her hand. "I'm not crying."

"Ms. Abigail Deane, do you not think that I don't know who and what you are?"

She eyed him warily. "What am I?"

"A child of the future, the key to my release, and mine to enjoy."

Abby gaped. "How do you know this?"

His golden smile filled with charm. He bent the power upon her and her world grew small. Only he existed for her, great and golden and alive. Abby weakened. Who could prevail against a god?

"I know this because within my prison, I sensed your approach and I sent you here to free me. I have been waiting patiently, my dear." He caressed her cheek and Abby swooned into it. "You are mine now."

Not nearly, Abby thought. This god hadn't reckoned on women's liberation.

But his touch seduced. "How often does a girl get to lie with a god?"

"Quite a bit if you believe my father Zeus." Dionysus chuckled. "And I confess, I have something of a reputation for it too."

Abby tilted her head. "You speak so strangely: almost archaic one moment, then like this time, then like mine."

"I am in all times and all places." His body took on an otherworldly glow, his voice echoing with his power. When he gazed down at her again, that supernatural cast had faded. "Now, let me show you how the gods do pleasure."

He leaned forward and kissed her. The simple contact of his lips sent a racing fiery line from her mouth to her belly. It bound her to him, made her his. Too late, she realized her mistake in allowing this.

Trapped. Her eyelids fluttered shut, drinking him in. She reclined, the god's heat and press of his flesh pursuing her. Cold, hard marble chilled her back, but Dionysus warmed her all the way through.

His mouth claimed hers, his tongue tangling with hers. Her heart rate rocketed through the roof. Her entire body throbbed with his kiss and a body she'd thought too used to be aroused again so quickly came to life.

Everywhere he touched created a delicious ache. Even in places she'd never thought erotic. The palm of her hand? The inside of her elbow?

She giggled with the sheer joy of the new sensations. His mouth left hers. Her eyes opened long enough to see his handsome face smirk at her before dipping to kiss along her collarbone.

He did more than kiss. He licked, sucked, and nibbled his way across her tender flesh, sliding his mouth between the valley of her breasts. She ached for him. Her very bones longed for his touch.

Dionysus stopped his blazing trail down her body, placing his hot mouth over her nipple, his warm hand covering the other one. He didn't remain idle, but worked his magic on her. He twiddled one nipple into aching hugeness, sucked and tugged on the other until it burned with the same fire.

She moaned and cried out, arching her back, wanting to show him she enjoyed his touch. More than any other man's, even Myles. She'd never experienced anything like it. She writhed against him, trying to find a way to find relief. All her senses were aflame. She flew beyond herself, beyond the bounds of her flesh, soaring on a golden plume. Reaching . . . reaching . . .

The scream came from deep within her, a long wailing cry. He'd made her come without even entering her, without even toying with her clit.

When he plunged his tongue between her parted thighs, she discovered how slick she'd become for him. Not merely moist or slick with need, but she gushed with it. One flick of his tongue propelled her into an orgasm.

Whimpering and trembling, she endured his oral assault upon her dripping slit. He licked up all she had to offer and demanded more.

His large, thick fingers thrust inside her convulsing cunt. He found the smooth spot within that drove her wild. She bucked against him, stunned by her response. What Myles coaxed into life, Dionysus incinerated. She came again, hard on the heels of her last orgasm. It was too much, too much. She couldn't imagine it any other way. Her next release came stronger and even wilder than the ones before. Arching her back, she delivered more of her juices into his waiting mouth.

A primitive cry burst forth from her lips. She'd never yelled this loud, not even at a football match. She drew in a deep, shuddering breath, expelling it in a groan. She blinked, dizzy and disoriented.

Dionysus rose above her, kissing her, his face wet with her sex juices. Her scent filled her nostrils, drowning her like an opiate. He kissed her hungrily, demanding of her even her breath.

And she gave it, willingly, trusting him to let her breathe in time. His lips lifted from hers and she sucked in air, his air, his breath.

It was a heady elixir: his breath, her scent mingled together. She found strength she didn't know she still had and wrapped her arms around his neck, pressing her palm against the back of his head, drawing him down for another kiss.

Lost in this second kiss, she wanted only to be a part of him. He granted her wish, fitting inside her. The length and breadth of his cock stretched her. Even as living flesh unlike gold-leafed solid stone, his cock remained implacable.

Abby sobbed beneath him, certain she'd never be able to take all of him in. One short thrust exploded that worry. She cried out, clutching at him, wanting him out, wanting him in.

He hauled her legs high over his hips and plowed into her, letting her body slide back and forth over the slick marble: marble made slick by her juices and their sweat.

She gave herself over to the ride, her body becoming used to his cock, her flowing wet easing his way. He fucked her harder and faster, grinding his hips against her groin.

Abby opened her eyes to find him gazing down at her. The wonder in his eyes left her even more breathless. Something else lurked in there, something that didn't belong in a god's eyes. Unable to put a name to it, she found it tugged at her heart.

He paused, deep inside her. "You are not a devotee and yet you surrender utterly."

She lifted a trembling fingertip and traced the length of his long nose, a nose that had worked wonders against her clit. "What other choice do I have?" she breathed. "I do not have the power to resist a real god."

Dionysus pulled her hand away from his face, smiling. "As long as you believe."

Before she formed the thought to reply, he thrust into her.

He plundered her body with his cock until her head bounced off the marble dais. He caught her head in his hands, holding her gaze with his own green eyes. Gold flecks flickered in their depths.

"Come for me," he groaned. "Come for me one more time." He ended the demand with a deep surge within her.

She came, on his command. Her wide, shocked eyes held his gaze while her cunt squeezed hard around Dionysus's cock. Squeezed and milked and demanded his own release.

His teeth bared and gritted together, his face twisting into a joyous mask. His breath expelled into her face and in the same moment the white-hot fire of his come propelled against her insides.

She sobbed, overwhelmed by the power of the god's release. She'd read that crazy euphemism in romances about the hero "filling" the heroine, but she never realized it was actually physically possible.

His coming filled not just her creamy cunt but entered into every fiber, every cell of her being.

It was then she knew she was truly lost.

13

Lucy woke from a deep slumber. At her side, she heard the deep breathing of her husband. Light shone through cracks in the drawn drapes. Aside from the rich colors the invading sunlight gave to the carpet and furnishings in its way, all else stayed in shadow.

Early morning yet. She closed her eyes, preparing to snuggle against her husband, her beloved duke, and resume her sleep.

Something nudged her foot. Lucy came wide awake. She froze. What had tapped her? Had a barn cat snuck into their room?

Lucy held her breath, reaching out with her senses while still pretending to sleep. She heard soft breathing. Not her husband's, but whose?

Her heart thudding in fear, she pretended to roll over and glanced down to the foot of the bed. She sat up, staring down at the base of the bed.

A young woman, naked but for her endlessly long, dark auburn hair, curled up at her feet.

"Who are you?" Lucy's voice sounded hoarse and shrill to her ears. "What do you want? How did you get in here?"

"So many questions." The woman's dulcet tones calmed and intrigued her. "I am here to serve you, my lady."

"Serve me how?" Lucy leaned forward, making sure her translucent shift remained hidden behind the covers.

"You wish to be satisfied, my lady, for more than your husband can deliver." The woman regarded the duke's sleeping form. "I can see why. He is old."

"Not so old," Lucy disagreed, keeping her voice low.

The woman rose onto all fours and crawled up Lucy's legs, straddling her body. The stranger reached out, her fingertips brushing Lucy's temple. "I see," she said, her eyes staring off into the distance, her voice sounding remote and otherworldly. "I see he is too much a man for you. You desire softness. Your own sex."

Her gaze snapped back to Lucy, staring into her eyes. "Me. I am Phoebe."

Lucy's jaw dropped, unable to believe what she heard. "How dare you?" she snarled. "It is not for you to say."

"Then let me show you." Before Lucy protested, the woman leaned forward and pressed her lips against Lucy's. Her soft kiss seemed like perfection to Lucy.

She'd never had anyone kiss her so willingly, so eagerly. In that one kiss, Lucy found the woman for her. The woman who wouldn't bed her for money, or because of her rank, but because Phoebe wanted to, wanted it, wanted her.

"That's all I want," Lucy breathed, nuzzling Phoebe's neck. "Somebody who wants me, really wants me."

"I do." Phoebe's hand trailed over her shoulder and cupped Lucy's breast, fondling it through the thin fabric, bringing Lucy's desire into sharp focus.

Phoebe glanced up at her through long, dark eyelashes. She

leaned in for another kiss. Lucy responded, wrapping her arms about the woman and drawing her down on top of her.

In a sudden frenzy, Phoebe pushed the sheets out of the way, shoving them aside into an ungainly heap. Only a fine lawn nightgown prevented their flesh meeting.

"I want you," Phoebe breathed. "I want to lie with that beautiful lush body of yours."

Lucy folded her arms over her breasts. "How do you know— how do you know I'm—"

Phoebe cupped her face in both hands. "I know."

Sitting up, Phoebe drew Lucy upright. With gentle hands, she gathered the hem of Lucy's nightgown, which was bunched around her hips and drew it up over Lucy's head.

"Beautiful," Phoebe breathed. Her fingertip brushed one of Lucy's bared nipples and then the other. Even that featherlight touch brought them into aching tightness.

Phoebe bent her head, drawing one of Lucy's erect nipples into her mouth. Lucy sighed, feeling Phoebe's tongue swirl around her taut flesh. She curved her hand around Phoebe's soft shoulder, pushing the wild tresses out of the way.

Lucy didn't want to stop her. Phoebe's feminine caresses seemed right to her. This is what she had dreamed of, hoped for, since a woman first touched her.

She bent to suckle Phoebe's neck, pressing long hot kisses down the slender column of her throat. Going any lower meant losing that sweet pleasure from Phoebe's mouth on her hard nipple.

Their mouths met again in a long, searing kiss. Their tongues slid along each other, tasting the other, enjoying the sheer pleasure of flesh on flesh.

Lucy lay back, Phoebe eagerly following. Their bodies remained joined, sliding against the other. Phoebe's thigh slipped between Lucy's legs, rubbing against her mound.

Lucy's heart pounded. This wasn't the deliberate demonstration of how to gain pleasure. Phoebe's enthusiasm was for her, not for the act. For her.

Lucy parted her legs farther, tilting her hips up to meet Phoebe's movement.

Phoebe broke the kiss, panting. "I want you," she gasped. She bent her head, laying a trail of kisses over the tender swell of Lucy's breast and then down, licking around her navel, dipping her tongue inside.

Lower, Phoebe went. Lucy lay back, gripping her pillow in preparation of receiving a great deal of pleasure. Phoebe's tongue flicked against her little clitoris. She gained an extra spurt of desire at the memory of seeing that anatomy book with the picture of a woman's parts and being told of the soul-altering effects of touching them a certain way.

Phoebe had the touch. Her tongue flicked again, never putting too much pressure upon the sensitive bud, just light and teasing. It drove her wilder than any mindless burying of face into her cunt. Too much pressure, too much sensation, and she went numb.

But Phoebe knew what to do.

Lucy moaned, curling her fingers into Phoebe's long hair. Phoebe's tongue explored further, dipping farther down her already moist slit, slipping its very tip into that intimate hole.

Writhing on the bed, Lucy sobbed her release. Her entire body became weightless, hovering above her corporeal self. She'd never experienced such bliss. She couldn't wait to return the favor.

"What is going on here?" The duke came awake beside her.

Lucy made an effort to cover herself, but the covers were pinned under her body and Phoebe's. She gave up, smiling helplessly at her husband.

His ire was not directed at her but at Phoebe. "You! What

are you doing here?" He rose up in the bed, preparing to throw her out.

"Pleasing your wife." The woman bobbed her head. "And you too, my lord. If you wish it."

Lucy clasped Phoebe to her bosom. "No. She is mine."

"I can see that, my dear. But a stranger?" His voice remained calm.

"She is already more dear to me than life." Lucy stroked Phoebe's hair.

"Is that so?" The duke reached over and pulled an ivy leaf out of the woman's auburn hair. "Where did you come from?"

Phoebe sat up, still straddling her body, her head bowed. Her hair formed a curtain in front of her face.

The duke grabbed it, pulling it out of the way. "Look at me, girl. Where are you from?"

Lucy stroked her husband's arm. "Don't terrify her, dear."

He ignored her. "Answer me. I command it." His hand curled about her hair, drawing her closer to him. Phoebe's gaze tracked to his grip in her hair and her eyes widened.

"You are of his blood?" she gasped, clawing at him.

The duke released her. "That was what I was afraid of."

"Husband?" Lucy sheltered the quivering woman in her arms. "What do you mean?"

He stroked her hair. "There is no need to worry, my dear. I will sort this out."

Phoebe moaned, curling into an even tighter ball. "No! Let us be!"

"What is she talking about?" Lucy asked, but her husband vanished into the dressing room, shouting for his valet.

Abby stumbled out of the Dionysian temple. She pushed past the ivy curtain, the sunlight blinding her. Her weak legs gave out beneath her and she fell to her knees in the mulch.

She looked up into the sky. The last of the morning mist trailed off into the high atmosphere, leaving the occasional scudding puffy cloud and endless blue sky. Good weather for England.

Pushing to her feet, Abby failed to find any joy in the day. She knew she ought to, yet everything seemed pale, almost colorless, despite the fact she knew she saw colors. Her mind grappled with the dichotomy, but the night's events had exhausted her and a cottony numbness filled her head.

Sleep. She wanted sleep.

Dionysus. She wanted Dionysus.

She stumbled back to the house, making a weaving path through the meadow's long grass.

Halfway there, she spotted a figure approaching, white hair blazing above darker garments. She paid the figure no heed, moving around him when he stopped to intercept her.

He grabbed her arm. "What have you done?"

Abby blinked at him, recognizing the duke. "Nothing," came her automatic, mumbled defense.

"Nothing?" The duke grabbed her by the shoulders and shook her. "Do you have any idea what you have done? You have awakened him, haven't you? You've woken the devil."

Dizziness hit her. Abby swayed. "Not the devil. Dionysus."

"Same thing." He shook her again. "Do you have any idea what you have done?"

"You keep sayin' that," mumbled Abby.

"Where is your husband? He is behind this, I warrant." He grabbed her arm and jerked her upright, his grip biting into her skin. "I should have known better than to allow you to stay. I should have known."

"Don't beat yourself up about it," Abby blithely replied with a drunken wave. "It will all come out all right."

"No, it won't. Not with Dionysus and his minions alive and polluting the world. Don't you see what will happen?"

Somehow, Abby managed to lift an eyebrow. "Everybody will have fun."

"Everybody will die." The duke ground his teeth.

Abby frowned, the concept too large to handle. "Die?"

"From an excess of lust: too much drinking, too much eating, too much sexual intercourse. The body overloads, ceases to function with all these wild humors racing through it. Don't you see? It's already happening to you!"

Abby had to accept the duke's truthful words. It explained a lot, including her inability to reason. "It's done." Her hand cut toward the ground to underline the finality.

"It's never done." The duke grabbed her arm and hauled her toward the house.

She let him guide her, stumbling over her leaden feet. In the rear courtyard, Abby heaved a sigh of relief. Her bed was not far. Sleep and then wake and . . .

She pitched forward, icy cold water numbing her head and shoulders. Spluttering, Abby pushed herself out of the water trough. "What was that for?"

"Are you awake now?" He still gripped the back of her neck.

Sense glimmered in the back of her mind. Without another word, she dunked her head into the water. Sitting back on her heels, she smoothed her hair, squeezing out water.

"All right," she said, gasping for air. "Tell me again what has happened."

The duke folded his arms, watching her with a bemused expression. "I think you should tell me. You woke the god. How?"

"It was a statue. I—" Abby halted, flushing. How could she explain what she'd done? On the other hand, the duke had seen her aroused. "I fucked it. It seemed like a good idea at the time."

"A gentlewoman shouldn't know such language," the duke

muttered. "And the god waked?" He stroked his chin, his steel-eyed gaze pinning her to the cobblestones. "Where?"

"The folly. There's a room beneath. I—I left him there."

The duke's eyebrow quirked. "I'm surprised he let you go."

Abby nodded. "So am I." Why *had* he let her go? She frowned. "Did you mean it? That Dionysus will destroy the world?"

"Yes." He extended a stiff arm. "Come, we will breakfast and plan his destruction."

She accepted his hand, rising without having to pull on his strength. "That sounds cheery."

Abby leaned on him though while they walked into the house and to the dining room. She slumped into a chair, letting him serve her a protein-rich breakfast of eggs, ham, bacon, and spotted dick.

Starving, she devoured the food, although it had only been the usual nighttime fasting. In her mind, she replayed the events of the previous night. It blurred, a miasma of constant fucking with both Myles and the god.

Dionysus. His golden glow embued everything with a richness she'd never before seen or experienced.

Abby set down her knife and fork. "How do you know about Dionysus?"

The duke nodded. "Good. I see you have come fully to your senses." He dabbed his lips with his napkin.

"You haven't answered my question." Abby folded her arms, swallowing a burp. She hadn't binged like that in ages.

"I think rather I am in the position to ask questions. Why did you release the god?"

Abby shrugged, touching her borrowed wedding ring. What had Myles really wanted? "Myles wanted to find the statue. It used to belong to his family. Some ancestor had brought it back from Greece, I suppose. Finding it would give him some sort of cachet with some club in London."

"The Dilettanti Society?" The duke snorted. "And you fell for that?"

Abby blinked. "What?"

"Did he tell you his family used to own this place?"

"Yes, he did. They lost the land because of the Civil War and didn't get it back after the monarchy was restored."

The duke's fingers formed an arch before him. "Yes, my ancestor made sure that it never returned to them. We don't know why they never reawakened the god, but they were his custodians."

Chewing her lip, Abby mused. "The knowledge may have been lost. Myles didn't know the statue's location. All he had was some nonsense riddle from his grandmother. It made no sense at all."

"Then how did he know to wake it?"

Abby closed her eyes, her heart thudding in anger—anger at Myles for lying to her, for getting her to agree to this ridiculous quest of his. "I want to believe he didn't know. It seemed entirely accidental."

"And you woke it by having sexual intercourse with it?"

Abby nodded.

"At whose suggestion?"

"Myles's." Abby defended him, her heart sinking. "I had with me a number of, ahh, sex toys, dildos and the like and Dionysus—the statue—just seemed like a life-size version."

"A newly married woman with sexual aids? With a man whose reputation with women surely precludes any such thing?" The duke's eyes narrowed. "Were they a wedding gift from him? Has he been preparing you for this task?"

"No!" Abby snapped. "They were mine before we even met." She flung up her hands. "This is absurd. It is done. What does it matter how it happened?"

"Because we need to find a way to undo it."

"How do you know it can even be done?" Abby demanded.

"Because one of *my* ancestors encased him in that gold and stone." The duke smiled with nostalgic satisfaction. "Now it is my turn."

"I think you need to explain this from the very beginning. Dionysus complained of—what was it?—some 'pesky Athenian.' Do you mean to tell me you're descended from that guy?"

"You assume 'that guy' is a man, but otherwise, yes. My ancestors trapped the god and guarded it until it was stolen."

"By Myles's ancestors," Abby guessed.

"Exactly so. They were merchants in the thirteenth century. My family failed in its duty, so when the Civil War came, we were in a position to resume custody of the statue. The statue was hidden and we were never able to find it."

"And lost from Myles's family too. Whoever stole it from your family kept the reason why a secret."

"You still defend him, despite what he has done." The duke regarded her with bemusement.

A lump formed in her full stomach. "He hasn't had a chance to tell his side of the story yet." Abby struggled to be fair.

"You speak very boldly to one above your rank."

Abby shrugged. "Rank isn't that important to me. You've got to earn my respect."

"And helping you recover from the Dionysian magic wasn't enough?"

She had to admit he had a point. She gave an abrupt nod. "I'm sorry I'm on the defensive. This is all my fault."

"Yes, it is," the duke agreed. "And you will help me fix it. My wife, my daughter, and probably my son are all enraptured by Dionysus's minions. You will help me free them."

"And Myles." Abby frowned, remembering the women ushering Myles away. "He is in danger too . . . Even if he's having a good time currently," she added wryly.

The duke leaned forward. "So you will help me?"

"Where do we start?"

Elaine crept away from the dining room door. She made a side trip to the kitchens, begging a large plateful of food and headed upstairs to her room.

Her satyr, Demetri, sat in the window seat, looking out at the woods. He looked over his shoulder at her entrance and he relaxed. "I worried it might be somebody else."

She smiled, at least she hoped she did. She didn't feel like smiling. "Nobody but my maid, and I've forbidden her my chambers."

"You looked concerned yourself."

Elaine rubbed at her arms. "My father is plotting to kill a god."

Demetri sat upright. "Dionysus? My master?"

Her smile grew thin. "I had a strong suspicion something supernatural was involved with your appearance. I didn't think your type ran wild in the bushes."

He grinned. "Or else you would have found one for your own by now."

Elaine smirked. She couldn't help it. "Something like that. What happens when my father succeeds in killing Dionysus?"

"Dionysus is a god. He cannot be killed. He can be imprisoned though, and me along with it."

The idea of losing Demetri sent her into a mild panic. "There's no way to stop it?"

"Do you want to?"

Elaine looked down at her hands. Did she want to keep this half-wild creature who satisfied her so thoroughly? *Yes, and yes*, her heart begged.

She didn't say.

The satyr slid off the window seat and trotted over to her.

He took her hands in his. "Elaine, you will never find another like me. I will love you."

"Love me?" she jeered. "Lying together does not equate to love."

"Holding you does." His thumbs smoothed over the backs of her hands. "Listening to you does. Who else will listen to your cares and woes but me?"

"I hate that you read my mind," Elaine grouched. He knew without asking that her father ignored her since the day her mother died. He knew she didn't get along with her stepmother. He knew her brothers blamed her for her mother's death.

He leaned forward and kissed her brow. "You are broken, my dear. You need me to complete you."

She ran her hands down his bared chest, stroking the mottled gray fur on his thighs. She wrapping her fingers about his stiffening cock. "I need you to complete me."

His head dipped to find her upturned lips. "Well, then," he breathed across them. "Then we have to stop your father."

Tucking her head lower, she released her grasp on his cock and hugged him tight. Squeezing her eyes shut, stopping the tears, she felt only despair. Her father always succeeded.

"We will find a way," Demetri whispered into her hair.

Myles struggled awake. A heavy weight lay across him. His eyes were sealed shut with some gooey mess. He forced them open. He lay in a grove of trees, the treetops shading him from the sun.

He tried lifting his head and slumped back. He looked down and found not one but two women sleeping across him. He nudged the nearest, trying to sit up.

The women shifted with grumbles. Myles rubbed at his head, overused muscles protesting even this simple move.

He looked around. Where was Abby? "Abby?"

Blinking to clear his vision, he didn't see her anywhere.

"Abby!" His shout echoed across the small clearing, fading into the blue of the sky.

He forced himself to his feet. He ducked under the lowering branches of a pine tree and into broad daylight. He winced, holding his forehead to keep his head together. This was worse than any hangover.

Not even looking back at the sleeping beauties, he headed for the temple, the last place he saw her. His toe caught on a rock. He avoided planting his face into the ground, grunting with the effort.

Rising again, he brushed the dirt from his palms and continued onward.

He slid down the open trap that led to the basement, landing in an ungainly heap on the hard floor. Groaning, he struggled upright. This shouldn't be this hard.

The god's booming laughter rattled his bones. Myles clenched his jaw.

"Have you tired of my bacchante already?" Dionysus called. He lounged on his dais. Someone had found some rich red velvet cushions. A royal green coverlet draped over a low fainting couch.

"There are more if you care to taste something new." The god gestured to the curled-up forms of women and satyrs. The population had depleted.

Myles remembered the god's declaration. How many of these wild, lustful creatures were out there? He drew nearer. "No, thanks. I'm looking for my wife." He didn't recognize Abby among the sleeping women.

"You mean Ms. Deane?" the god jeered. "She is not your wife."

Myles sucked in his breath. "How did you know?"

The god laughed again, a joyful sound. "I am a god. Of course I know. I brought her here."

Had he completely lost his reason? Did he just hear the statue say he'd sent Abby back through time?

"Time is relative. Now, then, it is all one. She is the key that freed me. And so I brought her here."

"Why to this time? Why not to when you became a statue?"

"I have not the strength of Zeus." He shrugged. "I did what I could when I could, harboring my strength until I had the power to reach her."

"And now you are free."

"Thanks to you and the lady." Dionysus munched on a grape. He held out the bunch. "Care for one?"

"No thanks. Is she here?" Myles took another look at the sleeping pile.

"No. But she will return. She won't be able to stay away from me. She is intoxicated by me."

"You? But—" His gut clenched, sickened he'd lost her already.

"You are going to say that you had her first. That may be, but she is mine now. One of the small benefits of being a god. How else do you think I came by my devoted followers?" He gestured to the sleeping mound of bodies.

Myles ground his teeth. "We will see about that."

"Most amusing." He waggled his fingers in dismissal. "Have fun."

Myles returned to the ladder, his spine itching with the god's regard. He had to find Abby, find some sort of cure before the urge to return to the god occurred.

The god's laughter followed him. He even heard the faint echo of it as he stepped into the house.

With the butler's assistance, he found her in the study, poring over books with the duke. On seeing her, his heart took an unaccountable leap. She looked her usual self. He hurried forward. "Abby, are you unhurt?"

Her glaring frown gave him pause. "I hope you are here to help."

"Help with what?" He reached out to touch her shoulder, but she jerked away. Had fucking the god put her off all other men? No wonder he still heard Dionysus's laughter.

"Perhaps Mr. Hardy doesn't care to," the duke put in, his voice like ice.

"Will someone tell me what's going on?" Myles's voice rose, even though it made his head hurt.

Abby closed a large dusty tome and reached for another. "We're going to stop the god, you idiot. If you're not going to help, please go away."

"Oh, I will help," Myles growled. "Hand me a book and tell me what I'm looking for."

The duke stroked his chin. "I am not so sure we should be so ready to have him help us."

Abby shot the duke an irritated look before returning her attention to Myles. "You better sit down and tell us everything, and I mean everything, about Dionysus."

He frowned. "He's the Greek god of—"

"I mean your grandmother's riddle and the real reason why you wanted to find the statue."

"I told you: to show it to the Dilettanti Society and win a place there, a place that was denied to my father." Myles frowned. Why did she ask such a strange question? "What other reason would there be?"

"To trick me into freeing the god from the statue."

Myles wiped his mouth with his palm. *Oh God.* "Is that what you think? Is that what you really think?"

Abby chewed on her lower lip. "It was your idea. To find the statue. To make me fuck it."

Myles noticed the duke didn't even wince. His lips twisted, thinking of Abby giving the duke an unedited earful in his absence.

"You're smirking," Abby accused. "You did trick me!"

"I did not. I was merely amused at your choice of language."

"What I say, or how I say it, isn't important, Myles. You *lied* to me."

"Is this how you end things in—" Myles broke off. He didn't want this to end. Not this way. "May I speak with you alone?"

The duke folded his arms. "I don't think that is wise."

Abby gave him an arch look. "I don't think you are in any position to tell me what to do either." She rose, dusting her hands on her skirts.

For the first time, he noticed the rumpled and torn state of them. What had she been through? He reached for her but she jerked away.

"I can manage."

How was he going to convince this stubborn woman that he told the truth?

14

In the hallway, Myles slumped against the wall. He faced incredible odds. Even to his eyes, the evidence against him looked damning. "I don't know what I can say that will convince you otherwise. I had no idea any of this was going to happen."

"And I'm supposed to believe you. I'm feeling used here, Myles."

"Used? By who? The duke? Dionysus?" Her face took on a dreamy expression. He snapped his fingers before her face. "Focus, Abby. I am just as surprised as you. I swear I had no idea."

"Not even from your grandmother?" Abby folded her arms, pushing her bosom to full advantage. He realized she'd abandoned her stays again.

"All I had was the riddle." He remembered his grandmother's warning. "She raved a lot, in her own little dreamland. But—but—some of what she says makes sense now." He sank to the floor in a long, slow slump. "Oh God, I should have listened closer. I should have believed her mumbled ramblings." He covered his face with his hands. "What have I done?"

"Did you know about—about using the statue?" He sensed her crouched by his side, her hand on his shoulder.

He shook his head. "I didn't have a clue. I was so excited that we found it. It was just a lark, just a bit of fun, I thought." He gritted his teeth and forced himself to meet her gaze. "Like we have upstairs."

Abby's hard expression melted. She kissed his forehead. "It's going to be all right. His Grace might have a solution, a way out, if we can find it among the family papers."

Myles pushed off the wall. "No, it's not all right. Dio—" He paused, remembering her glazed eyes when he said the god's name. "The god has his hooks into you, Abby."

She straightened, her nostrils flaring. "I know." She helped him up and he drew her into his arms. She held him tight.

Protectiveness surged through him. Dionysus may have brought her here for his own ends, but Myles promised to take care of her and he wasn't about to let her become one of the god's followers, crazed with desire. He wanted her to desire only him. Only him? He batted away the thought. Why set himself up for a deeper hurt? If they didn't succeed . . .

Abby drew back a little way. "Myles," she whispered, "I'm sorry."

"Perfectly understandable, but I'm glad you believe me." He tilted her chin. "I'm not ready to lose you, Abby. I'll fight this god every step of the way until you're safe again."

Her eyes filled with tears. "I'm supposed to say that I can take care of myself. I'm a modern woman, Myles." She sniffed, wiping her nose with the back of her hand. "But that was nice. Very nice."

He caressed her cheek. "Is there anything we can do to stop him?"

"The god?" Abby shrugged. "The duke thinks so, and all of his followers as well." She tugged on his arm. "Come on, there is work to do."

* * *

Lucy stepped out of the shadows of the upper landing. Phoebe, crouching behind the banister, looked up at her. "What does this mean?" Lucy whispered.

"It means I will not stay with you long if they succeed." Phoebe's sensual voice deepened with sadness.

Lucy stroked the woman's hair, soothing her. "We'll see about that."

Elaine rose from her bed, gazing back at the dozing satyr. From the waist up, he was in every respect a magnificent man. Although her body ached with his skill at pleasures she had never even dreamed of, she had to admit his bestial legs disconcerted her.

She hadn't really thought about his otherworldliness before, being so lost in him. Still naked herself, she flicked back the covers, bringing his whole body into view.

He lay on his stomach, limbs sprawled every which way, his arms wrapped about a pillow. She reached out, fingertips brushing his hairy hip—his flank?

Demetri's muscles twitched as if to dislodge a fly, his small tail twitching.

Elaine remained still. Would he wake and read her worried thoughts? She waited until she was sure he hadn't woken before touching him again.

This time his flank didn't shiver, letting her stroke his mottled gray fur. His fur didn't have the wiry roughness of a true goat, being soft instead. She loved the feel of it.

She sank her fingers into the thick coat, smoothing along well-defined muscles. She traced over the bones and tendons that made up his lower leg. Thick and strong, not weak and deformed at all.

Rather like his cock. Her lips twitched. That was a magnificent organ well worth further examination.

Her fingertips brushed the hard nail of his hoof. She brushed off a light smear of dust. Settling on the bed, she let her hand rest on his ankle.

Wanting him still filled her, despite his differences. It shouldn't matter. He understood her so much better than any other human had even tried to, even better than she understood herself. He saw through her walls, her devices for keeping hurt away, and crashed through them all. What could she do in return? She didn't know where he came from, but she didn't want him to be destroyed either.

She bit down on her knuckle. Truly, she faced her greatest challenge. Being slighted by her family? Nothing compared to this. All she needed was to give him her love, wholly and unconditionally.

Could she do it? Love this creature so different from herself, that had no place in this world?

Demetri rolled over, startling her to her feet. She covered her mouth to hide her shock. He regarded her with lazy green eyes. "What are you doing?"

"Looking at you." She sat down again. "You're so . . . so different."

"Am I?" His broad-lipped smile almost undid her. Looking into that gorgeous face, she'd forget anything was ever wrong with him. "There's nothing wrong with me."

Her skin turned hot. "Demetri . . ." She didn't know what to say.

"I am unusual in this day and age, I'll grant you that." He sat up, his goat legs curling awkwardly beneath him. It did nothing to hide them, only made them more noticeable.

She dragged her gaze away from them and back to his more pleasing face. "Demetri . . ."

"Come here." He patted the bed beside him.

She wriggled closer. She didn't understand what drew her to him. She ought to be repulsed by his deformities, even pity him, but she had to consciously think that. No, when she didn't think about it, the concern didn't exist. She tucked in her head, angling for his strong column of a neck.

Elaine wondered how she'd explain him to her father.

The satyr's lips found hers and he drew her down on top of him. "Go on, Elaine. Explore my workings. I know you want to."

"You know too much," she complained, not really meaning it. "I wish I knew more about you."

"Ask anything and I shall answer it."

"Anything?" she purred. She scooted down a little way and laid kisses on his chest. The tiny curls of hair tickled her nose. He smelled delicious, like sun-ripened peach. Her tongue flicked across his skin.

"Anything," he promised, his voice rough.

"How old are you?" Elaine looked up.

"About twenty-five years or so."

"But—but—" She sat up, folding her arms over her bare breasts. "You should be ancient!"

"I've been frozen in time. I am no immortal. In time, I will grow old and die. My mother was mortal, a bacchante, and my father a satyr." His faraway gaze seemed wistful. "They must be centuries dead by now."

Elaine patted his arm in sudden sympathy. She didn't have to tell him she considered herself without parents. "We are alike in that respect."

He smiled at her, a smile both wistful and pleased. "We are."

She scooted up to lie alongside him, her exploration of him forgotten. "I am glad you are not immortal," she said, stroking his chest hair. "I would not like to grow old and—"

He placed a finger over her lips. "Do not say it. I may end up as a fresco on the wall again if your father succeeds in his plans."

"Isn't there something we can do?"

"I am not the type to do murder and it pains me even to contemplate it, but perhaps we may be able to corrupt him." He smiled again. "And he will forget all about destroying Dionysus."

"How can you even destroy a god?"

"It's been done before." He gestured to himself as proof of evidence. "Now, weren't you doing something?"

"Ah yes." She beamed at him. "How remiss of me." She slid back down the bed, resuming her examination of the borderline of fur.

She swept her glance down his legs: truly misshapen, the knees making his legs bend in the reverse to how they ought to be, but they were not out of symmetry or balance with the rest of him.

It didn't take her too long to notice that the satyr's cock had hardened, a magnificent shaft, thick and a perfect balance to the lightly haired heavy balls beneath. Supernatural being or otherwise, Elaine didn't want to miss the chance of examining the male form.

She skimmed over his hard cock, marveling at it. The slight curve to it, the marbling of veins just beneath his skin's surface. Rising up to the tip, the protruding ridge seemed perfection for rubbing those delicious spots inside her that Demetri seemed to know about without asking.

Not that she had known of them either.

She pursed her lips and kissed the side of the head, the velvety texture hot against her lips. With the tip of her tongue, she licked the spot where she'd kissed him.

His hands curled into her hair. "I am not so horrible, am I."

He might be able to read her mind, but some things needed to be spoken. "Not at all." She flicked a sidelong glance up his form, past the furred groin, the flat stomach and prominent muscles of his chest to his amused face. "You are quite delicious, in fact."

She licked him again. She tasted the faint flavor of herself from their earlier lovemaking. She tasted him, starkly male, and not a hint of goat smell.

He laughed. Sometimes having him read her mind was an asset. Her lips, pressed against his cock, curved into a smile. She licked the whole length of him, laved his heavy balls. He tasted like red wine with a heady streak of brandy running through it.

His cock well tasted, Elaine sat back on her heels.

"Do not stop there," Demetri said. "Take me into your mouth. Suck on me."

Elaine stared at him wide-eyed. Why did he want her to do that?

"Imagine your mouth is your cunt," Demetri helpfully supplied.

Her mind raced. *Why?*

"It will give me great pleasure."

Elaine surveyed his cock. Could she take it all into her mouth? She doubted it, but she'd do her best to please him.

"Good girl," Demetri murmured.

She licked the head, wetting it thoroughly, parted her lips, and sank his cock into her mouth. She hardly believed she did this . . . but he tasted good, and having the pulsing muscle in her mouth made her cunt ache for it. If she sank her mouth down on him, could he not do the same with her cunt?

Elaine pulled back, his cock slipping free with an audible pop. She straddled him, wishing to surprise him but knowing that impossible. Already, his arms uplifted to support her downward journey upon his cock.

With him deep inside, Elaine rode him, bouncing up and down his cock in imitation of his fast-paced thrusts had he been in control.

A keening cry built up inside her. This position moved him deeper within her, something she scarce thought possible. She rotated her hips, swirling him around inside her, the golden heat rising up to flush the pale skin of her breasts and neck.

Through a curtain of red hair, she looked down at him and found him gazing at her with a strange intensity. He seemed awed, as if she were the goddess and he was her follower.

She liked that image.

From somewhere deep inside, her release hit her. She arched her back, screaming her joy to the bedroom ceiling.

The duke reluctantly accepted Myles's offer of help. Abby saw Winterton didn't quite believe Myles hadn't played a purposeful, key role in releasing the god from his stone prison.

The day passed in study. Abby would have much preferred to spend it in bed with Myles, but they had to save the world, after all. A little bit of lust was all right. But unbridled?

She shivered, imagining the world's greed and desire destroying the world like a nuclear war.

Abby read some obscure text of the duke's, a journal handwritten in scratchy angular black ink. It read like a fairy tale, hard to believe, and when the details became important, incredibly arcane.

Abby wondered if the duke's ancestor and Myles's grandmother had been smoking the same stuff.

She sighed, turning the page. With her thumb, she twirled the wedding ring about her finger. She'd spent the whole day at this, only getting more and more confused, especially when the three of them convened to discuss their findings.

Abigail... Her name sounded in her mind, a beguiling call of a golden voice. She knew at once who it was. She straightened up, looking around the room. Had he come for her? Had he come to destroy these precious books, the possible means of his destruction?

I hear your thoughts like rushing water, Dionysus said inside her head. *I am not afraid of such petty attempts by mere mortals to defeat me.*

Abby goggled, searching the room for some sight of the god. Both Myles and the duke looked up.

"What is it?" Myles started to rise from his seat, but the duke gestured he remain still.

"The god is calling her." The duke glanced out the window. "The sun sets and he calls his followers to join him in revelry and debauchery."

Abby gripped the book before her. "I don't want to go."

"Go," the duke murmured. "It will be harder for you if you fight him."

"I could hold her," Myles declared.

The duke actually considered it. "And so you risk having your skin flayed and your eyes scratched out. Dionysus's creatures become like demons possessed if they are prevented from heeding the call."

"If you know so much," Abby snapped, the god's will drawing her to her feet, "why can't you stop him?"

The god tugged on the invisible link between them and she ran from the room, rebounding off the walls in her desperation to get outside, to get to the temple, to get to him.

Sweaty and exhausted, she stumbled to her knees before the reclining Dionysus. Abby looked up at him. "Could you summon me a little more gently next time? I've ruined this gown."

"And you are thirsty."

She thought of drinking the god's come. Somehow, she guessed that thought wasn't original to her.

The god grinned, his handsome face lit by many candles. "Wine first, the nectar of the gods, and then you shall taste of me."

Abby swallowed, swearing never to touch another sex toy in her life, just in case another one came alive.

"Sex toy?"

He read her mind. She'd forgotten that.

She nodded. She no longer saw the need to speak, the god read her mind like tomorrow's headlines. Would he see the images in her mind? She strove to blank out the times she'd shared them with Myles.

"Myles," the god drawled. "When are you going to give him up?"

Abby raised her chin. "I am not permitted to even remember him? Even gods are jealous?"

"What do they teach people nowadays? Have you not heard of the legendary jealousy of Hera?"

"Who?"

"The wife of Zeus."

"Ah, the philandering god who came to women in the form of a swan and so on." Abby sat, cross-legged, accepting a cup of wine from one of the bacchantes. "So, you are a jealous sort too."

"I am a generous god. Generous and giving of my divine power."

"You mean sex?"

"It's more than just sex."

Abby sipped on the wine, not sure she wanted to get into a relationship discussion with a god. The rich liquid washed over her tongue and down her throat. She stared into the simple cup, eyes wide. She'd never tasted a vintage that good before. It was beyond description.

The god laughed. Hardly the maniacal cry of an arch-villain, it rippled, free and unfettered by anything but joy. "And so you have tasted the nectar of the gods, not tasted by mortals in over a thousand years."

She eyed the cup more warily. "What does it do? Put me into your thrall permanently?"

"It is but your first sip." Dionysus let a grape drop into his mouth. "And it will put you not in thrall to me but to the drink and the pleasurable sensations it evokes. Of course," he added, waving a hand, "I am the only source of this elixir. You can get it from nobody but me."

Her lips twisted. "So in thrall to you then."

The god shrugged. "Pretty much." He reached out to her. "Come, my delightful mortal. I have waited all day to enjoy your body again."

Abby wanted to resist. She rose, a derisive snort escaping her. "Typical. You just want me for my body, not my mind."

"Oh, I want all that," Dionysus drawled, his thick sensual lips curved into a smile. "And your soul too. But one thing at a time, eh?"

"My soul?" Abby didn't know if she dared believe it. But so far, everything recently went far beyond her understanding. That this adventure now imperiled her soul seemed too much to believe.

Her fingertips touched his, and all the fearful ice from his last statement dissolved into sexual heat. His fingertips slid toward her palm, his warmth firing up her senses. She forgot everything but Dionysus. One last memory of Myles Hardy trembled in her mind's eye before the god's golden light obliterated it.

Dionysus's large hand dwarfed hers. Within his grasp, a strong sense of safety filled her. He pulled her closer, embracing her. Her cheek pressed against the rough curls of his chest, the wiry hair imprinting on her cheek.

She breathed him in. He smelled delicious, like a hot summer's day filled with the sweetness of ripened strawberries, more complex than the odor of rich earth alive with growing.

He was more than that. More than the anchor upon which things grew, he was the pleasure resulting from that growth.

Dionysus cupped her chin, tilting her face up to his. "There are those of my followers who say I am more addictive than even the gods' nectar," he murmured.

"More addictive?" Abby breathed. "I might agree with

that." She reached up on tiptoe and kissed him. She gave no quarter, kissing him hard, twining her body around his larger one. He made her subject to him, both by the size and power of his body and by his godhood.

Still kissing him, her lips quirked. By that she didn't mean the size of his cock.

Although what man would have a cock that large and yet still be so pleasing?

Dionysus growled, rubbing his rock-hard cock against her, finding the curve of her belly, lifting her so that his cock pulsed against her thigh.

She grabbed his shoulders and hoisted herself up, the image of climbing a rock wall leaping into her mind. She sprang once up onto her toes and then again, spreading her legs and hooking them around the god's waist.

It brought her already juicy cunt into close contact with his hard cock. Dionysus lifted her hips higher, his cock springing free beneath her parted legs, the head probing her wet slit.

Abby tried to wriggle in his grasp, but he held her fast. She wanted him inside her. She wanted him to give her the wildest fuck of her life.

He edged her lower, his cock fitting against her slick entry. She sank onto him, gasping, surrounding him with her eager flesh. Her cunt muscles clutched at him, a butterfly-like embrace struggling to encompass him without squeezing him out.

Her pulse raced. She held her breath until he buried himself to the hilt. The air escaped her lungs in a rush. She hung limp in his arms, surrendering herself to him. He had charge of every part of her, to do with as he wanted.

Still embedded deep inside her, he crouched and laid her out on the coverlet-strewn dais. Her hips canted up at a steep angle, groin pressed against groin, her head and shoulders on the floor.

She writhed against him, panting with her need. He held still above her, letting her do all the work, letting her worship him.

"Please," she begged, wanting him to power deep inside her. "Please, oh please."

Dionysus cradled her with one arm, the other supporting one of her thighs. Abby blinked and found herself enraptured by the compelling, intense gaze of his sparkling green eyes flecked with gold. That intense expression did more to hold her than being pinioned beneath him.

He rolled, drawing her on top of him. Her hair swung out across her face, and when she blinked away the traces of hair stuck to her sweating skin, she saw the longing in his eyes hadn't changed.

He *longed* for her. He wanted her. He didn't need to say the words, and she didn't need to read his mind to see and feel that need.

The new position meant she straddled him, gazing down instead of up. It should give her a great feeling of power, but she thought only of pleasing him and finding that delicious release for herself.

"Yes," Dionysus growled. "You are mine."

He grabbed her hips, holding them steady while he fucked her hard from below, his buttocks lifting clear off the ground.

She laughed with joy. It was like riding a wild bronco, and although she'd never done so before, she waved her arm above her head, determined to keep her seat.

Of course, she had help. His cock anchored her, curling behind her pelvic bone, never sliding out far enough to be free of her.

His laughter joined hers. In the midst of their wild carousing, she came. Her back arched like a bow. She stared sightless at the dark basement ceiling, grinding down and around and down against his groin.

His come propelled into her, the incredible heat of it streaking through her body, a dazzling path of sparks up her spine and into her head.

She sank down upon him, biting and sucking on his upper chest, his neck, his mouth. Abby wanted more, and she knew Dionysus would deliver it.

15

The Duke of Winterton trudged upstairs to bed. He hadn't seen his wife the entire day, nor did he entirely expect her to be waiting for him in the room they shared. The bacchante had her hooks into his lovely bride. She might be anywhere with her new friend.

His lips stretched into a grim smile. Actually, he had found something, something that might put an end to this lecherous nonsense. The Wintertons didn't need ancient deities to have great sex. His Lucy should know that.

He'd found the solution and kept it hidden from Hardy. The poor woman he'd married might trust him blindingly, but he'd never dare risk his family so.

The duke opened the door. The bacchante lay in a tangle of bed linens, sprawled across *his* bed. "Lucy?" he called out in a low voice, not wanting to wake the woodland spirit. "Lucy?"

Had the bacchante fucked his wife to death? Did she lie somewhere alone, neglected?

His heart thudding, he scanned the room. Seeing no sight of her, he passed into her dressing room.

Lucy stood beside a large bathtub, wrapping her damp limbs in a translucent linen dressing gown. At the sight of him, she hugged her arms about herself.

He hovered by the doorway, not daring to approach. Despite her sagging shoulders, he noticed a fire in her eyes he hadn't seen before. "Lucy? Are you well?"

"That," she replied, "all depends on you."

He let his hands drop to his sides, palms outward. "Why is that?"

"You are plotting to destroy my happiness," she got out between gritted teeth.

He realized she came close to tears. "My dear, I would never do such a thing to you. Your happiness is paramount to me."

She stepped back, and he halted in his approach. "You want to take Phoebe away from me."

The duke froze, closing his eyes for a long moment. How to make her understand? "She puts you in danger."

"How?" Lucy demanded. Her arms fell rigid to her sides, her small hands curling into fists. "Explain to me how. Phoebe is harmless, a loving creature."

"Loving? Her fucking you will put you into an early grave, my dear."

"Her lusts have been unbounded," Lucy admitted, her face grave. "Have been. She needs only some care and consolation."

"She's blinded you," the duke retorted, his face growing hot. "She wants you to believe that so she can destroy you." The thought came to him in a flash. "Or to prevent me from destroying her."

A sob escaped Lucy's lips. "She's not like that. She isn't!"

"The god she follows has no such compassion," the duke snapped. "I have no objections to sharing you, Lucy, but I will not have you die."

"Die? I'm not going to die." Her lip curled. "Whatever it is you think she can do, Your Grace, you are wrong. She is as human as you or I, and has a sexual appetite no greater than yours or mine."

"How do you know that?" He folded his arms, his entire body stiffening with frustration. "How do you know?"

"She won't." Lucy flew across the small space between them and grabbed hold of his folded arms. Tears streaked down her upturned face. He wanted to give into her pleas, but something greater lay at stake. "Please. She's told me that if you kill her god, you kill her."

"I will not be killing the god—" Although he had an idea that just might work. "It is imprisonment."

"And what is her crime, to be imprisoned along with him?"

"I can't not do this, Lucy. It is my family's duty, handed down throughout the ages to keep Dionysus's passions well bridled. I have no choice but to do this. Don't you understand? Freed, Dionysus will destroy this world. There will be no Phoebe. Not you, not me, not your friend Portia."

Lucy sucked in her breath. He dared to mention the name of her dearest friend, Portia Carew? The woman who awakened her to feminine sensuality, only to have Society condemn her friend and banish her. The very thought that this Dionysus might destroy Portia and Phoebe into oblivion made her heart ache. "This is true?"

"All the old gods are gone, Lucy. There's no one to keep the balance. That is why. Please understand." He didn't want this duty to separate him from his wife, but nothing, not even her, kept him from this. He steeled himself.

Lucy shook her head, a strand of hair attaching to her damp cheek. "I understand it, but I don't like it. Isn't there some way Phoebe can be spared?"

"I'm having a most difficult time discovering a way to put Pandora back into her box," the duke admitted. "If I promise to keep looking and tell you if I learn a way, would that be enough?"

"Is it likely?" Her voice held little hope.

He unbent, capturing her hands. "I will do my best, Lucy. I cannot promise anything more."

"You know that if you succeed in your family's duty, you will lose me."

"Lucy . . ." Her cool pronouncement stunned him, stealing his breath. "Lucy, please . . ." He'd never had to beg for a thing in his life. Even Lucy had fallen easily into his lap. "I do not want to lose you."

She surveyed his face, her lips crumbling into a wilted pout. "Oh, my duke, I do not want that either. There has to be a way."

He touched her cheek, brushing away a tear he felt like shedding. "If there is, I will find it."

She rose up on her tiptoes and kissed him. "Thank you." She sidestepped him and disappeared into the main bedroom.

He turned, watching her progress. She crawled across their bed and spooned behind the sleeping Phoebe. The woman stirred, capturing one of Lucy's hands and making sure it covered a breast. Lucy kissed Phoebe's shoulder and subsided into sleep.

He expected the endless, rampaging sex he'd been taught that all the bacchantes did, not this gentle loving. Had he been mistaken about that?

Gnawing his lip, he let them sleep. Perhaps a few more hours in the study. He might find just the thing to save his marriage.

Abby didn't know how she made it back to the house after her all-night session with the Greek god. (And how often had she wished for that? A man built like a Greek god who would be all hers? Who knew it would be so exhausting?)

She woke with her head buried in a pillow. She peeled a lock of hair from over her eye and squinted into the room. Definitely daylight. Her stomach rumbled. And she'd missed at least one, maybe two meals. Grapes really didn't sit well if that's all one ate.

Nectar of the gods had made that seem unimportant.

She needed to get up, dress, find some food and Myles, not necessarily in that order. Just to see him again might bring some sense of reality back to this crazy hallucination she lived.

Abby leaned half out of bed and reached for a bellpull to summon a maid, unable to dress herself in these antiquated outfits. Living two hundred years ago did have its advantages when she felt too bone-tired to even lift a hand to get dressed.

She found Myles seated in the dining room, gazing morosely into his coffee cup. Her breath held for a long moment at the sight of him. Seeing him made her feel lighter, but his unhappiness deflated the sweet feeling like a sharp knife.

Confused and without a word, she touched his shoulder, her fingertips drifting across his shoulder blades as she passed.

After heaping food on her plate, she sat beside him. "Am I the last awake?"

Myles shrugged, still staring into his cup.

Abandoning her meal for the moment, Abby twisted in her seat and rested her hand on his shoulder. "Myles? What is it?"

He shook his head with such violence it almost jolted her hand away. "It is not your concern."

"It isn't?" Abby found that hard to believe. "Has the duke found something?"

Myles shot her a quick glance, his eyes dark and unreadable. "If he has, he isn't telling me. And why would he?"

"Because your family and his have been on opposite sides of this since the dawn of time?" Abby chirped, trying to jolly him out of his mood.

His brows lowered farther. "This isn't a joke, Abby. Why is

he blaming me for this when I wasn't even aware of my family's legacy?"

"Because he's lived with it." Abby patted his shoulder again and withdrew. Her stomach demanded food. She shoveled a forkful of eggs into her mouth. Around the food, she asked, "Is that all there is?"

"Isn't that enough?" He took a long draught of coffee, emptying his cup. He rose. "And why should you care? You're *his* now."

"Oh, unfair!" Abby choked out around dry toast. She examined his face, so shuttered, so remote.

"Yes, it is, but there's nothing I can do about it." With great care, he set down his cup. "Have you ever thought," he said, seeming to strive for a casual air. "Have you ever thought what will happen to you when Dionysus is destroyed?"

Abby frowned at him. The god's words from the previous night came back to her. "His magic brought me here."

Myles nodded. "From what I have read, you were destined to be part of the unbinding."

So the duke wasn't the only one keeping secrets. "What is a few hundred years to a god? But what should happen to me if he is bound again? He reached me while he was still encased in stone, remember."

"We do not know that for sure." His stern visage cracked, his voice gentling. "What if you go when he does?"

"To be trapped on the wall with the rest of his horde? You did say I was his now."

"Truthfully, not fully his." He took a deep breath. "To see you go to him at sundown without a fight made it seem so. It hurt," he admitted with a rueful twist of his lips. "But that time is running short."

"And if I remain so when the duke succeeds in recapturing Dionysus? What then?"

"Mayhap you will go back to your own time." Myles

shrugged. "The text is ambiguous. If the duke knew about the truth of our circumstances, I would ask."

Abby dropped her gaze. "I could ask," she whispered. Not looking at him, she reached out for his hand. Her fingertips grazed the back of his hand for the briefest of moments before he pulled away.

She looked up to see him stride from the room.

Abby half rose from her seat, knowing she should go after him. She sat again. She didn't want to rehash the argument of who was to blame. She just wanted it fixed. Didn't he know she missed him?

Fuming with frustrated anger at the hopeless situation before her, she finished her meal and went in search of the duke.

She found him in the study, searching through a fresh pile of rolled manuscripts. She watched him unroll the paper (or maybe it was older than that, vellum or parchment). "Your Grace?" she ventured, stepping farther into the room.

The duke glanced up. "Close the door and lock it."

She obeyed, setting the key down on the overcrowded desk. "You've found something." She thought he'd look joyous instead of retaining the continued strain on his face.

The Duke of Winterton set down the paper. "I found it last night."

"Then why do you still look?" Abby perched on the edge of the desk.

"For my own reasons," he hedged, focusing his attention on another tattered manuscript.

"Perhaps I could help," Abby offered, reaching for one of the fragile scrolls.

Winterton came near to slapping her hand, his narrow fingers frozen above her own. "No. This is for me to decipher."

"Then if you have found the solution to our Greek god problem, what is it? What do I need to do?"

The duke pierced her with a questioning look. "Why do you think it is you?"

"Because I am the key. You have called me that, as has the god. It makes sense that what unlocks, locks."

"You are a smart woman, smarter than most."

Abby gave a careless shrug. "I've had a better education than most, I bet." She waited for the duke to give her the answer, but he seemed to be lost in the scrolls again. "Your Grace?"

The duke stroked at his chin, still not looking at her. "Give me this day, Mrs. Hardy, before I tell you."

"Ah. About that, Your Grace. I need your help in a small matter."

"The small matter of a god and his followers running rampant across the countryside?"

She held onto the wedding ring. After this, she wouldn't have to wear it anymore. "The, ah, small matter of my not actually being married to Mr. Hardy. Or being born twenty-some years ago." No self-respecting female revealed her age even in the twenty-first century. What else were skin care products for?

The duke marked his place on his scroll with his thumb and let it roll up. His eyes narrowed in chilled anger. "Explain yourself."

"I was—will be—born about one hundred and"—Abby stopped to do the math—"seventy-five years from now."

To his credit, the duke gave no other reaction than a single blink. "From the future, Mrs.—What do I call you?"

"My name is Abby Deane. Ms. Deane."

"Mz? I know of no such honorary title."

"It comes into being about one hundred and fifty or so years from now," Abby supplied.

"What does it mean? You're married?"

"Not married, and it's none of your business whether I am or not." Abby bit her lip, realizing she sounded sharper than she intended. "It is so an independent businesswoman can do her business without being hit upon."

"Hit upon?" The duke's brow deepened.

"Wooed. Seduced. Whatever." Abby waved a hand airily. "So, now that you know I'm from the future—"

"I pity Mr. Hardy for marrying a madwoman."

"I told you we're not married." Abby huffed and folded her arms. "Look, I can spend the day trying to prove to you I am from when I say I am, but neither you nor I have the time." She took a steadying breath. "I need to know whether I will go back to my own time when we've defeated the god."

"I have read nothing about such matters."

Abby didn't trust that bland face. "Myles told me he read something in one of your books, but that it was ambiguous."

"But not so ambiguous to warn you of it. I see blood stays true to blood."

Abby snorted. "It has nothing to do with his family."

"What does it have to do with then?"

His cold words silenced her. She wanted it to be that Myles didn't want to give her up, but why would he when she'd given him nothing except evidence that gods trump hearts?

"Your Grace, I need to know."

Winterton shrugged. "I have read everything on the subject. The key is only mentioned in the act of unlocking. I have no information regarding whence the key comes or where it goes when its task is done."

Abby nibbled on her lower lip. "Nothing?"

"Nothing. If we had known what the key was and where it could be found, you may believe that I would have done everything in my power to prevent your existence."

"Hm." She didn't see the duke's powers extending into the supernatural. His political and personal influence maybe, and then how would he know which family might give birth to her?

"The Hardys, however, must have that information. How else would Mr. Hardy know how to best use you?"

"He didn't use me." The barb stung. Abby pulled herself to her feet. "Look, mister, I am not prepared to become the god's slave for all eternity, so you better just tell me what it is I need to do."

"All the old magicks of entrapment are lost," the duke told her. "The only way left now is for the key to act."

"Act how?"

"Only you know that."

Abby stamped her foot. "Dammit. Would I be standing here asking you if I did?"

Winterton pushed the scrolls aside and opened a heavy leatherbound volume. "There is but one key to unlock destruction and one key to contain it. One lock, one key, one way."

"That's it? That's all you have?"

The duke shut the book with a heavy snap. "That is all I plan to tell you before this evening, Ms. Deane. Now, if you please, I have work to do."

Her lip curling, Abby left the duke to his research. Why offer to help if all the help he offered was a stupid riddle? Besides, he didn't seem inclined to share his fresh problem.

She headed for the garden and some fresh air, kicking loose gravel off the path. Why was it that man insisted on being so uncommunicative? She longed for the authority of her job title, but that was two hundred years into the future and no help to her here.

Abby found a stone bench and sat on it, not really seeing the greenery around her. She stared down at the gray gravel path. What did the riddle mean?

As hard as she tried, her thoughts veered from the puzzle. She saw the hint of distress in Myles's face, heard the duke's cold words condemning him. Had she misread him that badly? Had he wanted her for more than her blueprints? How well might she be expected to read a man born two hundred years before her time? She'd bet he had a whole different mindset to the modern male. The overprotectiveness he'd displayed from the moment they'd settled their differences (that is, when he actually believed her) signified that.

But they had discussed him using her already. He'd seemed truly anguished that she thought ill of him. And didn't these gentlemen have some code of honor? If there was ever going to be an "us," she needed to trust him.

An "us"? Is that what she really wanted?

When there might be no opportunity to have that relationship? Was she nuts?

She combed her fingers through her hair, undoing all the maid's hard work, hairpins scattering across the gravel walk. She shook her head, letting the remaining pins fly and pulling out the last ones.

Abby didn't need to gain the duke's respect anymore. Her new unmarried low status took care of that, so why bother?

Only one thing left to do: vanquish the god and deal with the consequences no matter how it fell out. At this time, she shouldn't give her heart to anybody.

"Mrs. Hardy?" A girl's voice halted Abby's rise from the stone bench. Elaine. Her long red hair tumbled free down her back.

Abby straightened. "Your Grace," she said.

Elaine's eyes narrowed. "That's the wrong title. How common are you?"

"Pretty common," Abby cheerfully admitted. "Ask your father."

Pouting, Elaine folded her arms. "We are not speaking."

Abby mimicked her pose. "Why? Although I'm sure it's none of my business."

"Oh, it is your business," Elaine snapped. "You are the one who opened the Pandora's box—"

"More like Dionysus's box," Abby muttered.

Elaine steamed on, ignoring her interruption. "—and you brought Demetri into my life. And now my father is going to take him away from me." She took a shuddering breath, pointing a shaking finger at her. "And you're the one he'll use to accomplish it."

Abby blinked. "What makes you think that?"

"I eavesdropped."

"Ah." Abby examined the girl's features. A bruise welled on her neck, clearly a love bite. She had swollen, well-kissed lips, her eyes bright. "And who is this Demetri?"

"He's a . . . a satyr."

"A what?"

Elaine flushed red from her hairline to her neckline. Abby had never seen her blush, even though their acquaintance had been brief. "He's half human, half . . . half goat." Her eyes closed.

"I guess I should not be surprised that I'm not surprised," Abby murmured. "You do realize what happens if your father and I don't stop this god."

"I do not care." She stamped her foot.

"You don't care that this world will plunge into unbridled lust? That people will die because of unbounded greed and desires? That civilization will collapse? Can't you imagine that?" Abby could, but Elaine had never heard of nuclear war.

"You are spouting my father's words."

"He's right, Miss Winterton. I've not led a sheltered life. I've seen that greed in action."

Elaine shook her head, almost as if in wonder. "Who are you, Mrs. Hardy?"

"I am the key," she stated. "You have to expect a little oddness from such a person."

"What you plan to do means Demetri's death." Elaine glowered.

"If I do not, I become enslaved to the god forever, and I lose—" To Abby's surprise, she heard her voice choke. "And I lose my husband." Abby nodded back at the house. "Your satyr. I'll bet he's bewitched you, like the god is doing to me."

"No!" Elaine shouted. "No! He loves me! He understands me!"

"He *desires* you. He'll say anything to make you give him what he wants."

"He doesn't have to make me. I want him. And you are wrong, Mrs. Hardy. He does love me. I know it should be just desire, I know, but it isn't. He truly cares for me."

Abby shook her head. "You're blinded, girl, by your own hungry needs."

"How dare you speak to me in that way!" Elaine's hands closed into fists and she stamped her foot.

"Past time somebody did." Abby fixed her with a glare. "You cannot stop what is going to happen. It's the best thing for everybody."

Elaine stared at her. "How can you be so heartless, so cruel?"

"It's called facing the facts."

"If . . ." Elaine's lower lip trembled. "If you met him and you saw for yourself that he's sincere, would you reconsider? I am a good judge of character. I know you'll see I'm right."

"You're a duke's daughter," Abby grumbled. It wouldn't do any good but to mollify them both. "Aren't you always right?"

Elaine actually smiled. "You will come?"

"It won't change my mind."

"Please," she pleaded, her yearning eyes filling with tears.

Didn't Elaine expect her wish to be granted? Perhaps her wishes never really had. "All right," Abby conceded. It only delayed the inevitable. "Where is he?"

"Up in my room."

Abby followed the duke's daughter back into the house and up the broad, sweeping stairs. Elaine stood to one side to let Abby enter her room first.

Wary, Abby edged around her. The drawn curtains cast long

shadows in the room. *This is not a good idea.* She paused, scanning the room.

A curtain billowed and a dark figure limped into view from behind it. He pushed the curtain back, revealing himself.

Abby looked down and then focused most firmly on his face. "He's naked."

"Why did you bring her here?" The satyr spoke, his voice deep and rumbling. It was one heck of a sexy voice.

Elaine stepped around Abby, going to him. "So she would see and understand how important this is."

The satyr sighed. "Why her?"

"Because Mrs. Hardy is the key." Elaine stroked his hairy (furred?) chest.

The satyr looked at Abby with sudden interest. "Is that so?"

Abby didn't like that look. "Elaine tells me you love her."

He sent Elaine an affectionate look. "I do."

"Not lust, for which your lot are known for."

"Do not tar us all with the same brush, Mrs. Hardy. Some of us find love in our desires. Like my parents did."

"Parents?" Abby blinked.

"You think we were all created out of nothing." His lip curled. "My parents taught me what love is, horns and all."

Her lips twitched in amusement, and she saw an answering glint in the satyr's eye. "All right," she said. "I believe you can love. I even believe that you have feelings for her." A quick glance took in the tensed duke's daughter.

"That's good," Elaine ventured.

"No." Abby shook her head. "It just makes what I must do so much harder. I'm sorry, Demetri, Elaine, but I really have no choice."

"I understand." The satyr trotted toward her and passed within a hand space to reach the door. He held it open for her. "I hope you will understand also."

"Understand what?" Abby wished she stood closer to the door.

He slammed it shut. "That I love Elaine so much I can never let you leave."

Swallowing, Abby hoped she heard him right. He had said "leave" instead of "live," right?

16

Myles sat in the dining room. Either he'd missed the formal promenade into the room or they hadn't bothered, for the duke, duchess, and another woman already sat at the table eating.

No sign of Abby, but he didn't really expect it. Dionysus would have called for her at sundown. He'd avoided her since breakfast. With the duke not giving a sign of revealing anything, it was best, he'd decided, to make a break with her now.

Maybe it wouldn't hurt so much.

The guilt, on the other hand, would plague him for life.

Shortly after, Elaine arrived with a fantastical figure in tow. Myles recognized it as a satyr. He sucked in his breath in wonder. The creature moved with confidence. From the pictures and engravings he'd always imagined them as awkward animals.

The duke rose, flinging his napkin to land beside his place. "You dare bring him here?"

"I dare," his redheaded daughter shot back. "I dare because we will be married."

"Don't get your hopes up, girl."

She met his gaze with a serene expression. "Do not be surprised if matters do not pass according to your wish, Father. Demetri and I will be together."

"And where will you live?" the duke jeered. "In the woods?"

"With Dionysus's power, the woods will be the safest place," the satyr remarked. "And I intend to keep your daughter safe, Your Grace."

Elaine clasped her hands before her in dutiful submission. "Father, if you would give your blessing."

For a long time, the duke looked back and forth between his daughter and the satyr. At last, he glanced at his wife, who gave a slight nod. "Very well. If I do not succeed in containing Dionysus, you will have my blessing." His lips thinned. "Do not expect me to be happy for you."

Elaine beamed and dipped a curtsey before taking her seat. She gestured to Demetri to sit beside her. Somehow he arranged his limbs to do so.

The Duchess of Winterton lowered her fork. "Where's Mrs. Hardy?"

Myles shrugged. "I have not seen her all day." He glanced out to the window. "But I imagine she's with Dionysus."

"Oh." The duchess's face crumpled. "I had not thought it would break a marriage."

"They are not married," the duke interjected, cutting his roast beef into smaller pieces.

Myles stared at him. How had he found out? Had Abby told him? Why? He gritted his teeth. Had she already left him? Had Abby transferred her trust to the duke?

"Not married?" The duchess gasped.

Myles avoided looking at her. "I apologize for deceiving you." He speared a green bean. "We thought it would be best."

"Because you wanted to stay and release the god."

Myles met the duke's ice-cold blue eyes. "Because I wanted to stay and find the statue. I knew nothing about any god."

The duke harrumphed.

Myles changed the subject, tired of talking about his supposed wrongdoing. "Where is the young viscount? I have not seen him since this came to pass."

The duke lifted a single shoulder and let it fall again. "He is a Winterton. I am sure he is entertaining a bevy of bacchantes. I do not expect to see him again." He didn't sound too crushed by that, but Myles reckoned the duke still believed he would win. The duke's gaze narrowed. "Why aren't you with any?"

"I was," Myles admitted. "That first night, but . . ." He steered a forkful of food into his mouth. He wasn't about to share with the Wintertons his feelings about Abby.

He stopped mid-chew, staring off into the middle distance. His feelings for Abby? What *did* he feel? When all this was over, he'd think about it, not before.

Elaine broke into his thoughts. "Mr. Hardy is not married?"

Myles glanced her way in time to catch her stricken look before she masked it.

"No," he murmured.

Fire filled her gaze. "You lied!"

He blinked. "What does it matter to you? You have a satyr of your own."

Her temper fizzled into confusion. "And you have no one."

It shouldn't have hurt, but it did. Myles knew better than to show weakness. He smiled and returned to his food. He hoped she didn't see his fork tremble.

Of course, he needed women, but woman singular? That wasn't like him. He finished what was on his plate and pushed back his chair. "If you will excuse me, perhaps I should see if there are any of those bacchante girls roaming about." He grinned at the voluptuous woman next to the duchess. "Perhaps I have been missing something special."

"Perhaps you have," the woman replied, her low voice husky.

The duchess laid a possessive hand on the woman's arm, not saying a word.

"I will find my own." He bowed to the duchess, nodded at the duke, and strode from the room.

He headed outside, toward the temple. He'd find lusty bacchantes in that direction, as that was their source. One or two or three of them would make him forget Abby.

Trudging through dew-heavy grass, Myles reached the temple without seeing another soul. That gave him pause for thought. Did the bacchante have souls? He didn't remember enough of his reading of divinity from Oxford to know.

Best to leave that academic question to the scholars. His lips twisted at the thought.

He entered the temple. Torches had been lit, pushing back the gloom. He walked toward the rear of the temple, a glowing square of light showing the way below.

At the rim, he paused. Did he really want to see Abby in the arms of a god? He clenched his jaw. On the other hand, going down, picking up a Greek piece, might be the best way to show he didn't care.

No, he didn't care at all.

He descended the ladder and surveyed the scene. He saw mortals entwined with satyrs and bacchantes. The only difference between mortal women and Dionysus's female followers were the vine leaf crowns in the bacchantes' hair.

At last, he faced the dais where the god and his key doubtless made the beast with two backs.

Instead, he found Dionysus reclining amidst a mound of cushions, sipping from a large golden goblet.

"So nice of you to join us, Mr. Hardy," the god drawled. "Where is your lovely companion?"

Myles didn't hear the question. "What have you done with Abby?"

The god shrugged. "Not a thing. She hasn't answered my call. She shouldn't be able to resist it." He sounded puzzled.

"Perhaps she's tired of you," Myles remarked, on alert. He scanned the basement room. Nobody else paid attention to their conversation.

"She is not tired of me." He waved a hand down the length of his form. "How could she tire of this?"

He had a point. Myles's interests didn't extend in that direction but Dionysus displayed male perfection. The size of his cock alone was guaranteed to satisfy any woman.

Myles refused to feel inferior. "And yet, she isn't here."

The god stared at him, his green-eyed gaze piercing all of Myles's defenses. "You do not know her location either," he breathed. His thick lips spread into a delighted smile.

He shrugged. "She's her own woman. Always has been." Not that he knew that, but he knew of her independence. They had that in common, even though it meant nothing now.

"She will come to me." The god's confidence seemed triumphant. So triumphant, Myles turned to see if Abby descended the ladder.

Nothing.

If he stayed, he might come under the god's will. He'd be no help to Abby if he also became a puppet. Did he really want to see Abby come here and head straight for the god's arms, ignoring him? Her defection hurt bad enough.

"I will not disturb you any longer." Myles bowed and made his escape, wincing at the god's laughter echoing behind him.

In the temple above, he found two naked lovelies waiting for him. Had they been the ones he'd woken with the night he lost Abby to the god?

It didn't really matter. So long as they helped him forget.

He extended both his hands, palms up. "Ladies," he cooed.

Each of them reached for him, their hands cool in his clasp.

He drew them in, their bodies soft and lush against his. He kissed one, and then the other, with long lingering kisses.

Don't think about her. Just don't think.

"Ladies." He put on his most charming smile. "Shall we find somewhere more comfortable?"

He let the giggling women lead him away from the temple and into the woods. He recognized the shaded pine grove, the ground carpeted with pine needles from the giant trees overhead.

One woman, her hair long and midnight dark, sank to the floor, tugging on his hand. He released the second bacchante to unfasten his breeches, one-handed, falling to his knees before lush, willing curves.

Don't think about Abby. Just don't think.

The god's tug on her soul faded at last. Abby blinked tears from her eyes, trying to breathe around the gag in her mouth. Sagging against the tight knots, her entire body ached. Even her bones ached.

Her heartbeat slowed from its racing beat. The longing for Dionysus, her wanting him, the unbearable need for him, and not being able to go to him, wreaked agonizing havoc in her body. Every muscle strained toward him, her skin tearing against its bindings. The agony stole every breath from her lips, her breath winging its invisible way to him, while she sat, tied and trapped. She'd thought her heart would rend in two.

What did it mean? If she resisted the god's call long enough, she'd escape Dionysus's clutches?

Elaine and Demetri entered. Abby glared at them, struggling against her bindings. Where had a duke's daughter learned to tie such tight knots? Her saliva had run dry, soaked into the gag. Still, she let out a muffled scream.

Elaine caressed her cheek. "So you are not Mrs. Hardy after all."

Abby's eyes rolled. Did everybody know now? She shook her head, jerking away from Elaine's touch.

She leaned forward, right into Abby's face. "But you want him," she whispered. "You want him, don't you?"

Trying to swallow, Abby refused to give away her answer.

Laughing, Elaine straightened. "You poor, deluded woman. Myles Hardy will never commit. He will as soon waltz out of your life the same way he appeared."

She turned away, falling into her satyr's arms. They fell onto the bed.

Abby looked in the other direction. She remembered the first time she saw him, looking like a disheveled stablehand. Arrogant, belligerent. She smiled—or would have if the gag hadn't prevented her. She had to admit it had been fun exchanging words.

The smile faded. Not that she'd have the chance to do that again.

Moans drew her attention. She looked before she thought better of the idea. Elaine and Demetri lay entwined on the bed, skin, pale and dark, merging.

Breathless, Abby found she couldn't look away.

Demetri slid down Elaine's body, his mouth pressed against her skin. His goat haunches quivered, his little stump of a tail twitching in excitement.

He tongued her nipples. She moaned again, arching up, rolling her body against his.

Abby swallowed, feeling an echo of her aroused heat spark to life in the pit of her belly. Why was she always the one witnessing the sex acts of the Wintertons? Even that wry thought didn't enable her to look away.

It was like a porn film, only live. Abby supposed she ought to be grateful she didn't have a remote to switch between multiple angles. Her position at the foot of the bed seemed the most demure viewpoint in the room. Short of being out of the room altogether.

Demetri tugged at Elaine's nipples with his teeth. From Abby's vantage point, she saw the tiny pink points of flesh grow large and red.

Elaine writhed and whimpered beneath the satyr's touch, her sounds alone increasing Abby's own arousal. Too bad she was tied up, otherwise she might do something about it.

Like leave?

She smirked beneath the gag. Like take care of herself.

Abby stilled. She didn't have to take care of herself. All she needed to do was find Myles. He'd take care of this particular itch.

She struggled at the bindings, trying to ignore the groans and sighs coming from the bed beside her. Her wrists, behind her back, already rubbed raw from the rope binding her, but Abby couldn't give up. She had to escape, else witness the intimate scene on the bed and maybe . . . maybe they would put an end to her life.

Her struggles hadn't been successful with the power of Dionysus's call upon her, and they didn't work now without that supernatural pressure. Tears filled her eyes, and she let them run unhindered down her cheeks.

Not the first time she'd cried with frustration tonight. She had to be grateful Elaine hadn't noticed.

Elaine squealed. Abby inadvertently glanced their way again and froze, riveted. Demetri crouched between Elaine's legs, his face buried against her pussy.

He made grunting noises. Abby held her breath and heard the sound of wet tongue licking wet flesh. If her legs hadn't been tied to separate legs of the chair, she would've squeezed them together to eke out a little pleasure.

Abby rocked her hips, mimicking Elaine's motion. Was it

the echo of Dionysus's power that made her want to get off on what she saw or the similarity to porn films?

Her bunched-up skirts provided a friction point to rub against. For once, she was glad of the gag. It kept her own sounds well muffled.

Elaine's heels pummeled Demetri's long back, her hands lost in the satyr's dark curls. She squealed and sobbed, her entire body writhing and focused on an impending climax.

With a loud cry, Elaine bucked hard, her pale flesh reddened by the flush of release.

Abby tried to swallow. A low ache, her own arousal seemed destined to remain unsatisfied.

Demetri lifted his head and turned to catch Abby watching. His face and beard shone with Elaine's juices. He didn't seem surprised by her voyeurism, smirking.

Abby's face turned hot.

"Roll over," Demetri growled. Elaine scrambled to obey, presenting her pink, rounded arse to him. He ran his tanned hands over her smooth flesh, crouching behind her. "I'm going to fuck you," he growled, sparing a side-glance for Abby. "Fuck you the way you want it."

Elaine trembled. "Yes, oh yes."

Bending over her, he took firm hold of her shoulder. For the first time, Abby caught a glimpse of his cock: massive and dark, it jutted out of the mottled gray fur of his lower half. A long trail of semen hung suspended from the end of his cock.

What it would be like to capture that long skein of come into her mouth. What did he taste like?

She took a steadying breath. No wonder Elaine wanted to keep him.

He rubbed his cock along her exposed wet slit, making his cock gleam with Elaine's liquid arousal. Abby watched his buttocks clench and release, his hips gyrating.

"Give it to me," Elaine begged. "I command you, Demetri. Give it to me hard."

Demetri slipped inside her with one long, slow motion, his moan mingling with hers. If either of them heard Abby's, they gave no sign.

With one hand at Elaine's shoulder and the other at her hip, he pumped in and out of her in hard, short thrusts. Abby watched, amazed. His lower half seemed built for this, a powerful base from which to thrust hard, his hooves gripping the bedcovers by Elaine's knees.

Abby knew she'd never see the like again. The satyr was built to fuck from behind.

Harder and harder, he thrust into Elaine, her body shaking and her cries becoming staccato with each thrust temporarily robbing her of breath.

Abby's cunt muscles clenched, longing for a cock or one of her sex toys to fill her. She squirmed in her bindings, her view of the copulating couple growing dim while she strove to find some sort of release.

Demetri plowed into Elaine, not slowing at all. If anything, his pace grew faster, a violent frenetic bucking that showed no mercy at all to the almost prone, moaning form beneath him.

Abby wondered how many times Elaine had come under this sensual assault. Her cries had peaked at least twice. She saw Demetri's hand slide around Elaine's hip and move to the front.

Elaine sent up a fresh bout of moaning, exhaustion tinting the edges. Still, her hips gyrated against his pounding cock. Her shrieks and whimpers grew louder, coming more quickly. He released his grip on her shoulder to find the apex of one of her breasts and tugged on the nipple.

Her breath coming hard and fast, Abby wondered if the satyr planned to fuck Elaine into insensibility.

Screaming, Elaine bent her back like a bow, frozen for a long moment in a position of extreme release. Demetri's cry ran as an undercurrent beneath the scream, his thrusting hips stilling.

He released her, and she slumped face down on the bed, his cock sliding free of her. He crouched there for a long moment, stroking her back and thighs with incredible tenderness.

Abby expected him to lie next to Elaine, but instead he hopped off the bed and approached her. She tried to slow her breathing, but seeing his cock still hard and dripping with both his come and Elaine's only made her pant faster.

He stood before her, forcing her to look up at his horned head. His massive cock bobbed in front of her face. She saw it with her peripheral vision.

"You liked watching that, didn't you?" he growled in a low whisper that sent Abby tingling afresh.

She didn't want to answer him, but she nodded, once.

He moved, cradling his cock in his hand. "And you want to taste this, don't you?"

Abby looked at him. She thought only the god had the ability to read her mind.

"He gifts his followers with that as well. It is how I came to know Elaine so quickly and deeply." His erect cock bobbed. "You want this, don't you. You want what I give Elaine."

She stared up at him, drawing her gaze away from his still-hungry cock.

He bent over, whispering. "You can have it, you know. Have any man you want if you join us. Dionysus allows his lovers much freedom."

His hands disappeared behind her head. She inhaled the scent of him through her nose: raw man and raw sex. Heat radiated off him, and had she not been gagged, she needed only to lean forward to lick the sweat from his hairy chest. "I do not expect you'll scream."

He removed her gag, letting her lick her lips but once before he covered her mouth with his. He kissed her hard with a strong yearning that found an answer inside her. He kissed her until she whimpered in protest and in the need for more.

"That's why you're the key," Demetri breathed. "You are as insatiable as the god."

Abby mulled that over in her mind, trying to bury the need her voyeurism had sparked. She'd had a lifetime of practice in not following her desires, so often inappropriate in the modern world. Here, though. Here with Dionysus at work, she may follow them to her heart's content.

The image of Myles flashed through her mind. He'd satisfied her every need. Would be doing so still if they hadn't awakened the god. But he wasn't here now, and he hadn't come to her rescue or even tried to stop her from going to Dionysus. What kind of man didn't fight for his woman? Perhaps because she was not his?

She met the satyr's dark-eyed gaze. "I want to taste you," she croaked, her throat still dry.

He brought his dripping cock closer. Abby leaned forward, sticking out her tongue. The musky scent of Elaine mingled with the much-darker arousal of the satyr. The tip of her tongue touched his hot flesh, tasting him, tasting her.

Her sigh escaped. She licked the circumference of his head, tasting him, tasting Elaine. He moved even closer, and she drew him into her mouth.

Suckling on his head, Abby closed her eyes. Tied to a chair and yet she had power over him, the power to make him come. That he'd been the one who put her in this position didn't seem important.

Bit by bit, she drew more of him into her mouth, until she took no more. She slid her mouth up and down his shaft, her eyes flickering open to see how much more of him there was. She moaned at the sight of his still-visible inches, the sound vibrating his already-sensitive skin.

He clutched a handful of her hair, drawing her closer.

Gagging, she drew back, letting his cock pop free of her wet lips. "No," she moaned. The idea came to her. She might win free this way. "It's too much. Release my hands, let me pump your cock. Play with your balls."

His Adam's apple bounced in his throat, his eyes narrowed. She gazed up at him with all the need and wanting no longer hidden from her expression.

"You forget I can read your mind. You cannot escape." He untied her hands, giving her a few moments to rub life back into her nerveless fingers. She winced at the bloody welts around her wrists. Painful sensations rushed into her numb hands, and she bit back a cry.

She reached out for Demetri's hairy balls. Huge, loose, and heavy, Abby'd easily suck one of them into her mouth if she weren't still tied to the chair. She played with them, drawing the head of his cock back into her mouth. She pumped his shaft with both mouth and hand.

It didn't seem possible, but he grew even larger in her mouth. The tension within that long muscle grew, but it held and didn't break into a gushing flow down her throat.

Abby glanced up, reading his taut body. So the satyr couldn't come, eh?

Her hand that still stroked his balls moved farther back, pausing to tease the smooth spot behind his balls. His cock jerked but no come came.

Exploring further, Abby discovered the tight bunch of his arsehole. She swirled her fingertip over the puckered skin. He grunted but didn't protest when she probed in deeper.

Too late, she realized she should've licked her finger first, but she was in now and he seemed to be accepting her intrusion.

His cock pressed against the back of her throat. Her finger wriggled in deeper, searching for the spot to massage his prostate.

Demetri choked. His come poured into her mouth and she

let it flow out again through her lips, trying not to swallow. He stopped thrusting and stepped back, his wilting cock dripping with his come.

"I shall teach Elaine that."

Abby wiped her face. "Please do."

His eyes narrowed at her. "It hurt when Dionysus called for you and you couldn't go, didn't it."

"You know it did. You witnessed the start of it." Abby rubbed at her wrists at the memory of it. That hurt, so she stopped. "And unfair considering I don't know how to stop him."

"The duke knows."

Abby sighed. "He hasn't told me yet."

"He told you something."

"A riddle." Abby dared to bend and untie her ankles from her chair. "Without an answer." She stretched her legs out before rising. Why didn't he stop her?

Demetri watched. "You cannot leave. If you find out the answer . . ."

"You have given me another day to find it," Abby bargained. "If you had let me go when Dionysus called, I'd be wholly his by now."

The satyr ducked his head for a moment. "I cannot lose her." His gaze warned her that he meant to kill to protect his relationship with Elaine.

Abby wondered if anybody would hear her scream.

17

Behind the satyr, the door swung open. The Duchess of Winterton stood in all her undress, her bacchante, Phoebe, at her side sans any clothing but her long, long hair, not very strategically draped.

"You will not," Lucy said, favoring a small smile at Abby. "You may go, Abigail."

She didn't dare move. She reckoned those small horns on Demetri's head might do some serious goring. "But . . ."

"Go." Lucy stepped into the room, clearing the doorway for her. "Your actions will no longer affect us."

The satyr shot her a puzzled stare. "How?"

"I will tell you when she's gone." Lucy fixed Abby with a firm look. "Go, Abigail."

Abby fled.

First, to the room she shared with Myles. She didn't find him, but the duke. He'd taken a seat on a tall-backed, uncomfortable-looking chair by the door.

His thin, unwelcoming smile gave her pause. "You didn't succumb to him utterly then."

"I didn't go." Abby opened the door and stepped in. It was empty. She didn't think Myles'd allow the duke to stand guard at their door. She turned back to him. "Your daughter tied me up."

"You stink of sex." The duke reached out and took her arm, pulling back the sleeve on her gown to reveal her bloody wrist. "You fought hard."

Abby snatched her hand away, blushing. "It's done now. I suppose you're here to tell me how to put a stop to all this."

Winterton managed a small smile. "Now that I've determined a way to keep my wife happy."

"So she can keep her playmate?" Abby guessed. Why else would Lucy have allowed her to escape?

"Yes." Winterton looked less than happy. "It won't be easy for her, but if she truly wants this Phoebe . . ." He straightened. "Enough maudlin."

"How is she going to do it? Keep whatsername, Phoebe?"

"She needs to hold her bacchante in her arms until the change is over," the duke ground out between gritted teeth. His nostrils flared in distaste.

Abby knew she should let the subject drop, but chances were she'd miss hearing their stories if her mission failed. "How are they going to know?"

"Oh, they'll know. As for you, what you have to do is have sexual intercourse with Dionysus."

Abby blinked. "I do that already. Every time he calls me, in fact."

"Ah. How do I phrase this delicately?" Winterton pursed his lips in thought.

"You don't have to, I'm a modern woman." The solution came to her at his hint. "And you don't have to tell me, I've worked it out."

The duke's eyes widened. "You have?"

"I used Dionysus the statue as a giant dildo, a perfect key–lock metaphor. Therefore, I have to use a dildo on him."

The duke swallowed. "Your frankness is going to take some getting used to."

"If I'm still here," Abby reminded. "If I undo everything, I undo my being here. That's what Myles found out."

"That's not certain." His lips twisted. "Likely, but not certain."

Abby squared her shoulders. "I need to get some things and . . ." She took a deep breath. "And say good-bye to Myles."

"I have not seen him." The duke held out his hand. "Good luck, Ms. Deane."

She shook his hand, hoping she hid her disappointment. "Thank you."

She stepped inside her room. It felt strangely empty without Myles. Well, perhaps it was better this way, without a proper good-bye. She pulled the wedding ring off her finger. It didn't belong to her by rights and it should go to whomever Myles ended up marrying.

Digging her handbag out from under the bed, she made sure she had all her essential items: purse, ID, nonfunctioning cell phone, change of underwear (essential as she wasn't actually wearing any). Everything might go back with her, or not. Would she find herself in her plane, flying over the English countryside, or in the folly, painted on the walls?

She didn't like leaving behind the blueprints and all her bags, but she reckoned the credit card could handle a hit when she got home.

Abby took one last look at the room. She didn't really see it, remembering Myles: how he had sat in that chair; how he'd lain naked in that bed beckoning her.

She bit down on her lip. She better go before she started to cry.

One last thing for her handbag. She dug out her suitcase and scrounged around in it. She pulled out a seven-inch dildo made of bendy silicone, pale pink and realistically detailed.

She didn't plan to use it on herself tonight. She just hoped to convince the god to have it used on him.

Leaving the house behind her, Abby didn't look back, striding purposefully across the large green grass meadow toward the woods and the folly temple. One way or another, she'd see that building again.

She ducked under a hanging pine bough, entering the woods, not slowing her pace at all.

Grunts and soft cries off to the left gave her pause. They came from a thicket of pine trees, the branches hanging low. It had to be some of Dionysus's minions doing what they do best.

Well, that'll be soon interrupted.

A male groan followed by a protest of "Ladies, ladies!" stopped her progress again.

She turned, disbelieving, toward the grove. *Myles?*

Abby investigated. Far too soon, she came upon Myles, propped up against a pine tree trunk. He was naked, but he didn't seem to mind the rough bark at his back, and who would blame him? A woman, a bacchante, sucked at his cock while another distracted him by dandling her heavy bosoms before him.

"How idyllic," Abby sneered.

Myles turned toward the sound of her voice, blinking from the light or his sexual daze. Abby didn't want to guess. "Abby?"

"Starting on the process of forgetting me already?" Abby slung her bag farther over her shoulder and folded her arms.

The bacchantes paid her no heed, continuing with their respective tasks.

Myles's face looked a mite strained. "Abby, I can explain . . ."

"Do you need to?" Abby snapped.

"No," he agreed, shaking off the persistent bacchantes and getting to his feet. In this case, his erection wouldn't help him smooth this one over. "Because you are right. I am trying to forget you. Why are you not with Dionysus? I thought after last night—"

"I didn't go last night. Your ex-fiancée and her satyr tied me up."

"And that stopped you?"

Abby presented her damaged wrist for inspection, hiding it again before he even moved.

"Abby, if I'd known . . ."

"If you'd known? Would you really have freed me to go to the god?"

Myles grimaced. "I would have kept you company, eased your pain."

"But not freed me."

"No. You don't belong to him."

What did he think she was? A pocket watch? "I don't belong to anyone, Myles. Not you, not a god, not anybody." Abby twitched her head in the bacchantes' direction. "If you want to keep either one of them, I recommend hanging on to them when the time comes."

Not waiting for an answer, she about-faced and stalked away.

"Where are you going?" Myles called. Abby glanced over her shoulder to see him follow her.

She cut him off with a sharp downward slash of her hand. "To Dionysus. Good-bye, Myles."

Not going to cry. Not going to cry. She chanted the mantra in her head. What else should she have expected? She'd been foisted on Myles, why shouldn't he be relieved to be finally rid of her?

She'd known him only for a short time, so why did she expect him to actually miss her, the way she would miss him?

She dashed away a stray tear.

Forget about it. Forget about him.

She had things to do.

In the shelter of the folly, Abby leaned against an ivy-covered column. The leaves rustled at her back, and she welcomed the damp coolness of the secluded space.

She had to get herself together. Dionysus mustn't suspect anything, so she shouldn't be anything less than enthusiastic and eager.

Pushing off the column, she headed for the trap door. Making sure her handbag was slung over her shoulder, she hiked up her skirts in one hand and descended the ladder.

Myles ran his hand through his hair. One of the bacchantes curled herself about him, hooking her leg around his thigh.

He shook her off. "Leave me," he declared.

"You're not supposed to resist me," she complained in a soft, sexy contralto.

"Or me." The other bacchante attached herself to his other side, her hand swooping down to collect his drooping cock.

Myles tried to pry her grip free. The last thing he wanted was damage done there, although perhaps he deserved it. "I need to think."

"Nobody needs to think." The first bacchante slipped her tongue into his ear.

He shivered and almost gave into the temptation. Abby had washed her hands of him after all. Why not?

From the very beginning, Abby had resented the need to have him around, giving her countenance and guiding her through this strange world. She hadn't objected to the sex though, and she had enjoyed it.

They had been getting closer . . .

And then he'd ruined it all by finding his precious, all-important statue and setting chaos upon the world. Worst of all, losing Abby to a Greek god.

Why not walk away? Why not let her end the mess he helped make and go back to her own time? A time she undoubtedly belonged in. She was used to being in charge, used to her independence, even to dressing herself. She didn't belong here.

Not even with him.

He covered his mouth with his hand, hiding his emotions. The thought of not seeing her again punched him in the gut. A raw ache that not even meaningless sex could erase.

He should have held her, should have kissed her. He should have apologized and made things right between them before she departed.

Why walk away? He knew why not.

He succeeded in freeing his cock from one hand and his body from both of them. He stepped away, holding them both off. "Ladies, find somebody else to play with. I have someone to save."

Abby shook out her skirts and stared across the folly's basement at the lounging god. "You called?" she teased, her voice ringing out across the enclosed space.

Dionysus rose from his cushions, uncurling himself to stand upright, majestic. "You dare come before me now?" he bellowed.

The few followers in the room twisted and writhed out of the path of his anger.

"I got tied up." Abby bared her wrists, extending them before her for him to see while she walked toward him. "See?" She wondered how many more times she'd have to tell that story. Once more when she returned to her own time.

"You will not be returning to the future." The god stepped off his dais and met her halfway, taking her forearms in his large hands. "Bonds should not have prevented you."

"Isn't this proof enough that I tried? It was a heavy chair." She turned a pleading gaze up to him. Had she come so far only to be destroyed here and now by a god?

"Who would do such cruel things to my beloved?" His warmth calmed her, filling her with a sense of well-being.

Beloved? Abby ducked her head in momentary shame at her deception. Her eyes widened at the sight of her wrists. The weeping, open sores closed to thin pink lines.

Her wide eyes shot up to his golden face.

His lazy smile would send any woman's heart thudding, and Abby's was no exception. "You know I have powers." His head cocked to one side. "Why have you come now?"

Abby slipped free of his loose grasp to trail her fingertips down his well-defined pectorals. "I came because I wanted to be with you. I came because I didn't want to wait for evening to see you again."

"You came because you plot my end." His gaze tracked her every movement.

She sucked in her breath but forged ahead, pressing her body against his, circling his neck with her arms. "Do you want me to go?"

He beamed down at her. "Now why would I want that? I can stop any of your puny attempts. Plus, you are mine." His hands smoothed down her arms and back to her shoulders. His fingers brushed against her handbag's leather strap. "What's this?"

She smirked up at him. "I brought you a present."

His green eyes widened. "You . . . you . . . A gift? For me?"

Her lips twitched. "Come now, you're a god. Shouldn't you be used to getting presents?" She kept sucking his chest, relishing the sensations. She caught her lower lip between her teeth.

"Being a god is complicated," Dionysus told her. "It is very sweet of you to bring me something. What is it?"

"You'll have to wait until later," Abby said, going up on tip-toes to reach his mouth. She pressed a chaste kiss against his lips.

She'd never really gotten a chance to know this personification of a god, or a true god, whichever, but this first glimpse of vulnerability gave her pause.

How could she put him back into his prison?

His eyes glistened with the knowledge of her thoughts. "Then don't," he whispered.

Abby cupped his face in her hands. "I'll give your gift to you later." She reached up to kiss him again, and this time Dionysus was not content to let the kiss remain innocent.

Easily, he parted her lips, deepening the contact and possessing her mouth utterly. He hoisted her into the air, arms tight around her body. He carried her back to the dais.

Breathless, Abby hooked her legs around his hips, rubbing herself against him. He never broke the kiss for a moment, and Abby loved every minute of it. She shouldn't, she couldn't get lost in this, but, god, he was good.

He laid her on the cushions, covering her body with his. Pressing kisses down the curve of her neck, Dionysus pushed her bag strap off her shoulder.

Sighing with pleasure, Abby realized his purpose. She gripped his shoulders. "Later, I said." She struggled into a sitting position, watching the god's abashed expression with some amusement of her own. She tossed the bag to the edge of the dais.

"Later," he groaned. "First, I will have you."

She ran a risk coupling with the god again before carrying out her plan, but really, how else could she get him relaxed enough to do what she, ah, needed to do? If it meant losing her freedom and suffering the same fate as his followers, at least she'd saved the world, right?

Right?

If Dionysus noticed her sudden trembling, he gave no sign of it. He knew her thoughts, knew her plans, and yet he still wanted her. He kept kissing her.

The warmth from his body had just been the start. His

kisses sparked something wild in her. Each time she came to him, she had the same reaction: that illicit thrill and anticipation of something unique, something forbidden.

She returned his kisses, demanding as much of him as he did of her. His cock leaped in response, prodding her thigh, making her aware of his nakedness and her substantial clothing.

Dionysus created a small space between them, keeping her away from him. With his bare hands, he ripped the fabric from her body.

He drew her to him, his lovely cock prodding her belly. Abby gasped, rubbing against his hard cock. His mouth slid down her throat, kissing and nibbling his way to her breasts.

Abby arched her back, eager for his attentions. He flicked his tongue over her nipple, but Abby wanted more. She begged him, words incoherent, for more.

Entering a golden haze, Abby surrendered to the god, his magic touch rendering her insensible. His hands and mouth seemed to be everywhere, making erogenous zones where she thought none existed. The slightest connection became heaven.

He slid farther down, nuzzling her belly. She wanted him to go faster, to reach her clit and make her come. She pushed on his golden curly head, but he resisted with a soft laugh.

Dionysus gazed along the length of her body. "You came to me of your own free will, even if your motives were less than pure. Allow me to reward you at my own pace."

His remark chilled her, but she refused to let it show, even if the god could read her heart. "Shouldn't it be at my pace as a reward?" she teased.

He smirked. "You never stop, do you. Tell me, do you want a small orgasm or a big one?"

She propped up on her elbows, chewing her lip. "That shouldn't be a difficult choice . . ."

"I like you, Abigail Deane." He chuckled, dipping his tongue into her belly button. His teeth grazed her tender skin, tugging on the lower ridge of her belly button before continuing his slow path down.

His tongue flicked across her clit, and a burst of pleasure flooded her. She stiffened, surprised to be so close to the edge so soon. Had she become the god's already?

Dionysus shifted, hovering over her. His mouth drew near to hers, and she smelled her own scent on him. She wrapped her arms around his neck and drew him down for a long, wet kiss.

He lifted her hips, lying between her legs, and his cock slid inside her wet cunt. She gasped, the shock of his entry reminding her of her mission.

Would she lose herself in him forever?

He pulsed in and out. She trembled, unable to stop the flow of her lust for him, not sure if she even wanted to. She wanted him, even if it meant hurting herself. His immortal touch made sure of it. It was hard to remember anyone else, even Myles, who had so freshly torn at her heart.

She cupped his buttocks. Her fingertips brushed the top edge of his arse. He didn't stiffen or still in protest, rocking gently into her while she explored him.

Tears in her eyes, she pried her mouth away from his. "Dionysus," she breathed, his name punctuated with a pleasured sob. "I wish—"

Dionysus tugged on her nipple and her thoughts scattered. Her hands buried themselves into his hair. "What do you wish?" he breathed, the warm air from his lips over her wet nipple making her shiver.

"That I could please you the way you please me," she got out.

He broke off his tonguing attentions to her breast, looking down at her. "But you do. You please me immensely. You gave me my freedom."

She flushed. "Anyone could've done that."

"No," he informed her, his usual good-humored expression disappearing beneath a frown. "No, only you."

"You brought me here to do so," she remembered. She stroked his cheek. "Dionysus, can I not give you something freely?"

He blinked. "Such as?"

"I brought things from my time. I'd like to . . . to pleasure you with them." She held her breath. Would he agree?

"You think that will bring about my end?" Dionysus chuckled. "I assure you, there is nothing in the future that will surprise me. Your generation thinks you have invented everything. On the contrary, they are just reinventions."

"Oh," Abby said in a small voice. Was that a no?

"But if it pleases you," he murmured, kissing her forehead.

Don't be nice to me, she thought. *But I'll take any opportunity you'll give.* "It's your surprise," she said aloud.

"And perhaps yours." He grinned down at her, grinning wider when he read her fear. "Show me."

She wriggled out from under him. Even now, so close to betraying him, she didn't want to lose physical contact with this god. "Close your eyes," she warned him, forcing a smirk.

He obeyed. Abby delved into her handbag. Her fingers closed around the thick silicone shaft.

"Keep your eyes closed." She glanced over at him. He sat cross-legged with an expectant expression. His eyelids squeezed shut.

Sliding her hand down the dildo, Abby found the flat dial at its base and turned it on.

Dionysus's eyes opened at the sound. "It's motorized and it works?"

"Battery operated," she confirmed, adding, "Eyes closed" in mock severity, keeping the dildo hidden.

He closed his eyes, covering them with a hand. "This will be fun."

Abby hoped so. Myles had liked its affect after all. "Just keep your eyes closed."

Removing the dildo, she crawled toward the waiting god. She let it vibrate, tip to tip. His hand dropped from his face, revealing a beatific expression.

She circled the head of his cock, watching his face and the tense and release of his muscles for a sign of displeasure. He seemed to enjoy the sensations, his pre-cum coating the vibrating dildo's tip.

Abby rolled it down his immense length, his cock pulsing and jerking at the vibrating touch. She slipped it below, keeping it on the shaft. From the base to the tip and back again, letting it vibrate against his hanging balls.

A groan burst from Dionysus's lips. "Oh yes. Oh yes. That's good," he managed to get out. "That's incredible."

She teased his balls some more. His legs parted, giving her more access. She lifted his heavy balls and let the dildo roam below and behind.

His cock quivered, the head streaming with clear, viscous liquid. He groaned again. "I want to put it in you, woman." He shuddered. "Thank you for your gift."

Abby let the vibrator slowly slide along the length of his huge, rock-hard cock. One last swirl across the tip and she released him.

She switched off the vibrator and placed the tip of it, wet with Dionysus's pre-cum, against her wet hole. Her cunt pulsed against it, wanting more. Ever so slowly, she slid it in, their juices commingling.

Dionysus sagged. He took a breath, opened his eyes, and made to rip the dildo from her, but stopped. "What," he whispered, "what are you doing?"

With slow strokes, she pumped the dildo in and out of her eager cunt. She'd been close to coming again, and she hovered on the verge. All of a sudden, she wanted to do nothing more than to pleasure herself before him.

But the martial glint in his eye warned her she didn't have much time.

Conceding, Abby pulled out the dildo, closing her parted thighs before Dionysus ravished her. She held up the large silicone dildo between them.

Seeing his gaze upon it instead of her, Abby gave the drenched sex toy one long lick. She imagined it being his cock and saw his cock jerk in response to her thought. "There is another place for this," she purred. "Are you willing to try?"

Dionysus's heavy-lidded gaze turned amused instead of aroused. "There is little that will surprise me. I am the god of lustful desires, after all."

She forced a grin. "That's true."

"So you want it in your arse?" he inquired with a polite tone and the most devilish grin.

"Oh no!" Abby exclaimed. "It wouldn't fit! Maybe we can improvise something smaller later?"

"Later," he promised. "So if not there . . ."

"To use your words," Abby took a shaky breath, "in your arse."

To her surprise, he didn't protest at all, rolling over onto all fours and turning at the same time so he presented his arse to her. "I've had men galore," he told her. "If it gives you a thrill—"

"Only if it gives you one," Abby interjected.

Between her wet cream, her saliva, and his pre-cum, it was well lubed. Positioning it against his puckered arsehole, she tickled his dangling balls, running her fingertips over them and taking the weight of them in her palm.

"You should've been born a man," he remarked, groaning. "You have the touch."

Abby laughed. She leaned over and kissed his right buttock. "I have been well trained. Lots of practice."

She bent lower, licking his balls so they bobbed above her

tongue. "I never dreamed," she whispered, "that I'd experience something like this."

The dildo wavered.

She had to do this. The world counted on her.

"Do your best, little one." Dionysus chuckled under his breath.

She pressed the dildo against his arse. It inched in. Abby didn't want to hurt him, part of her not even wanting to do this.

"By all the gods, Abigail, put it in," Dionysus groaned.

She kissed the little dimples just above his arse. "And now I make love to you."

The dildo slid in. Abby withdrew it and shoved it into his arse again. Far enough in to rub and press against that special spot so close to his prostate.

Dionysus cried out, a wordless throbbing cry. It filled the small underground space with his joy and pleasure.

In the next heartbeat, his cry transformed into an outraged roar. "No!"

"Sorry, sorry," she whispered, continuing to fuck him with the dildo.

Then her world exploded.

18

By Elaine's bedroom window, Demetri collapsed onto all fours. "It has begun," he managed to get out between gritted teeth.

Elaine flung herself from her bed, rushing to him. "Are you sure?"

"Argh!" His face twisted in a rictus of pain, his teeth bared. "Yes, yes."

At once she wrapped her arms about him, hugging him to her. His back muscles corded and twisted against her cheek. "I'm going to hold onto you," she cried, her voice full of tears. "I'm going to hold onto you forever."

Her satyr screamed, a hoarse cry that tore at her heart. He curled into a huddle. "It hurts, oh, it hurts." He clutched, not at her hands clasped about his chest, but at his middle.

"I don't want you to be a painting on the wall," Elaine sobbed. "I will not let it happen."

"I feel it happening," Demetri managed to get out. "I feel it changing me."

"No," Elaine begged. "No!"

* * *

Lucy sat on the small velvet sofa next to her husband. The duke took her hand into his. "Are you sure you want to do this?"

She kept her gaze steady and her chin uplifted. She squeezed his hand. "Only if you stay here with me."

"I cannot help you. I cannot touch you. If I do, I lose you."

Lucy nodded. She'd heard the warning a hundred times. The duke knew, for he had told her. She had to know the risks. "She's the one, my love. We will both enjoy her when I've saved her."

His lips twisted. "She's more yours than mine, but I thank you. I look forward to taking you up on the offer."

He glanced across their bedroom to where Phoebe lay, the bacchante's lips thinned in dread anticipation.

In the next instant, Phoebe screamed, her back arching high off the bed.

Lucy jumped, startled, half rising from her velvet chair.

The duke held on to her hand. "It is beginning," he murmured.

She bent down and kissed his forehead. "I know." She dipped lower, claiming his mouth. "Thank you."

He released her and she ran to the bed, leaping on it and holding down the writhing Phoebe with her own weight. Lucy gripped her flailing wrists, pressing Phoebe's hands against the pillow.

Phoebe stared up at her, wild-eyed, terrified. "This is the end," she sobbed.

"No." Lucy's voice remained firm, calm. "No, it is just the beginning." She released Phoebe's arms to wrap her own about Phoebe's slender waist.

"Let me go! You must!" Phoebe's sobbing wails rent the air.

Phoebe fought Lucy with all her strength, tearing at her hair and arms. Blinded with tears, Lucy squeezed her eyes shut, holding on with everything she had.

Blood poured from her biceps from Phoebe's attack. Lucy kept her face pressed between Phoebe's bosom, the bacchante's large breasts almost smothering her.

But Lucy held on.

Then the transformations began.

From his position sitting in the wing chair, the Duke of Winterton watched his wife wrestle with the bacchante. His knuckles turned white, gripping the arms of his chair.

Her determination near broke his heart. He wanted to help, wanted to go his wife's aid, his dearest, most beloved Lucy. But the text forbade it. If he dared, then the bacchante—Phoebe—would be lost, and maybe his wife also.

The duke swallowed his tears. The bacchante shifted beneath Lucy, her desperate clawing limbs changing from pale olive skin into golden furred limbs, the knee twisting backward. The golden fur rippled and bunched with new muscles.

Giant claws grew where Phoebe's toes had been.

Lucy screamed, blood blossoming across her shoulder and thighs in long, red streaks.

The duke gnawed his lower lip. Phoebe's cat claws left long, red gaping wounds.

The duke shot to his feet, taking a step toward the wrestling couple. His fists clenched. If he went to her aid, he'd lose Lucy. If he didn't, the monster clasped in her arms might well kill her.

Phoebe mutated, her feet shrinking into the hooked claws of chicken feet. The claws curled about Lucy's legs, trying to pull her away.

Lucy cried out, more in anger than in pain, he judged from its raw sound. Feathers of pale yellow gold rose up from the bed as Phoebe's arms became wings, beating hard to free herself from Lucy's grasp.

The wingbeats lifted them from the bed, Lucy hanging on, struggling to find purchase over the slippery feathers. She hooked her arms around Phoebe's neck, dangling precariously. Her feet kicked in the air, trying to find some sort of purchase.

The duke leapt into action, hefting a side table and placing it on the bed, under Lucy. Her toes found it, and Lucy used gravity to draw the winged Phoebe back down.

Phoebe changed again, her limbs transforming from feathers to scales.

The duke whipped the small side table out of the way just in time, the grappling pair crashing onto the bed. He heard the breath whoosh out of Lucy, but she held on. He stumbled out of the way.

Beneath her, great green scales shifted with a dry hissing whisper. Phoebe's lower limbs, all that the duke could see, formed into one large serpentine tail, the barbed end whipping across Lucy's thighs and calves.

Her flesh ripped and tore, but somehow Lucy held on. The Phoebe-serpent rippled beneath her, its scales turning varying shades of gold and orange. Phoebe squirmed, her lower half wriggling free.

Lucy gave a desperate cry. She reached out with her leg, hooking the scaly tail around her knee and ankle. The snake tried to unwind, but the barb caught on Lucy's foot.

The snake's head rose over Lucy's shoulder, looking at what prevented it from escaping. It turned its translucent green oval-shaped eyes toward the duke. The transparent eyelids flickered over the icy gaze. It loomed closer to the watching duke.

Its tongue flickered out, tasting the air. The duke retreated another step.

Hissing, the Phoebe-snake arched its neck and sank its bared fangs into Lucy's shoulder.

Lucy stiffened, not even crying out, and her body convulsed, squeezing the serpent. Bright red blood, arterial blood, streamed down her shoulder, escaping from between the snake's lipless mouth.

A roaring wind filled the room, whipping the bed curtains into a frenzy. It took Lucy's hair and wound it upward in a long blond tornado coronet.

The wind blew the duke back against the wall. He held his hand before his eyes, shielding them while trying to keep his wife in sight. What more could he do?

A bright light blinded him, the following heat sucking the moisture out of his pores. He slumped to the floor, still trying to see Lucy.

The bed caught fire. He made out Lucy's dark shadow, kneeling on the bed, her arms flailing. He blinked and her image became clearer. Blood crusted dry on her pale skin, but the fire didn't seem to harm her.

Her cry, a dried-out croak, shook him with its misery. "How am I to hold fire?"

What could he tell her, that Phoebe, her bacchante, engulfed her, burned her alive? How *do* you hold fire? Would it consume her as it had Phoebe? Had he lost them both?

The very air itself exploded, a piercing white light that rendered him blind. Frantically, he rubbed at his eyes. "Lucy!" he yelled. "Lucy!"

"I am here." Her voice came low and quiet in the sudden stillness. "I am still here."

The duke blinked, tears running down his cheeks. Dark spots still prevented him from seeing. He cocked his head, using his peripheral vision to espy the bed.

Lucy lay upon it, locked in Phoebe's embrace. Not wanting to see the damage, he approached the bed.

He swallowed. There had been too much blood.

Not a mark marred Lucy. There should have been horrible gouges where the serpent's fangs had sunk into her neck, or the horrible claw marks on her legs, but not a hint of them remained. He saw not a trace of the fire on the sheets.

He reached out his hand to her. "You are well."

Lucy's smile might have beamed had she not been so tired. "I am. I saved her, my husband. I saved her."

The duke crawled onto the bed and took her into his arms, giving Phoebe a stern glance. Lucy would be his, if only for a short while. He kissed Lucy's hair, holding her tight. "I was so sure I had lost you," he whispered.

Lucy pulled back, blinking away tears, and cupped his face in her hands. "You will never lose me." She covered his mouth with her own.

Frightened beyond words, Elaine held on to Demetri, his body warping into something new and strange beneath her. First he had become a giant cat and she'd ridden him about her small bedroom, refusing to be bucked off.

She squeezed her eyes tight, the jolting images of the room making her dizzy.

Demetri sank to the floor, growing soft beneath her, the hard muscle of the great cat sinking away. Slime coated her cheek pressed against his hide.

Elaine opened her eyes. Wet, gray skin greeted her, dark valleys encircling each raised portion of skin. Black spots decorated its ochre flesh.

She raised her head, looking along the length of this creature that Demetri had become. Two fleshy horns rose from his narrow head, eyestalks twitching to look at back at her.

A slug! Her handsome satyr was a slug!

She reacted without thinking, releasing him and trying to wipe the slime off her arms.

"Elaine . . ." She heard his voice fade and sigh.

She reached for him, but too late. He vanished, leaving a silver trail where his sluglike body had lain.

Elaine curled into a ball and sobbed. Stupid! So stupid! He'd warned her it may not be pleasant, even dangerous, and she'd failed him.

She'd failed their love.

She covered her face with her hands. Demetri's slime came into contact with her face. She screamed. In a frenzy, she rubbed her hands onto the rug, springing away and ringing for a maid.

Myles strode across the green meadow, trailing Abby to the ivy-concealed temple. He'd wasted enough time already in his debate on whether he should follow her.

He might have lost her already.

Fear quickened his step, making him stumble over the worn low risers to the temple floor. He grabbed at the ivy to keep his balance, sending sheets of it to the floor.

He slid across the damp, dark green leaves, arms flailing, seeking to regain balance. He skidded to a stop in the middle of the temple floor, his breath sounding harsh in his ears.

Myles knew exactly how he would save her. Hadn't Abby told him to hold onto his bacchante lovers if he wanted to keep them? That's all he'd have to do for her.

He hurried down the trapdoor's narrow ladder, the wood burning his palms in his haste. He faced the interior of Dionysus's domain, muscles tensing for a fight.

An unearthly golden light brought the dais into clear view. There had to be some hidden skylight above he hadn't seen before, even after that initial search of the folly.

Centered in that light lay Abby and Dionysus, limbs entwined. Myles watched Dionysus worship Abby's body with his mouth and hands, bringing her into gasping, eager joy.

Myles glanced up the ladder. He should leave. He didn't want to see this. He didn't want to see this woman, his Abby, the woman he loved, being bedded by another man, even one who called himself a god.

He rocked back on his heels. Love her? Abby?

He'd loved before . . . a little. Nothing to jerk him out of his well-planned life. But Abby . . . Abby had the same independent spirit of adventure as he did. He out and out *liked* her.

He rubbed at his face. What did it matter anyway? He'd lost her to a god, and he'd already proven he was no good for her.

Dionysus's laughter made him look upon their idyllic scene. One last time, Myles looked at the lovers.

He blinked. Abby pulled a dildo out of her purse and applied it to the god's cock.

Myles turned away from the scene, his head lowered. His stomach roiled. She'd done that for *him*. Now she did it for another?

He gritted his teeth. Well, he wasn't going to stay and watch this, no—

His gaze met Dionysus's and the god's little smirk almost pulled his heart out of his chest.

No. He didn't want her to do this.

The god rolled onto all fours, presenting his arse to Abby.

No.

Myles swallowed. He stood riveted to the spot, longing to leave but not able to shift a single foot. Magic didn't prevent him, but disbelief.

He wanted to close his ears to the god's moans. He wished he didn't feel compelled to witness this.

The god's angered roar changed everything. The warm golden light surrounding Abby and Dionysus blazed with a sudden fierceness. The air grew heavy and thick with all the weight of water.

She had done it.

Abby had defeated the god.

But did she belong to the god now?

He remembered what she'd said: "If you want to keep either one of them, I recommend hanging on to them when the time comes."

Myles sprinted for the dais. The thick air turned his dash

into a jog, the air coming hard into his lungs. The walls blazed with color, bright ochre and viridian green.

He reached the dais, dashed up the three broad steps. Shadows appeared on the walls, flickering human figures. A wailing filled his ears, a high counterpoint to the god's roar.

Despite Dionysus's anger, he hadn't moved to stop her, kneeling rigid on all fours, his buttocks moving in spasms against the inserted dildo.

Myles fell to his knees beside Abby. He grabbed her shoulders, trying to pull her away, but she resisted. The curse had her in its grip.

Choking back a curse, he wrapped his arms around her. His cheek pressed against the back of her neck.

Her skin seared him, burning him with a white-hot heat. He jerked his head away, the heat seeping through his fine woolen evening jacket.

Wide-eyed, he stared at Abby's skin. It looked flushed. With that kind of heat, her flesh ought to be burning, blistering. The impression of a blister swelled on his singed cheek.

It hurt like the very devil. He imagined the charcoal-dark odor of burnt flesh, his burnt flesh, filling his nostrils. At least he hoped he imagined it. His sore cheek warned him it might be otherwise.

But to let go meant losing her: watching her become a statue entwined with Dionysus—although this was a particularly embarrassing position for a god to be immortalized in—or watching her become painted brush strokes on a wall.

He gritted his teeth, eyes streaming. He looked away from the blazing golden light of the god. The shadowy figures on the walls coalesced.

The paintings grew clear: satyrs and bacchantes, locked in position, being chased or lying in each other's arms. Myles recognized Demetri among them, a tear glistening on his cheek while he merrily played a flute.

He glanced down at Abby, wondering if he'd see the brush-strokes on her skin or if she'd simply fade away. It didn't change from its faint heated flush.

Dionysus roared his anger again.

Myles caught movement in the corner of his eye and tensed. He wouldn't let go.

It was the god. He pulled free of Abby, the inserted dildo still locked in his arse, and faced them. His handsome face convulsed with anger. Dionysus grabbed her outstretched hands and pulled on them.

"Leave her!" Myles snapped over the top of Abby's head.

"She's mine!" Dionysus bellowed. "She made her choice."

"She made the choice to imprison you, not to stay with you."

"She came to me of her own free will." Dionysus tugged on her arms and Myles braced himself against the dais's steps.

"To destroy you." Myles shook his head. "Ask her! She has a voice of her own."

Dionysus's gaze dropped to Abby's face. "Speak."

Abby's head flung back, almost catching Myles on the chin. "Sorry, Dionysus, I had to do it."

"No," growled the god, his face paling to a jaundiced hue. His lip curled, his eyebrows drew together. "No!"

Myles gripped Abby tighter, her breasts squeezing beneath his forearms. If the god's last act was to destroy her, they would go together.

The god lunged, pushing off with his legs and diving for them. Myles had no chance to react. The blow knocked them backward off the dais.

They rolled—Abby relaxing from her crouched position— down the broad steps, each edge digging hard into Myles's back under their combined weight.

Landing in a heap in the bottom, Myles twisted his head toward the dais.

"Begone!" Dionysus boomed. He knelt, his outstretched hand dismissing them.

Myles ducked, twisting his body to shield Abby in his arms. He prepared himself for the god's killing blow.

Thunder roared, sounding like the earth cracking. A blinding flash of white light seared through Myles's closed eyelids.

The basement blacked out.

Abby opened her eyes. At least, she thought she did. She blinked. The impenetrable black remained. Had Dionysus banished her to hell for her treachery?

She took silent inventory. Her legs felt chilled, and her hips. Her back and waist were warm. Her head nestled on some something firm.

"Abby."

She recognized the hoarse voice. "Myles?"

The warmth nestled closer. "How do you feel?"

"Tired. We're not dead, are we?" She resented the wobble in her words.

Myles shifted. "There's light coming from behind me. We're still in the basement."

"Oh." She lay silent, gnawing her lip. "Dionysus?"

His shoulders shifted against her. "Let's find those torches." He sat up. "Are you sure you are unhurt?"

"Yes." Abby patted his arm. She lifted herself into a sitting position. She sensed his movement away from her before she saw it, a shadowy outline against the gray-green light filtering down the trapdoor.

He picked up a torch from a pile left by the ladder and struck something against the wall. The torch flared into life.

Myles came back toward her, his evening clothes dirty and rumpled. His uncertain smile made her feel unexpectedly good inside.

"Myles," she breathed.

He gave a sharp jerk of his head, gesturing to something behind her.

She twisted. Dionysus knelt in gold-leafed marble perfection on the dais, hand outstretched.

Abby rose, ascending the dais in slow wonder. She reached out, her fingertips brushing the god's cold hand. "He's gone."

"Locked up inside," Myles corrected. He ascended the dais and placed a hand on her shoulder. "Do you regret it?"

Abby sucked in her breath and let a long sigh escape from between her lips. "No. No, I don't. There was no . . . balance." She patted his hand and faced him, capturing his hand in hers. "It looks like I'm stuck here."

Myles's thumb smoothed over her palm. "Is that really so bad?"

Abby pulled her hand free. "I don't know. I've said some things, done some things. My staying isn't fair to you."

"I've done things I've regretted too. Saving you isn't one of them," Myles told her. It eclipsed all else. He'd cared for her enough to keep her with him. Her heart warmed. "Let's get you dressed and back to the house before it gets too dark."

Abby pulled on her clothes, Myles helping her to pull the shreds together. She tried not to think about him standing so close behind her. She retrieved her handbag from the dais and looked around her.

"Ready?" Myles prompted, standing close to the exit.

"Just one more thing." Abby ducked behind the statue. The dildo lay on the floor. She held it up for Myles to see. "At least he didn't freeze with this in him."

She started to put it in her handbag.

"Leave it," Myles said. "I don't think we need a reminder."

Abby surveyed the dildo, twisting her wrist to see more of it. "You're right. It's not something I'd want to use again." She glanced at the frozen statue's face. "I don't know how he handled it. It might have done a lot of damage. But I had to do the inverse of what he had done to me." The god's bravado had undone him, almost as much as her bravado in mounting the statue had been his freeing.

She laid the dildo on the floor before the kneeling god. "Let the archeologists figure that one out." She flashed Myles a quicksilver grin. "What are you going to do with him?"

"The statue?" Myles gazed beyond her into the looming darkness.

"It was your dream." She kept her voice casual. Something in her tore at the thought of the god being on display in some museum.

"It was my father's dream." Myles joined her, settling an arm about her shoulder and gazing upon the supplicating statue. "And I am not even sure he really knew why he must find it. He had a passion for archaeology—as do I—but this . . . Dionysus is too magical to risk on the world."

Abby took a cleansing breath. It felt so right to have Myles hold her. She quirked a grin. "Do lots of people have sex with statues in museums and galleries?"

Myles choked. "I am sure I don't want to think about it. It is best to keep him hidden."

His wistful voice made her realize Myles had given up his dream of success. And for her. Abby leaned against him. "But it is your dream."

His grip tightened on her shoulder. "There are other statues, other treasures to find. I'll make my father proud by doing the hard work myself instead of finding the easy way."

"This was easy?" Abby squeezed his arm in reassurance despite her teasing.

"Well, I learned that the easy way is often the hardest." His chest expanded, and a sigh wafted across her hair. "Are you ready?"

"I'm ready." She took one last look at Dionysus and crossed the dark floor with Myles's arm still slung about her shoulders.

He gestured to the ladder. "After you."

Abby arched a brow. "Are you ever going to give up looking up a girl's skirt?"

Myles's smile broadened. "Every girl's but yours."

Abby rolled her eyes and hitched her skirts, ready to ascend.

19

Abby stepped into the gloomy and dark entry hall. Only a few lit sconces gave a hint of life. An unnatural quiet settled over the hall.

"Where do you suppose everyone is?" Myles stood beside her, his arm slung around her shoulders.

She leaned into him. "After a night like this, maybe everyone thought it was better to stay in bed." Abby traced a dusty path on a side table. "Myles," she said in a strange, suffused voice.

He picked up on her worry at once. "What's wrong?"

"Myles, I don't think we're in the nineteenth century anymore."

"What?"

Abby watched his frantic examination of the hall.

"I do not see any difference." He rubbed a hand through his hair. "How do you know?"

Abby folded her arms and smiled in smug self-satisfaction. "Just kidding."

At his blank incomprehension, Abby giggled. "It was a joke."

He came at her. "I should strangle you."

Laughing, she dodged out of his way, heading for the stairs. "You'll have to catch me first."

She couldn't explain her light-heartedness. Just that Myles was with her. Just being in his presence (so long as he wasn't fucking other women at the time) made her ridiculously happy.

At the landing, she glanced over her shoulder at him. He closed in behind her, his boyish grin not hiding his eagerness.

"I think I have better plans for you besides strangling." He caught up with her, gazing into her upturned face. "Although you do deserve at least a spanking."

She darted away, but he caught her arm. "Let me go," she said, injecting a breathy note.

"I caught you. Fair is fair." He drew her near, his arm going about her waist. "Now it's time to claim my reward." His head lowered.

For a long moment, Abby wavered. She wanted to kiss him. She wanted everything to be light-hearted and back to normal as if the entire god thing had never happened.

However, it had. Abby pushed against his chest. "Myles, we need to talk."

He kept her within his arms, loosening his embrace. "Do those words still strike fear into the hearts of men two hundred years from now?" Myles smiled at her, but the smile didn't reach his eyes. Concern lurked there.

Abby couldn't help smiling back. "Pretty much." She eased out of his embrace. "Myles—"

A throat cleared. "Mr. Hardy, Ms. Deane. Please join us in the drawing room for tea." The duke stood in the drawing room doorway beneath them. "There is much to discuss."

"What's to discuss?" Abby retorted. "It is done."

"Humor me." The duke stepped back into the drawing room.

"We should go," Abby murmured. She tapped Myles's chest. "Don't think you're getting out of this."

Myles took her arm. "I would not dream of so doing."

They descended and stepped into a room full of waiting Wintertons.

The duke sat on the arm of a sofa, his wife Lucy and her bacchante Phoebe nestled together, the latter looking uncomfortable in a high-waisted day dress. Elaine curled up in the window seat, dressed in unrelenting black. She took one look at them and turned to gaze out the window.

Winterton gestured to another sofa. "Please, sit. I would like to know what happened. For the family records, you understand, in case this happens again."

They sat. Abby resumed her clutch on Myles's arm. "I recommend acid-free paper and ink. If such things exist. At the very least, make sure what you have is kept legible. Rewritten, if necessary. Maybe printed."

The Duke of Winterton accepted her advice with a simple nod. "What happened?"

Glancing at Myles, Abby relayed the facts in plain, simple words. She didn't bother with euphemisms. After all, she'd seen enough of the Wintertons—literally—to know such terms would be wasted. Lucy blushed at her frankness.

When she had done, Elaine flung herself from her seat by the window. "You've killed him!" she shrieked.

"Demetri is not dead." Myles rose, interposing himself between her and Abby. "He's trapped in the wall paintings again."

Elaine stood before him, clenching and unclenching her fists. At last she spun away, covering her face. "I couldn't hold on to him! I couldn't!"

Lucy extracted herself from her bacchante's embrace, crossing to pat her stepdaughter on the shoulder. "Then it wasn't meant to be. The right one will come, you'll see."

Abby remained silent. The bravado and the vulnerability of the god in their last hours together gave her an idea of what Elaine might be going through. Abby gripped Myles's arm. What would she have done if she'd lost him?

Elaine twitched away, retreating to the windows.

Lucy gave an apologetic look to Myles and Abby. Her gaze focused beyond them, and her features transformed into surprise. "Gareth! Are you all right?" She flung her arms around the startled young viscount. "I am so sorry."

Young Winterton managed to extricate himself from Lucy. "I am well, stepmother." He looked at the assemblage. "What's going on? Who is this?" He pointed at Phoebe.

"Your stepmother's new companion," the duke replied, not stirring from his position. "She's a bacchante."

"What?" The viscount's confused gaze canvassed all of them. "Aren't they mythical?"

Abby rested her arm on the back of the sofa, twisting to face him. "The women you've been having sex constantly with for the last few days and then just mysteriously disappeared. Those were bacchantes."

"What women? Sex?" The viscount's face crumpled in incomprehension. "I've been up getting the hunting lodge ready. Caught some partridge, by the way."

Abby covered her mouth, suppressing giggles. She'd heard about the randy viscount from her maid. "He missed it. He missed the whole thing!" She glanced across at Lucy to see her amusement mirrored there.

Rising, Abby gave the duke a brief curtsey. "I think I'll leave it to you to explain everything to your son. I have matters to discuss with Mr. Hardy."

"Just one more thing." The duke held up his hand for attention. "Mr. Hardy, this ends here."

Abby knew exactly what "this" was and looked up at Myles, wondering if he agreed. The crinkling around his eyes had faded.

The duke continued, "I do not want any descendant of yours hunting for that statue. They will not know of it."

Myles frowned. "I cannot promise for actions beyond my control, but not one word of this will pass my lips."

"One word of what?" the viscount burst out, face reddening further. The duke waved him off.

"Are you going to seal the temple?" Abby asked.

"I have half a mind to tear it down." The duke glowered fiercely.

"No!" Elaine wailed, stuffing her hands into her mouth, blinded by tears.

"I cannot." The duke relented, hushing his daughter with a curt wave. "The statue is a magical thing. Best to properly entomb it."

Myles nodded, and without further words, he escorted her from the room, pausing only to deliver a polite bow to the duchess.

Abby halted on the stairs, close to where they had stopped last time. "Myles, we've been through a lot, and after everything I said to you . . . I—I never thought you would rescue me."

The smile disappeared from his face. "You told me that if I wanted to keep someone from succumbing to the spell, I should hang on to her." He lifted and lowered his shoulders. "So I did."

"But why?"

Myles sat on the broad wooden steps and drew her down to sit next to him. "Why?" He rubbed his hair. "I couldn't have us end the way it did. You didn't give me a chance to explain . . ."

"About your bacchantes?"

"I thought you had been summoned to Dionysus already

and that you wouldn't be coming back." He sighed. "Maybe it would've been better if I'd gotten drunk instead."

Abby rested her folded arms on her knees and rested her head on them, looking sideways at him. "So it was revenge sex?"

He thought it over and nodded. "Except I never expected you to find out. I thought you were gone already." He stared out into the hall. "I thought I'd never see you again. It hurt." He rested his head on his hand. "I promise it will not happen again."

Her breath caught in her throat. She wanted to believe him. What he said made some sense, after all, hadn't she felt the same? "And I can trust that?"

Myles looked affronted. "I made a promise."

"You made a promise to Elaine too." His broken engagement with her, would Elaine demand its renewal? Biting her lip, Abby didn't think she could go through losing Myles again.

"And got ran out of town by her father," Myles reminded her. "I think if the duke had any idea she'd end up with a satyr, he'd have accepted me."

A chill shivered through her heart. "Did I see Demetri on the wall?"

"Yes." Myles folded his hands before him, fingers pointing out into the great hall's empty space.

"Doesn't that mean . . . ?"

"I was released from that promise. I doubt very much if Winterton will permit any renewal of my suit. Besides, Elaine is a mite annoying."

"She's young yet," Abby allowed. "Give me a year and I could whip her into shape. Of course, I'd have to find a job for her."

"Yes, but would you want to?" Myles shot back, a grin lurking at the corner of his lips.

Abby conceded the point. She thought over everything they'd said before they'd fallen into the comfort of teasing each other. "So if I release you from your promise to look out for me in this world, then we're even."

"Release me, Abby, and I'll just promise over again, and keep promising until you realize—" Myles shot to his feet and descended a few steps. He turned and looked up at her, staring wide-eyed down at him. "Abby, if you haven't figured it out by now, then you'll never—"

"A woman likes to be told," she murmured, refusing to let him off the hook just yet.

"I love you." The quiet force of his words convinced her.

"When did you know?"

His cheeks reddened. "I had a strong inkling after we lay together the first time. But it was after we woke the god and I discovered I might lose you . . ."

Abby stood and went down to stand at eye level with him. "And you screwed it up."

The wide flash of his eyes led her to believe he'd been expecting her to soften. "I did. I apologize."

"Technically, I screwed around too." How could she hold him accountable when she'd made the same mistake? She bit her lip and then smiled. "So I guess we're even."

"And that means?"

"I'm willing to give this another try." She brushed his cheek with her palm. The trust wouldn't be restored overnight, but she wanted to give their relationship another chance. Seeing him walk away from her was not an option. I like you too much not to." She gathered his hand in hers. "Shall we go to bed?"

Myles ascended the stairs with her, hand in hand, not saying anything. He undressed her and she shivered, her skin becoming exposed to the air. He needed to do very little to free her from her ruined clothing. He stood behind her, hands smoothing over her shoulders and down, his fingertips brushing the sides of her breasts.

Her gown puddled to the floor and she stepped out of it, turning to face him. Abby laced her hands behind his neck and drew his head down for a kiss.

His cool lips warmed against hers. After Abby began to wonder if Myles really wanted to do this, he banished her worries by deepening the kiss, starting a gentle exploration of her mouth.

His cravat long since lost, Abby pulled his pine-pitch stained shirt over his head. Her eyes feasted on his flat stomach, the dark line of hair rising from the waistband of his breeches.

She flattened her hands against his chest. When had they last made love? Days ago, and the surge of affection at seeing him half-naked, at being able to touch him, stole her breath. She bent forward and pressed a kiss against the center of his chest.

Looking up, she saw Myles gaze down at her, his long eyelashes concealing his eyes. His unreadable expression gave her fresh concern. Did he feel duty-bound to do this because of that damned promise?

Abby vowed to make it worth his while. She kissed her way up his chest, tasting his tangy warmth. Nestling her mouth in the hollow of his throat, she licked and kissed him there, enjoying his closeness. She breathed him in, her hands snaking down his chest to unfasten his breech buttons.

Easing the breeches off his hips, Abby stood back to admire the view. His half-erect cock rose sluggishly to greet her. She sank to her knees, sitting back on her heels to tug the breeches off his lower legs.

"Boots." She frowned at Myles, hands on hips. "I forgot about the boots."

Myles sat on the bed and pulled them off in short order, removing his breeches also.

Before he might rise, Abby got up and straddled his lap. She stroked his chest, hands rising upward over his skin until she cupped his face. "There's something you need to hear."

His forehead crinkled and he waited for her to continue.

"Do you know why I imprisoned the god?"

"Because you had to." His even gaze disconcerted her, so she lowered her own to his pecs.

"Yes, I had to. I didn't want to leave you, but I don't belong here."

Myles opened his mouth to protest, but she cut him off by placing a fingertip over his lips.

"When I saw you with those women—I just had to run."

He found her hand and took it in his own. "Abby . . ."

"I know, I forgive you." She met his worried gaze. "That's just it. I forgive you. I spent almost an entire day without you and I missed you. I don't want you to feel honor-bound to fuck me. If you don't want me anymore, just let me go."

Her head bent forward and met his forehead halfway. "Myles, you stole my heart. I never really let myself give in to what I felt. And now I'm here, and you're here, and there's this long road ahead. I want to travel it with you, Myles, wherever it might lead."

Myles tilted her chin up so their gazes met. "So what you're saying is . . ."

"I love you." Tears filled her eyes and spilled over. "I do, Myles."

He came to life, the old vital Myles that she'd fallen for. He rolled, trapping her beneath him, his cock surging between her legs. "Say it again."

She gave him a watery smile. "I love you, Mr. Myles Hardy."

He slid inside her. Abby moaned, clutching him. This is what she wanted, him deep inside her, where he belonged. He began a slow rocking, pelvis to pelvis, surging in and out of her.

Abby hooked her legs around his waist, letting him ride her, letting him guide her to satisfaction. Emotion and desire rose and crested, Abby rocking in Myles's bliss.

Here, two hundred years from her own time, in this charming man's arms, she had found the key to her balance.

Feel the heat of
NIGHT FIRE,
by Vonna Harper!

On sale now!

1

Feeling more than a little disconnected from the crowd, Hayley McKeon stood off to one side taking in the large, brightly lit event room. Maybe she wouldn't have felt out of it if she hadn't worked late last night—Friday, of course—but then maybe being alone among so many chattering groups was responsible.

You can't do anything about it, kid, she reminded herself. *Getting divorced means turning into a "one" again.*

Determined not to go down that road today, when singlehood was what she'd wanted emotionally, financially, and in every other way, she took a deep breath. Unfortunately, the air was warmer than she liked and smelled too much of people and whatever they were offering at the food booth. Still not moving, she concentrated on her surroundings. She hadn't been to a gems and minerals show for a couple of years and had forgotten how exciting yet overwhelming they could be.

As a rough guess, she estimated there were at least forty separate booths in addition to the elaborate, glass-enclosed displays in the middle of the cavernous room. People filed slowly past the central displays while some of those in front of the booths showed no interest in moving on. Much as she wanted to see what was for sale on the various tables, getting close enough to do her own gawking and purchasing was going to be a challenge.

A challenge she had to meet unless she wanted to spend the foreseeable future and beyond gritting her teeth every time her boss at Galpan Enterprises asked/ordered her to work late.

It's your fault, sis. If you were here, we'd be pushing folks aside and damn the consequences, and I'd be filled with courage, not fear.

However, not only was being scared of her future an all but permanent condition, Saree had called her on her cell phone just as she was arriving to say she'd be a little late—something about needing to pick up a new outfit. Laughing under her breath, Hayley imagined what would happen if her knock-'em-dead younger sister walked in wearing a red latex body suit with openings for her breasts and crotch. No doubt about it, gems and minerals would come in a distant second to that little show. Thinking about the difference between the way she and her sister paid their bills got her moving. She had no—well, probably no—interest in becoming a porn star. Of course, if she could make enough baring everything she had to get out of debt—

Forget debt today, damn it! Take chances, take control!

Now that she'd joined the milling throng, she took increased note of the throng's composition. Not only did there seem to be equal numbers of men and women, but all ages were represented, including children, who were repeatedly being told to keep their hands to themselves. A large number of older couples were in attendance, and although her parents had been dead for two and nearly one year, respectively, Hayley still mourned what she'd lost. At least they hadn't had to see her marriage implode or explode, depending on how one looked at it.

She hadn't paid much attention to where she was heading

since she figured that as long as she went in one direction, sooner or later she'd see everything there was to see—and hopefully make some *put your money where your mouth is* purchases. When she'd first heard about the show, she'd told herself to go to it with her mind and imagination and creativity open, that her love of and skill in jewelry creation would guide her.

Well, maybe. However, at the moment, she was stuck behind a noisy group of six women, and waited for them to move away from a booth in the far right corner. Sure, she could come back to it later, but something indefinable kept her in place. Other attendees were interested primarily in what was on display, but going by the women's animated conversation with whoever was manning the booth, something important or educational or entertaining was being said.

She'd just about given up when a man with a toddler in a stroller backed away, and she took the vacated place. The moment she looked down, she was glad she'd waited because the table was devoted to fire opals. Some had been made into jewelry, and necklaces, earrings, and rings were arranged on a variety of displays, but the majority of the opals had been spread out on velvet in cases with locked glass tops. Lighting had been designed so each box was touched by a slightly different hue, adding to the presentation. For the most part, the boxes had been arranged in color groupings ranging from a translucent crystal to opaque milky white to bold red with a predominance of the orange that was so common to fire opals.

Was it the fire lurking deep in the stones that had always drawn her to opals? Probably, since there was something sensual about finding so much color in such small stones. True, the stories about opals' place in history was fascinating, particularly the ancient Persian and Central American belief that they were symbols of fervent love, whatever that was, but even without the legends, she'd always loved working with them. Creating a faceted or cabochon piece to display the most fire possible gave her a sense of satisfaction she doubted would ever get old, and she loved holding the finished product in her palm, becoming part of it.

Unfortunately, she hadn't done as much work with opals as she wanted to, both because she hadn't had enough time what with life's recent curves and because she'd been discouraged by the large number of inferior or manufactured stones on the market.

There wasn't a single marginal gem or opal figment held together in a clear plastic cast here, nothing but the real deal. A virtual gold, or should she say fire, mine.

Excited, she leaned over for a closer look. As she did, she almost swore heat was coming up from the cases and touching her with warmth and energy, calling to her. If only the owner or distributor or whoever hadn't locked them up, not that she could blame him. Unlike her ex, she'd never taken anything that didn't belong to her, but Lordy, did her fingers itch to hold one, or more. For the gems to become part of her.

"Be careful," one woman said as another slipped on a ring. "You don't want to wind up with bad luck."

"You don't really believe that nonsense, do you?" the ring wearer asked of her companion.

"All I know is, I'm not taking chances. What about it? Do you think there's anything to that business about opals bringing bad luck?"

For a moment, Hayley thought the woman was talking to her. Then she realized she had to be addressing the man behind the table.

"Quetzalitzlipyollitli were sacred to the Mayas and Aztecs," a deep, strong voice said. "Gifts from the gods."

Almost of its own will, Hayley's head came up. The voice—that rich, strong voice—settled in her. More than that, the masculine tone seemed to be spreading out, seeping into her veins and racing through her.

"What was that you said?" the woman asked. "I can't begin to pronounce that word."

"Quetzalitzlipyollitli. It means the stone of the bird of paradise."

Forget birds of paradise and tongue-twisting syllables. Forget everything except deep eyes, eyes as dark as the darkest cave, and yet filled with a rich glow. Forget the crowds and noise. Absorb this man's energy and the look of raw disbelief and desperate hope in his gaze.

Even as her body heated, Hayley told herself this wasn't happening. Hell no. She didn't believe in like at first sight, let alone love in that particular instant. Fine. Fine and good. But what about lust? What about a communication that went beyond words?

Now her arms and legs were going numb and what was that buzzing in her lips? Just because the owner of what might be the world's sexiest voice was a good six foot three with shoulders that would make a football coach drool and a lean, hard body encased in a skin-skimming black shirt and faded jeans that more than hugged the territory they were responsible for was no reason to—to what?

The women were still talking to him, but if he heard, the man gave no indication. To her disbelief, his eyes had found hers, latched onto them, bonded with them. He'd cocked his head to the side as if trying to convince himself that he was truly looking at her, maybe wondering whether she was getting whatever message or order or command or tidal wave of sex appeal he was giving out. If he did that much longer, she just might melt.

Either that or jump over the display and launch herself at him.

Fuck. That's all there needs to be, fucking. Mating like a couple of animals in heat. Whether he or she was expressing those sentiments, she couldn't say. Didn't give a damn. Neither did she know how the hell she was going to keep her legs under her and her pussy from melting. Disconcerted, she dropped her gaze from pure magnetic power before said power ripped her to shreds.

Her attention snagged on a display she hadn't noticed before, probably because it was at the back of the table and near him. None of these stones had been cut and polished, but she saw their potential within their plain host rocks. Her heated fingers truly itched to touch and turn and explore, briefly distracting her from the man's unnerving eyes—either that or she'd found a connection between the opals and him.

"Blacks," he said and ran a strong, dark finger over the case.

"I, ah, I know." Much as she wanted to, she didn't risk looking up.

"What else do you know?"

About what? Wondering if he was referring to the connection already forged between them, she nevertheless refused to bite. Some things a woman needed to keep to herself—like the wet heat between her legs, like her tightening nipples and the pressure on her chest. "Blacks are rare, and thus quite valuable," she heard herself say. Then she lifted her head.

Looking slightly more relaxed, he gave an approving nod. "Yes, they are; I'm delighted you know that. Your knowledge says a great deal about many things."

"What kinds of things?"

The way his head came up, she knew he wasn't going to answer. Instead, he took a deep breath. "The most valuable have deep red captured in the black. They're considered depth instead of light, mystery over glow."

She'd never heard it expressed like that before, but he was right, so right. "Where are they from?"

When he didn't answer, she surrendered to the pinpricks of fire spreading over her spine. Animal magnetism was a buzz term, right? Then what the hell was this?

"They're from the Mexican highlands, on the site of an extinct volcano. The Indians call the area Pico de Orizaba. These"—he indicated the spectacular case—"came from a labyrinthine passage that winds through the open-cast mine there."

"Oh." She'd seen pictures of opal mines carved from isolated and desolate-looking land, and of the Mexican Indians who toiled there. Those laborers were short and solid, their bodies protected from the relentless sun by broad-brimmed hats and ragged clothing. They'd seemed part of the land, as if hardened by it.

This powerfully built man was larger and taller with dark, deep eyes undimmed by physical labor, and yet he made her think of those native workers. Maybe it was his rough-looking hands, his sun-weathered skin. And maybe it was because, like men who made a living from the earth, he seemed to be part of something ancient and enduring.

Don't do this. Don't get carried away!

But how could she help it? This man was passionate about some of the same things as she was, and his voice was like a strong wind surrounding and burrowing deep inside her. She couldn't remember when she'd last had sex or wanted more than her vibrator. She wanted him, now—rough and raw and loud and messy.

"Am I the only one feeling the heat?" one of the women asked.

"Hell no," another laughed. "Enough to burn down the place."

Vaguely wondering what they were talking about, Hayley tore her gaze off the ageless man. All six women were dividing their attention between her and him, smiling, fanning themselves, one pulling her blouse out and blowing down her front. "Don't worry about it, honey," the first speaker said on a giggle. "We aren't scandalized, just jealous."

It took every shred of civilization in her not to clamp her

hand over her crotch and push against the hungry heat there. Maybe it would have been easier if *the man* was looking at something else, doing anything except leaning toward her with his beautiful strong hands resting on the table and his lips slightly parted. Thank goodness, the table hid him from the hips down. If she'd been able to see—

Knock it off! You want to catch fire?

Well yeah, truth be told, she did.

His gaze intent, his breathing deep and rapid, the man called Mazati studied the woman. It was too early to know whether she was *the* one, his reason for living. But if instinct bore him out, his desperate and determined search had come to an end.

But, before entrusting her with his knowledge, came stripping her down, exposing her deepest vulnerabilities, teaching her how much she needed from him.

And once he'd accomplished that . . .